if this bed could talk

Liz Maverick

Kimberly Dean

Lynn LaFleur

if this bed
could talk

red

A V O N *An Imprint of* HarperCollins*Publishers*

IF THIS BED COULD TALK. "Agent Provocateur" copyright © 2006 by Elizabeth Edelstein; "Unrequited" copyright © 2006 by Kimberly Dean; "Victim of Deception" copyright © 2006 by Lynn LaFleur. All rights reserved. Printed in the United States of America. No part of this book may be used or reproduced in any manner whatsoever without written permission except in the case of brief quotations embodied in critical articles and reviews. For information address HarperCollins Publishers Inc., 10 East 53rd Street, New York, NY 10022.

HarperCollins books may be purchased for educational, business, or sales promotional use. For information please write: Special Markets Department, HarperCollins Publishers Inc., 10 East 53rd Street, New York, NY 10022.

FIRST EDITION

Designed by Joy O'Meara

Printed on acid-free paper

Library of Congress Cataloging-in-Publication Data

Maverick, Liz.
    If this bed could talk / Liz Maverick, Kimberly Dean, and Lynn LaFleur.—
1st ed.
        p. cm.
Contents: Agent provocateur / Liz Maverick—Unrequited / Kimberly Dean—Victim of deception / Lynn LaFleur.
ISBN-13: 978-0-06-088536-6
ISBN-10: 0-06-088536-X
1. Erotic stories, American. I. Dean, Kimberly. II. LaFleur, Lynn. III. Title.

PS3613.A885I35 2006
813'.6—dc22   2005057198

06 07 08 09 10 RRD 10 9 8 7 6 5 4 3 2 1

Contents

Liz Maverick

AGENT
PROVOCATEUR

One

They say you only get a few seconds to make a good first impression. Vienna James needed to make a great one.

It all came down to numbers. Numbers and time. How many strikes do you have? How many years did you get? When should you make your move? How long do you give it before you run like hell?

She gazed up at the shadowy figures of the men in the glass booths encircling the top tier of the auction round. They watched her as if they were spectators at a sporting event. As if she was the sport itself—with just seconds remaining in the final period.

Numbers and time. How many men have told you in so many words that they could fix your world if you just gave them long enough? How many actually have?

The odds of finding a buyer on a three-strikes sentence were practically nil. But not impossible. Seething inside that her life had come to this pathetic crossroad—where the best possible scenario would be another human being purchasing her for unknown service—Vienna did her best to smile on the platform. Not an easy thing to do when a pissy attitude, wrist shackles, and a grubby prison uniform were your only props.

The loudspeaker instructed her to turn in a circle. Vienna did exactly what she was told, her heart rate picking up again as she finished the 360 and came back around to face the front, where a row of green lights were extinguishing one by one. When the entire line of lights on the wall went out, the auction would be over. Two out of six dots left.

Smile, Vienna. Smile for the silly boys . . . oh, for God's sake. This is ridiculous!

She was just a weapons specialist. A gunrunner. A target shooter. End of story. This . . . this *preening* and putting her . . . *girliness* or whatever on display . . . it just wasn't her game. But you had to do what you had to do. Working this hard to impress men might not have been part of her old job description, but it apparently was a requirement now. And if this was what it took to convince a buyer to get her the hell out of this mess she was in, then this was what she was going to do.

Vienna looked up and scanned the booths again, noticing that in one of them, two men had leaned forward on the window and were staring intently down at her.

You there. Buy me. *Buy me and you won't be sorry.*

And I won't be sorry either, because once you get me away from here, I'll get away from you.

{͡⊶}

Michael and Devlin Kingston leaned against the glass of a cramped auction booth, glancing between a folder describing Docket 664291 and the woman down below—the real thing, Vienna James.

Blond, blue-eyed, and working serious bombshell curves that even the most ill-fitting uniform couldn't hide, the girl could not have been closer to the specifications of Devlin's ex-fiancée, Julia, if she'd been custom built that way.

She's perfect, Michael thought.

"She's a mess," Devlin said abruptly.

Michael glared at his brother. "Are you joking? Look closer."

Devlin folded his arms across his chest, his mouth a grim slash.

"I have a feeling about her," Michael said. "And, come on. Blond. Blue eyes. You know she's perfect." He slid the auction file over to his brother. "Vienna James."

Devlin arched an eyebrow. "How much do you want to bet it's not her real name?"

Michael chuckled. "It's the name attached to the crime, so I expect it's the only one that matters."

"*Three* crimes caught *three* times. And now she's looking at automatic execution, aka Three-Strikes policy, if somebody doesn't buy her." He tossed the folder back at Michael. "We'd be better off with somebody whose line of business had more to do with seduction than common illegal weapons handling."

"I disagree. I think Pierce would detect a professional seductress in a second."

"You don't plan to train her?" Devlin asked.

"Of course I'll train her. I'm just saying that a little rough around the edges is a good thing." He pointed at the row of green lights. "We need to make a decision."

Devlin was silent for a long time. Finally, he said, "She has Julia's coloring exactly."

Michael studied his brother's face. Though anyone else would probably miss it, he always caught the change in the set of Devlin's jaw when he said Julia's name. Julia's or Pierce Mackey's. Devlin hadn't forgotten. Hell, Michael hadn't forgotten either. And neither of them had forgiven.

Michael looked down at the girl who was busy complying with a litany of automated requests blaring from the platform speaker. She turned in a circle, modeling for the prospective buyers in a strange kind of Simon Says that would have been laughable if her life hadn't been on the line. "Maybe *you* need to be running the job," he suggested to his brother. "Maybe it would make more sense if you were the one with her. A kind of repeat that he wouldn't be able to resist."

Devlin winced. "I'd rather not. You're better in the field and Pierce will jump at the chance to wreck you. It would make his victory complete."

The final green dot began to pulse, indicating only thirty seconds remained in the auction. Michael picked up the red line. "I'd like an opportunity to question the prisoner on the block prior to bidding." He hung up, and a moment later an all-call message went out to the booths that a buyer was interested in one Vienna James and that the courtesy of questioning her was extended to any who were interested.

Watching her face as the guard announced buyer interest, Michael saw the moment her courage failed. As she took in the news, her lips parted in surprise. She closed them again and swallowed, and he could see uncertainty move like a shadow over her face.

With no competing requests filed, time ran out and the pulsing green light turned a solid red. The girl was unceremoniously yanked off the block and the clock reset for the next prisoner.

"Well, then. You're the people person," Devlin said. "If you find her satisfactory for the job, buy her." He opened the door with one hand, yanking at his perfectly knotted tie with the other. "I'm off. Fucking claustrophobic."

Five minutes later, the guard ushered Vienna James into the booth. "You want me to stay?" he asked Michael, per protocol.

"No, thank you," Michael said.

The guard shrugged his meaty shoulder. "Then I'll just wait outside." He left Vienna standing there, still shackled.

Michael looked up and watched the booth camera switch on. The girl turned and followed his gaze. "Is that for my protection or yours?" she asked.

Michael just smiled. "Hello, Vienna. I'm Michael."

Her eyebrow arched in surprise. "Hello."

She stared at Michael, her almond-shaped eyes widening as he gave her a very blatant once-over. In person, Vienna was taller than he'd expected. Her looks less common than he'd first imagined when he'd checked off the details he was looking for in a blond bombshell stereotype. Maybe it was as simple as the fact that she didn't have access to the goods, but there was a natural quality to her, a far cry from the plastic sameness the women in his social circle were buying for themselves these days.

He grabbed her shoulders and swept his hands down her arms. Her toned body proved she'd been exercising, and that she'd bothered indicated either boredom, or better yet, confidence in her ability to score an auction interview and a desire to impress. Good. She'd need both self-confidence and desire to pull off this job.

"Everything should be in my file. I don't have any major scars or anything like that," she said with a slight tremor in her voice.

"Nerves, Vienna? Or have you just not felt a man's touch in a while?"

"It's not nerves, and if you're suggesting I haven't been *pawed at* recently, I'd have to agree."

Michael laughed and suddenly pulled her in even closer, ducking his mouth to her ear. "Not nerves. How about a temper?"

She went silent, but her eyes sparked with an intensity that wouldn't have fooled anybody.

"A hot temper," he murmured, pulling the hem of her uniform shirt up just enough to place his palms on her bare back. She gasped in surprise as he continued moving his hands downward to follow the tight curve of her ass. Michael smiled. *Hot inside and out.* And if his own reaction to her was any indication, that heat would translate well to the kind of passion he was looking for.

Breaking away before she could feel the quickening of his pulse, Michael took to the chair, leaning back casually as he said, "You know, there's something I like about you, Vienna James."

Her surprised laughter filled the air between them. She shifted her weight, pushing the shackles against her body to adjust the heavy metal and stared right back at Michael, giving him no ground. Her mouth opened as if she had a mind to speak, but then she simply fell silent once more.

"Something on your mind?" he asked.

"I was just wondering what exactly your line of business was."

"Import/export."

"What do you trade in?"

"Agents."

She nodded. "I'm a trained shooter. An ace."

Michael gave her a slow smile. "I don't need a shooter, Vienna."

"Then what kind of an agent do you need, *Michael*?"

"Shall we say . . . an *agent provocateur*?"

She blinked rapidly, like she was trying to process what he'd just said, the momentary ease between them vanishing as quickly as it had arrived. "We're talking about sex?"

"Seduction."

"That's just sex, all dressed up."

"If you like."

"I don't know if I like," Vienna said after a long silence. "A professional seductress?" She took a step backward, absently rubbing at a raw spot on her opposite wrist. "This is not some-thing I had mapped into my long-term career plan."

"Did your long-term career plan include dying long before thirty?"

Her face went pale. "How long would you plan to . . . use me on your job?"

He steepled his hands together on his knee, watching how she pressed her back against the door with a kind of trapped look about her. "I couldn't say."

"How about we put a time limit on it?"

Michael had to marvel at the balls on this girl. Maybe she didn't quite understand who was boss here. "You're actually try-ing to negotiate with me?"

"I can turn the buy down."

"In favor of death," he said. "Time isn't for sale."

"I shouldn't be either."

"It's not a perfect world, then, is it?" Michael said cruelly.

Vienna winced. "Just promise me that indentured servitude with you won't be forever."

"That's out of the question, on principle alone. Not to men-tion, I haven't done anything to suggest I'm untrustworthy. I may be a businessman buying a product that doesn't want to be sold, but I've done nothing to earn your distrust."

"It's my default position."

You sound like Devlin. "I'm sorry for you, then."

Her eyes narrowed. "I don't want your pity. Just your word."

"You'd take it?"

"Sure, because if you break it, I'll know for certain you're a liar. That's a good piece of information to have about someone."

"Yes," Michael said thoughtfully, "It is. Though in your case, if I'm a liar, either you're not going to figure it out for a long time or you're going to be dead."

She lifted her chin. "I don't think dead's going to happen."

"Why not?"

She slowly pushed off the door with her elbows and leaned over him. "Because I have a lot of raw talent, and I learn quickly."

Michael reached up, took a fistful of uniform and pulled her down even farther, their mouths separated only by a whisper. "Then prove it," he said. "Kiss me as if it were the one thing that could save your life, and I'll judge your talent for myself. But make it good, because I don't have the inclination to spend any more time on this interview."

"Time and numbers," she whispered.

The tease of her lips just barely moving against his made Michael's head reel for a moment. Time for her to put up or shut up. He pushed back the chair and stood up. "Make your move, Vienna. Or shall I throw you back into the swim?"

Vienna sprang forward like a wildcat, driving him backwards against the glass wall so hard it reverberated around them. She swallowed hard, her eyes wide, and something about the mess of emotions in the blue of them . . . well, it got to him. Made him almost want to apologize without having a decent reason.

With her heart beating so fast he could feel it through the fabric and her cuffed hands caught between their bodies, Vienna leaned in and gently pressed her lips to his for only a second. Then she pulled back just barely, her tongue flicking across his mouth as she moistened her own lips. An act without artifice, to be sure, and it ignited the anticipation down to Michael's very core. He might have green-lighted her right there if he weren't craving to know what was to come.

Her lashes fanned downward and in the breathy sound of her sigh, she bit down gently on his lower lip and deepened the kiss. In a flash, the languid sensuality of her mouth over his began escalating into something more urgent.

Raising the loop of her arms up and over Michael's head to rest on his shoulders, Vienna eased the full length of her body against him. The top button on her uniform slipped its hole and her shirt slid down to reveal bare shoulder and the full swell of her breasts.

Michael sucked in a quick breath, working hard to steady himself. His body was already thinking too many damn steps ahead. He hadn't planned on giving her the satisfaction of a hard cock as proof of a passing grade, but she had his mind fogging over as much the glass around them.

She kissed him again, harder now, and Michael could feel a kind of frenzy build up inside of him. The simple, gorgeous scent of her, the smoothness of her back under the uniform, the hot-sweet taste of her mouth . . .

Ah, God. So easy to pull her clothes away, sample her body with his mouth . . . *enter* her. He wanted to take full control and drive his cock into her very core until she threw back her head and screamed out her pleasure.

He'd played his part as long as he could. The small amount of control he'd given her—demanded of her, really—he wanted it back. He pushed her arms up and away and whipped her around, throwing her up against the damp glass. She raised her cuffed hands above her head, the metal striking hard against the pane, and he just moved in on her, taking her mouth this time with total domination.

She moaned softly and followed his lead as he swept his tongue in and out, licking and biting her bee-stung mouth. Logic vanished somewhere in the heat and the wet, the urgency of Michael's desire growing as she pressed her undulating body into his in the same unmistakable rhythm.

He moved his hand down to the zipper on his pants, ready to take her, but the harsh sound was like an alarm. *Enough, Michael. Enough!*

Michael pushed her away, a little rougher than he meant to, but his body was torqued at such a high level his self-control wasn't all there.

Vienna leaned back against the glass, her breathing raspy and uneven, the two of them panting at each other like a couple of animals.

Then she raised her chin, her blue eyes burning like the eye of a flame, all defiance and lust. "Did I save my life, Michael?"

She might be nearly identical to Julia in build and coloring, but the similarity ended there. She looked like Julia, yes. But she didn't remind Michael of Julia. She didn't remind him of anyone.

What a brilliant lie of a kiss.

Without giving her an answer, Michael pulled himself together, reached over to the controls by the phone and pressed the buy button, scanned his paycard, and took his receipt.

A knock sounded at the door. The guard reclaimed Vienna and the glowing, wanton look of her vanished immediately, though her nipples still pressed through the fabric of her uniform. "I have other skills!" she yelled as the guard pulled her out the door. "I'm a weapons specialist. Try me out!"

"Stop panicking, Vienna," Michael said, fighting a smile. "I'm buying you. You're mine, now."

And dear God, you're all the weapon we're going to need.

Two

Once she had arrived at the Kingston compound—blindfolded in the back of a limousine—Vienna had hoped things would all be fairly simple. She'd imagined training with a squad of other auctionees. She'd imagined blending into the group until she was forgotten and then using the scheduled training runs in Center City as opportunities to get away.

But she wasn't in a squad. She wasn't taken to Center City with the others. And she wasn't forgotten. She was isolated in a dorm room and marked as Michael Kingston's personal responsibility.

Granted, it could be worse; for a slave driver, Michael took Vienna's breath away. And five days after she thought she just might have tasted some brand of heaven on his lips, even though she knew he had been manipulating her, she still felt a kind of breathless anticipation at the possibility of recreating that sensation. Once he finally called for her, anyway.

And, finally, he did. With a summons in hand and instructions leading her to building 4G, Vienna was allowed to cross the grounds for the first time since her arrival.

What she found on the other side would have been more appropriately called a theater. It was pitch black as she stepped into the lobby, then through the double doors. A tiny glow of light emanated from somewhere up front and Vienna headed in that direction.

The seating area looked like it was designed more for a fashion show than for a play: the wide stage had a catwalk that protruded from the left side and then curled around to run horizontally through the audience. Spotlights hung from the rafters, pointing at the front lip of the stage.

A perfect setup for a casting call.

Suddenly, the silhouette of a man appeared, backlit. But she knew immediately who it was, the shape of him, the head cocked.

If she gave him what he wanted during training, he'd begin to believe that it would always be so. Eventually, he'd provide her with an opportunity to get away.

Michael beckoned her forward and then disappeared into the back. She headed backstage. There were no props, no scenery, no special rigging for curtains to be raised or lowered. Just rooms labeled COSTUME and MAKEUP and CATERING.

Michael held the door open to Makeup. Vienna had heard people in the dining hall refer to a brother named Devlin, and as she entered the room she knew she was looking at him for the first time. He was unmistakable. Physically, the two men were nearly identical—black hair, green eyes, and a taste for expensive designer apparel.

"Devlin, this is Vienna," Michael said. "Vienna, Devlin."

"Hi," Vienna said.

Devlin Kingston pulled himself away from a gorgeous redhead at the makeup mirror and studied Vienna for a moment. Then he stood up and grabbed her chin, roughly turning her head to one side. Vienna had to bite her tongue to stop herself from telling him to piss off. Though Michael had done much the

same thing, Devlin's actions seemed incredibly impersonal compared to the warmth of Michael's touch.

"Easy," Michael muttered. Vienna wasn't the only one who
looked over at him in surprise. But he and Devlin just exchanged
a look, revealing evidence of some kind of power struggle.

Devlin let her go and walked to the door. He turned back to
the redhead. "Genn, put her in blue." And then he walked out.

That was an alpha dog moment if ever I saw one. Vienna had
spent quite a bit of time analyzing the dynamics of people with
power; her job in the weapons trade depended on it; the times
she'd guessed wrong were the times she'd been arrested for
weapons crimes. And if she was guessing right, there was under-
current of something between the brothers, a sense of obligation
or guilt.

"Sit down," Michael said.

Vienna took a chair at the cosmetics counter, looked helplessly down at the mess of makeup and just shook her head. "I'm
from Bordertown," she said. "I've never . . . this isn't my—"

"You'll be fine." He reached out and swept her hair back from
her face, tucking it behind her ears. "Genevieve will show you."
On his way out, he turned back at the door like his brother had.
"Genn, put her in *black*," he said, and then disappeared from view.

Vienna just threw her arms up in surrender. "I don't know
what to make of that guy."

The redhead laughed. "I'm not entirely sure he knows what
to make of you. But that's what I'm here to help with." She
pressed her palm against her carefully coiffed, retro '40s glamour
hairdo, then addressed Vienna's hair, swiping a curler through the
ends and sweeping it back from her face.

"Devlin didn't exactly warm up to me," Vienna mumbled.

"I wouldn't expect it right away. Especially not if you're playing Julia in some way," she said as she began to apply makeup to Vienna's face.

Vienna frowned. "What do you mean 'playing Julia'?"

The redhead's expression changed. "I shouldn't have said anything. If they haven't described the job, I shouldn't be the one."

"Who's Julia?"

"Well, that's no secret. She was Devlin's fiancée. She's the one who came between them all."

Vienna was just getting more lost. "Where is she now?"

The mascara wand in Genn's hand stilled. "She's dead. But she's what put the strain between the boys."

"How did she die?"

No answer. "They look similar, but they aren't, are they?" Vienna asked, switching to a more gossipy tone in hopes she could keep the woman talking. The more she could find out about what made the Kingston brothers tick, the better. "Devlin and Michael don't seem anything the same. Devlin is like . . . ice. Michael is like . . ."

"Fire?" Genn supplied, with a smile. "You like him, I think. That's good."

Vienna frowned. "I don't like him. Why would I like him?"

"Well, I hope you'll at least learn to like him," she answered suggestively. Then she added. "You look very much like Devlin's type, very much like his love. But your personality is not Julia's at all. I think Michael must like your roughness. You should get on well. They come from the streets, too, you know."

"I didn't know," Vienna said, frowning a little at the slight. "But it explains the way he talks. It's like he's conditioned himself to talk like old money but the rhythm underneath, the pattern of the words . . . we talk like that in Bordertown."

Genn nodded. "Bordertown is where they were born. Where

they met Pierce Mackey. I understand why they picked you. You're a local girl. And a very lucky one at that."

"I suppose I am," Vienna said. "Are there many former strike-prisoners here?"

"Several at the moment."

"Do they ever bail out?"

"If they did, I doubt they are still living," the redhead said, her voice suddenly cold and hard.

"You're very loyal," Vienna noted.

"I'm *very* loyal. It's important here." Genn leaned over and stared into the reflection of Vienna's eyes. "I would warn you, new girl, not to be rash in your decision making. This may be a bad field of business, but these are good men. You'll see." She snapped the last makeup container shut, her head cocked as she studied her work. "I think you're exactly what Michael wanted. Let's go to wardrobe."

Vienna stood up from the chair and pulled the clip from her hair. "So which one wins?"

Genn stared at her, not understanding.

Vienna gave her a big smile. "In other words, blue ... or black?"

❦

Michael called up to the control booth and a few moments later the house lights went down. From his vantage point in the audience seating just behind the horizontal extension to the catwalk, he could hear the uneven click of several pairs of high heels against hard surface.

Next to him, Devlin shifted impatiently in his seat. "Why the lineup?" he asked. "We've already agreed she's perfect."

"I thought it would be helpful," Michael said. "Just so we're sure. This is for both of us."

Devlin made a choking sound.

"Are you laughing at me?" Michael asked.

"Absolutely. Come on, admit you just want to see her in the lineup."

After a pause, Michael said, "Okay, fine. I just want to see her in the lineup. *And* I think it would help us make sure that she'll really stand out to Pierce. Out of a group of perfectly gorgeous women, would he pick this one?"

Devlin's face turned cloudy. "You know he'd pick her out."

Without warning, the spotlights flipped on, revealing four of the most beautiful trainees in camp. Red curls, a shiny blue-black bob, brunette waves . . . and under the third spotlight, Vienna, the blonde. The lot of them wearing nothing more than obscenely expensive lingerie.

Michael noted immediately that she was wearing baby blue and shot Devlin an annoyed glance.

The corner of Devlin's mouth curved up in a smile.

"I think she'd work better in black," Michael muttered and turned back to study her again.

"Pierce will prefer light blue. God, in blue she'll practically be Julia's twin."

Michael studied his brother, hesitating a moment before he dug in and asked, "Do you really think we should offer him something he already had?"

"We're giving him what he thinks we have now," Devlin said, flexing and curling his fingers into a tight fist. "I like the light blue on her. Julia wore it all the time."

"So blue is what you had. Black is what I'd have. Pierce will want what I'm having. I'll tell wardrobe to put her in black," Michael said, surprising himself with the hostility lacing his voice.

"Fine," Devlin spat out.

Michael studied his brother's face. "I'll ask you one last time. Do you want to run this job?"

"No." Devlin switched on the intercom and then said, "Will number three please walk the stage?"

None of the girls moved. Finally the redhead in the fourth spot turned her head and said something to Vienna. She gave a start of surprise, then awkwardly stepped forward from the lineup.

"Walk it," Devlin called out, beckoning her forward with a graceful curl of his fingers.

Wearing a baby blue bustier with white lace trim, and a matching satin mini wrapskirt slung low enough to show the top of her garter belt, Vienna walked toward the brothers under the harsh lights.

She stopped a couple of feet back from the edge, cocked her hip and rested her weight on the heel of one stiletto, a totally blank expression on her face.

"Closer," Devlin said.

She arched an eyebrow and walked to the edge of the stage.

Devlin swept his hand in the air, and she continued along the catwalk moving to the horizontal section until she was standing right above the men.

"Stop there," he said.

Michael eased back into his seat. With a defiant smile, Vienna widened her stance.

She wasn't wearing any panties.

The sound of Vienna's dossier slipping off his lap broke the silence. He cleared his throat. "I guess she'll do."

"I guess she will," Devlin said. He leaned over and pressed the speaker button once more. "Numbers one, two, and four . . . you can go." Sliding past Michael into the aisle he added, "Have fun."

Vienna looked over her shoulder and watched the other girls

file off the stage. She turned back and looked down at Michael. "Can I change now?"

"No."

She stared at him in silence for a moment, then said, "When I sit down, this skirt is going straight up."

"I realize that," Michael said. He leaped up on the stage next to her. "Come with me."

He led her behind the stage back to the wardrobe room and held the door for her, watching the white lacings crisscrossed along the back of her corset sway as she passed and headed directly for the wardrobe racks.

She reached out and ran her fingers down the rack of lingerie like she was running her fingers across a picket fence.

"You like them," Michael said, his head cocked to one side.

Vienna turned and looked through the options. She pushed two sides of the rack aside to expose a black lingerie set—garter belt, thong, bustier, deceptively simple, gorgeous pleats, lace detailing. Michael smiled to himself as she pulled it off the rack and held it up against her body.

Her eyelashes fluttered against her porcelain skin, then flicked upward in a quick instant as she pierced him with those blue eyes. "I guess I'm supposed to protest, tell you I hate shit like this, say that I don't want to wear it." She shrugged. "I don't know that we're going to have a problem with this. I think my problem is going to be looking like I'm used to wearing it."

Michael took the outfit from her hands and hung it back up, then led her back to another makeup chair. He took a hairbrush and slowly stroked it through her hair, the pressure of the metal tines a strange reminder of his power over her.

"There is a man," Michael said, pulling a set of ornate rhinestone hairpins from a white cup and setting them on the makeup table in front of her. "He double-crossed my brother and me. His name is Pierce Mackey."

He twisted his wrists and expertly put up her hair with a kind of cold efficiency.

"He took our family's business." Michael took the first pin and stuck it in her hair.

"He took our family's loyalty."

He tucked another pin carefully away. "And he took our family's love. We would like him to experience the same."

"Revenge," Vienna said, looking into the reflection of those green eyes.

"Revenge. We will work on the business. You will work on the man. You've heard the name 'Julia'?"

Vienna nodded.

"Pierce Mackey keeps Julia's engagement ring on a chain around his neck. He wears it like a trophy for anyone to see as proof that he has bested the Kingstons. That he has won. That was my mother's ring. She gave it to Devlin when he and Julia became engaged. My brother loved her more than anything. She betrayed us all for Pierce Mackey. And we would like you to betray Pierce Mackey for us."

"So you want me to sleep with him?"

"I want you to make him believe that you would leave me for him. And I want you to make him believe that you could fall in love with him. I want you to put on the performance of your life. I want you to do all of that. Subtle, clever, compelling. And then I want you to take the ring away from him and bring it back to us."

Vienna stared at him in the mirror. "That's my mission? That's why you bought me?"

"You're the spitting image of Julia. Devlin wanted that. He thought the idea of stealing Julia once again but from me this

time around, would be too hard for Pierce to resist. You see . . ."
His voice faltered a bit, and Michael had to clear it to continue.
"He's damaged everyone personally except me."

Vienna had turned away from the mirror and Michael gently
moved her head to face it again. "This is the look I want for you.
Julia always wore her hair up. He won't be able to resist." He
frowned and said a little absently under his breath, "Personally,
I like you better casual. The way you were before."

"The way I was before?" she echoed. "What happens to me at
the end of all this? When the job is done."

"Assuming you're still alive," Michael said harshly.

Vienna jolted away from him. "That's cruel," she whispered.
"You don't know me. I wouldn't expect you to. But this is my life,
not a game."

He searched her face. "You were sentenced to die, Vienna.
You'd be dead already if it weren't for me. That's just a cold, hard
fact."

Michael ran his fingers down her cheek. "Everything's just a
game in the end. Julia was supposed to be in love with Devlin.
Pierce was supposed to be our best friend. And you and I are supposed to be falling for each other. Why do you think I'm so convinced that Pierce will believe what we need him to believe?
You'll sell it. You play a good game," he said softly, running his index finger down, over the soft of her neck and between her
breasts. "Maybe you don't want to admit it. But I think you play a
very, very good game.

With that, Michael slipped out of the room. In the mirror she
saw him pause outside leaning his palm against the wall and staring blankly at the floor.

And then he just collected himself and in the next minute he
was gone.

Three

Blindfolded, wearing a white satin evening gown, and sitting thigh-to-thigh with a gorgeous man in the back of a limousine, Vienna laughed to herself thinking this had all the trappings of a fantasy evening out . . . except that it was a job.

A setup for the job, anyway, at a political fund-raiser for Center City's elite. When the limousine finally stopped and Michael removed the black ribbon from her eyes, what she saw was hard to believe. Vienna stepped out onto red velvet carpet leading up to a stately Romanesque event hall, a far cry from the brick and dirt of Bordertown. Guided inside on Michael's arm, it was all she could do to not let her jaw drop at the sight of crystal chandeliers, parquet flooring, and walls painted with delicately shaded cherubs.

It would have been easy to let the sheer luxury of the event shake her focus. The fact was, a girl could easily get lost in a place like this. *She* could get lost and somehow never make it back into Michael's arms.

"I'm going to use the ladies' room," she said to Michael, turning away.

He grabbed her by the wrist. "I'll show you where it is."

She snatched her wrist away. "I'm sure I can find it on my own."

They eyed each other for a moment, then he finally said, "Come straight back here."

She smiled. "Of course." Walking purposefully through the crowd she found the ladies' room easily, went in, and reapplied lipstick that didn't need reapplication. After counting to five, she snapped her evening bag shut and went back out to the party where the halls were already swarming with people.

Vienna looked around for Michael, then headed in the opposite direction from where they'd been standing. She found a fire escape exit, but the alarm system made it a no go. Picking up the pace now, and flush with excitement over the prospect of freedom so close, Vienna craned her neck over the crowd to pick the best route.

The front of the party was even more congested, and Michael was hopefully still in that mess. She headed to the back, but saw as she got closer that it was likewise wired . . . it was a side exit she needed.

Glancing over her shoulder, she spotted Michael looking for her over the crowd. Cat was tailing the mouse already. *Dammit*.

Moving faster now, Vienna slipped into a parallel hallway and started pushing more blatantly through the crowd. And as the door loomed closer and the air turned colder, tears sparked her eyes.

She hadn't been free, truly free, in over a year.

The doorman saw her coming, his expression registering her distress. He swung open the door and she could smell the strange, glorious scent of wet pavement as a slight drizzle fell out of the sky.

Vienna's stiletto heel smashed down hard on the metal runner that ran like a seam across the threshold. Then a hand wrapped around her upper arm and whiplashed her around so hard she almost fell over.

{∘∘}

"Training camp isn't over, Vienna," Michael said, his voice cold and flat.

"I suddenly felt faint. I was just going for some air."

"Don't lie. And don't try to escape. I bought you. I own you. And you have a job to do."

She resisted, tried to pull away; he caught her tight by the wrist.

"I don't want this life," she said, in a voice so small he could barely hear her. "I don't want this bullshit, these games."

"Look at me."

Vienna raised her eyes to his face.

"I cannot understate how important this is to me and my brother. I need you to do what I ask you to do without questioning, without blowing cover, without a misstep. Please do *not* give me a hard time." He finally let go of her, noticing with a frown how she rubbed at the red around her wrist as if she were still wearing shackles.

"I'm sorry if I hurt you."

Vienna stared at him, a kind of wounded expression on her face. Then, she shrugged, a disdainful little slip of the shoulders, and in the next moment her face broke into a beaming smile as she went into character.

Michael tried to relax.

He'd done this sort of thing on missions many times before. Both he and Devlin had. To prevent suspicion that all of their women were operatives, they'd also take nonoperatives, gorgeous women visiting from out of town or from the city's society scene, and bring them to parties and dinners and shows.

In that way, they used business to conceal pleasure and pleasure to conceal business. Tonight should have been no different. But the job was different; having Vienna on his arm was somehow different, and they could both enjoy themselves tonight if she were willing to play the game properly.

Michael smiled and affectionately smoothed a strand back against Vienna's updo, nuzzling her ear. Her scent made him dizzy. She looked like a porcelain doll, so perfect that she should have seemed cold; but the fire in her eyes, the smoldering pout of innocently curved lips . . . he already knew something burned hot inside the carefully costumed shell, and he knew Pierce would be able to see it, too.

"Laugh. Swat my shoulder or something. Pretend I said something amusing and perhaps a little suggestive."

Vienna smiled. "Then why don't you *say* something amusing and perhaps a little suggestive."

"Don't act up," he said, planting a light kiss on the exposed expanse of her neck. "Unless you plan to act out a little more flirtation with me. As it is, I think you should turn it up just slightly."

"Whose benefit would that be for exactly?" she asked, laughing and then swatting his shoulder as if he'd just said something deliciously scandalous.

"I'm going to pretend to go to the restroom. Take the opportunity to look around. Catch his eye. Linger only a moment too long. And don't think I'll stop watching you for a second this time." Michael ran his finger down the vee of her bodice, stroking between her breasts, then he moved away.

Once out of the doorway, he quickly headed down the hall, turned the corner, and waited in the shadows at the opposite end of the room.

Vienna moved slowly through the crowd as if she were people-watching. Michael sucked in a quick breath as Pierce

Mackey started toward her. And when Vienna finally looked up at him, the man was already staring her in the face.

She gave him the extra moment Michael had asked for, and in fact, gave him longer than he would have liked. Michael studied his family's nemesis; he probably wasn't at all what she'd been expecting. Pierce looked boyish, underdressed for the occasion. He always had; he thought it projected a higher magnitude of his power, sending the message that his wealth gave him the right to do as he pleased, etiquette be damned.

Pierce threaded his way through the crowd until he was standing right before her. Michael's hand clawed into the plaster wall as the man boldly stared down Vienna's décolleté, then looked up at her and smiled his approval.

She raised her eyebrow just slightly, parting her lips in a bit of surprise, projecting a subtle attraction. She was perfect. Too perfect. Michael couldn't stand the sight of Pierce looking like he was ready to eat her alive—and Vienna being forced to look like she just might want him to.

He headed back around and swooped in from the side to pull Vienna away, looking over his shoulder at Pierce who smiled and raised his champagne glass in cocky salute.

The look of him, the taunting look of him . . . it ignited Michael's anger as nothing else could.

"She wants to fuck me later," Pierce mouthed.

"Is everything all right?" Vienna asked.

"You were perfect," Michael said, shaking her a little. "Press your palm against my chest like you're trying to put some space between us."

Vienna complied and Michael bent down and took her in a brutal kiss. On display for just one other man, Michael swept his tongue into Vienna's mouth, savoring the heat and the sound of her gasp.

Then, tearing his lips from hers, he nuzzled her ear, and whispered, "Flick a last glance in his direction."

She did so, and Michael pulled her out of the room, mouthing to Pierce behind him, "She wants to fuck me *now*."

He passed several smaller drawing rooms before he found one unused, small and dim. Leaving the door cracked open, he drew Vienna in behind him, pulling her against his body as he leaned against the far wall.

Vienna drew in a sharp breath as he pushed the supple fabric of her long skirt away from her legs and ripped her panties off, throwing the lace to the ground. His mouth came down on hers once more and she answered his kiss with an almost violent intensity that sent him burning even hotter than before.

He slid his hands around to run his fingers along the crease of her ass, the laughter and movement of partygoers walking by the door blurring as his mind and body focused in on her and only her. Her taut body pressing against his, his fingers stroking between her legs, the urge he had to forget this was a mission and just take her for the sake of pleasure alone . . .

"Someone will walk in," Vienna gasped as Michael pushed one strap of the gown off her shoulder. He drew his mouth down her burning skin to run his tongue between her breasts.

"Someone might *see*," he murmured, hitching one of her legs up to him at the knee, white satin spilling behind her as he drew up the front hem of her dress. "No one will walk in."

The possibility of discovery spurred them on, and when Vienna ran her palm down his body, tracing her fingers over the shape of his cock pressing hard against the front of his trousers, he didn't tell her to stop. He didn't tell her that it wasn't necessary, that this was just part of the game, that he'd let her fake it if she wanted to.

She unzipped his trousers. Michael slammed his head back against the wall, reeling with anticipation and found Pierce Mackey watching them through the slight opening of the doorway.

Michael pressed a kiss down on Vienna's shoulder, biting down slightly until he felt her shiver, then managed a slight "fuck you" smile for his rival as her hand wrapped around him. Her eyes closed, completely unaware of Pierce's presence, she brushed her thumb over the head of his cock, leaving a slight damp on his skin.

He couldn't take it any longer. Moving his hands under her smooth, tight ass, he lifted her up. She swept back the folds of her dress, letting it flow behind her like molten angel wings, exposing her delicate cunt, and moved the head of his cock across her wet center.

A sweet moan escaped from her lips. Pressing just the tip of him inside her, Michael felt a wave of lust slam straight into him. And in the second before he surrendered to the sensation completely, he could feel himself pulse against her, like the most intimate heartbeat.

Suddenly insane with want, he braced himself against the wall and let Vienna's body go just slightly. She slid down on him, tight and fast, made slick with desire, tossing her head back.

She crossed her ankles behind him, the sharp point of one of her stilettos striking the wall as he pumped her body over and down his own.

One hand around his back, the other holding her dress away, Vienna boldly revealed everything; the place where their bodies joined, the raw thrust of his cock.

The desire inside of him built, first like a dull roar, then like a blinding force that seemed to swamp all his senses. The smoothness of the fabric, the hotness of her skin, the perfume at her neck, the laughter just over the threshold . . .

She moaned, her eyes closed, lips parted, jeweled clips falling to the ground as her hair spilled down. Michael buried his face into the curve of her neck, and when she arched her back and cried out through parted lips, he came hard inside her.

When he finally opened his eyes and recovered enough to lower her gently to the floor, Michael realized that somewhere along the line, he'd stopped watching the door. He'd stopped thinking about throwing Vienna in his rival's face.

He'd forgotten about Pierce Mackey entirely.

Four

Vienna couldn't stop thinking about that night. What he asked her to do, how she'd done it . . . Pierce Mackey's face, Michael's reaction . . .

God, his *reaction*. She'd never been taken like that. Wanted like that. Every time she thought about it she sucked in a breath and felt herself go wet.

But the end, the end of the evening was strange. They'd left immediately, Michael suddenly moody and distracted. And when they were finally back in the limousine and he'd blindfolded her for the return trip, she could tell by the change in the pressure around the seat that he'd scooted far to one side.

For a moment, she'd forgotten what this was really all about. Hell, she'd forgotten about her plans to escape. All Vienna could think about for the entire ride was the tension in the few feet between her and Michael—and that it was a waste of a perfectly good limousine.

But she remembered now. She remembered that she'd tried to escape and he'd stopped her.

The sooner she got herself away from Michael Kingston's control, the sooner she'd be able to get away. Which meant that the sooner she could convince Michael to let her go after Pierce Mackey, the better.

When Michael knocked on her door a few days later, she let him have it and told him she didn't need any more training. That if her weaknesses had to do with makeup application, wardrobe selection, and table manners, it was a pretty sorry reason not to get on with things. He knew firsthand how well she'd be able to wield sex as a weapon.

He had the nerve to say that he hadn't seen her shoot yet.

Michael called her to the shooting barn as he had done before for everything—when none of the training teams were around, when they'd be completely alone. It was a long building, filled with side-by-side target booths, its utilitarian nature far removed from the glamour of the theater.

She'd been supplied with a training code and told to select something to wear from the costume room. She was supposed to dress for Pierce Mackey. She found herself dressing for Michael Kingston and picked a strapless leather minidress accessorized with just a pair of thigh-high stiletto boots and a tiny black lace thong.

After making her way across the compound ground, Vienna typed her training code into the keypad by the door and pushed her way into the shooting barn. Pausing a moment to register the total silence of the place, she punched in the code once more at the vending machine. A few seconds passed, then she heard a whirring sound, a click, and then the thump of something heavy sliding down into the retrieval door.

Vienna pulled the weapon out of the slot; it was the first weapon she'd held in over a year. And though it wasn't loaded, the sense of control she felt while holding it was a welcome change from the servant role she'd had to play both for the prison officials and for the Kingstons. If only this thing had ammo . . .

"Over here."

Bobbling the weapon like an amateur, she turned and found Michael leaning on the side of the vending machine with his arms crossed over his chest, a blank expression on his face.

He walked off without commenting on her appearance which riled Vienna more than she would have expected. There was nothing to do but follow him alongside the booths toward the far end of the darkened building.

He chose the last booth, unlocked an ammunition crate, and handed her a box of bullets and a pair of protective glasses.

With the weighty silence still between them, Vienna loaded her weapon and flipped the safety. Testing the heft of the weapon and lining up her body with it a few times, she looked over at Michael for the okay and then just started blasting away.

Bull's-eye. Bull's-eye. Bull's-eye. Too easy. How about a cluster on the left 40. Now on the right 30. Adrenaline surged through her body as the bullet casings showered down around their feet. *You have no idea what I'm capable of Michael Kingston. No idea.*

Already out of ammunition, Vienna lowered the weapon and pushed the recovery button, sending the target paper flying back in at top speed. She handed the paper to Michael; there was no disputing she was a brilliant shot.

His expression never wavered. He seemed totally unimpressed. Vienna frowned as he put the paper down and handed her another box of ammunition. "Do it again."

She loaded up, momentarily distracted by the heat of his breath on the back of her neck as he crowded her from behind.

So he was testing her. No problem. Smiling to herself, Vienna repositioned her body, legs braced wide, upper body set to cause as little strain as possible. She squeezed the trigger.

Michael's hand came down hard on the barrel of her weapon. She nearly dropped it, and an arc of bullet holes missed the target completely, instead cutting through the white edge of the paper as they sprayed out of control all over the far back of the booth. "What the hell?" she blurted out.

"You're pretty pleased with yourself."

Vienna looked over her shoulder at Michael, a self-satisfied smile on her face. "I'm hitting all the damn targets. Yeah, I'm pleased."

He pushed the recovery button this time and reeled in the messed-up target, then ripped the hole-ridden paper from the clasp and slammed it down on the counter. "It's not just about hitting all the damn targets. Anybody can do that just standing there with no provocation, no sound, no sight distraction."

She studied his face. He was spoiling for a fight and wanted to argue with her. But, why? "What's wrong?"

"You're operating in a vacuum. Shoot like you'd have to do it in the real world."

"No, I mean, what's wrong with *you*?"

His face softened. Clearly maintaining the blank, emotionless face he'd walked in with was a bit of a struggle. *Oh, Michael. I'm getting to you. I'm actually getting to you.* She should have been silently reveling in this triumph as it could only aid in her escape. But Vienna couldn't help but remember how his indifference toward her pricked so badly when he appeared to take no notice of the sexy outfit she'd put together for him.

"Why *does* the fact that I'm succeeding in your training program bother you so much?" she asked gently.

"It doesn't bother me," Michael said tightly. "Except that you think you've already got it conquered when we've hardly even begun."

Vienna shrugged. "It's too easy."

"Make it harder on yourself, then."

"You make it harder," she said, raising her palms up in surrender. "You're the trainer."

He folded his arms across his chest, cursing under his breath. Then he suddenly went to the far wall, took out a key and opened the control box, then pressed the lever down. The lights went out, a drone sound escaping as the power went out. Vienna watched as ceiling-mounted cameras blinked, flatlined a blue streak, and went out.

"Turn around and shoot," he said, behind her once more. A simple phrase, but the look in his eyes: complicated.

Slowly, she slipped the protective glasses off and tossed them into the corner of the cramped space. Then she took the completed target paper and crumpled it in her hands.

Then, she waited.

Michael was silent for a long time. At last he reached over and reloaded the weapon. He pointed it straight at her, then used the muzzle of the gun to sweep a fallen lock of hair back behind her ear.

Vienna's heart pounded as the metal grazed her temple, but the dangerous look in Michael's eyes didn't yield that kind of threat.

"Take your weapon back and approach the counter," he ordered, his voice dripping with suggestion. A delicious little shiver went down Vienna's spine as she did as he demanded.

"Now, concentrate, Vienna. What if there was someone up in your business while you were trying to make a hit?" Michael asked. He moved in from behind, so close she could feel the heat of his body all around her.

She made a perfect shot.

He put his mouth up to her ear, running the tip of his tongue around her earring. "It's night," he murmured.

"I guessed that," she said harshly, refusing to give in so easily.

"Brace your legs, hold your arms up straight, and shoot," he ordered.

You're going to have to make it harder than that. Deliberately trying to mess with him as much as he was messing with her, she ran her tongue slowly over the cupid's bow of her lip, then turned to the target and very systematically began shooting off rounds, every bit as accurate as before.

"It's night, the target is dim, and there's distraction every-where. It's hard to get off a shot."

She pulled off a round and hit the target. "Not that hard."

Michael slid his hand over her bare thigh, setting fire to her skin in the space between her boots and dress. But he didn't stop there. His fingers moved around to the front and up her body, grazing the edge of her lace thong.

Vienna closed her eyes for a moment, swallowing hard. Her finger hesitated on the trigger. "Take the shot, Vienna," Michael said, the strain in his voice telling her he wasn't immune to all this.

Steadying herself, she took the shot, hitting the target once more. Michael was hard and wanting against the back of her skirt. Vienna could feel his cock pulsing, and she couldn't help arching her body slightly to press back against him.

He sucked in a quick breath.

Goad him on. Break him. Make him want you.

Staring straight at the bull's-eye, she purred, "You didn't like it, did you?"

"Like what?"

"You hated the idea of me with Pierce. It made you feel . . . jealous."

He didn't answer her, tantalizing her instead with the slow, rhythmic pressing and sliding of his pelvis up against her ass. For a moment, the shushing of crumpling leather was the only sound between them.

"Focus on the target," he finally whispered into her ear, biting softly on her earlobe. "Part of your brain is somewhere else. What if you've been drinking, wined and dined; your lover is in the room—perhaps he's sliding his finger inside of you . . ." His fingers moved across the small triangle of lace between her legs. ". . . And you've still got to make the shot."

"You mean my lover *Pierce*, for example?" she asked, her voice coming out in between two gasps.

Michael put his hand on Vienna's back and pushed her down hard, bending her over the shooting counter. She nearly dropped the weapon as his fingers moved under the thin string of her thong and slipped inside her.

Closing her eyes, she cried out in sheer ecstasy as he stroked through the wet.

"Pierce, *for example*," he spat out. "Let's say he is distracting you from a shot. He wants you. You are a very beautiful girl; perhaps he can't wait."

Her legs trembled, and Vienna spread them wider, wanting to feel him press up against her, inside her. He'd backed off and just the sense of him so close behind her remained.

"Take the shot, Vienna," Michael said, moving two fingers slowly inside and out of her body.

Suddenly, he pulled them away; Vienna gasped in dismay before she could stop herself. But his hands moved up to her back, unlacing the back of her dress just enough to let him slip his hands inside and cup her breasts.

"You're not paying attention," he said, his voice strained and demanding. "Take the shot."

"You know I'll make it," she said, pressing back and grinding against him.

Michael's groan elevated her own excitement even higher. "Make it harder," she said, breathy with desire. "Make it harder."

The sound of his zipper, the feel of his knuckles on the round of her ass as he moved his hand down on himself . . . suddenly Vienna felt like she could barely breathe much less make a shot.

An errant bullet pinged off the metal lining the seams of the booth. Vienna swore, tried again, and this time hit the target, a rivulet of sweat trickling down between her shoulder blades as Michael worked her nipples with his free hand.

Vienna lowered her weapon; she had to squeeze her eyes shut hard then open them wide to achieve any semblance of focus.

"Keep shooting, Vienna. Keep the pace."

She raised the weapon again and started shooting, but he'd nearly won the game. A kind of desire she'd never met before had her and good; she wanted to feel what he made her feel more than she wanted to prove herself on the range.

He's working you over. It's just a game. He'll stop any moment now . . .

Please, please, don't stop.

She pulled the trigger over and over, the target swimming before her eyes. Against the inconsistent staccato of her gunfire, she heard the dull thud of Michael's belt hitting the ground. A moment later she felt him skin-on-skin as he gently spread her legs even wider and rested the head of his cock against her asshole.

Her shooting went all over the place.

Do it, Michael.

She arched her back; Michael's hands came up around her, sliding down her bare arms, his fingers curling over hers around the weapon.

"No, no, Vienna. Don't lose your form. Arms up . . . and legs wide," he whispered.

She widened her stance, running her tongue over her trembling lips.

"Make everything around you nothing but white noise or you *will* miss your shot."

He ran his hand up the inside of her leg. Her form slipped again as he ran his index finger in a circle over the delicate ring of her asshole and shifted his cock to the slick, wet of her cunt underneath.

She felt the head press just barely inside her. Skin on fire, mouth going numb, head spinning with want, Vienna gasped and let herself give in a little to desire.

"Eyes on the prize," Michael murmured into her ear. "Give everything a rhythm or make it all white, make it blank."

Doing her best to focus on the target as he slid all the way inside, Vienna allowed herself the luxury of closing her eyes for just a moment. Pure, delicious sensation rocked her body. Clenching every muscle she had to try and still herself enough to make a shot made Michael groan with ecstasy when her body closed in even tighter around him.

And as he worked in and out of her body, she pressed the trigger hard until the ammo ran out, then just let the weapon fall over the side of the counter. It clattered to the ground, metal on pavement echoing around them with Vienna thrusting back to meet his movement with her own.

Michael pressed his hot mouth against her neck then moved her fingers to join his cock, bringing her to the point where white, blank focus was out of the question.

In an electric haze of lust, Vienna arched her back, crying out as she came hard. Michael followed her lead, emptying himself inside of her. She could have sworn she heard him say her name on a whisper but maybe she just wanted to believe this all meant something more than the mere physical act between them.

He held her for a moment longer, the heaviness of his body

strangely wonderful, then he pulled away, too soon for Vienna's taste, and quickly set himself straight.

Vienna stood upright, looked at the target sprayed liberally with stray bulletholes, and had to smile, though Michael was already all business again.

"We're going out tomorrow night," Michael said very suddenly.

Pulling her dress back into position, she looked over her shoulder. "Really?"

He ran his sleeve over his sweat-streaked forehead. "Yes. Don't you want to get out of here for a little while?"

"Of course," she said, a little startled by his wording. Did he mean something not on the job?

"Good," he said, and she thought she could detect a smile in his voice. Without another word, Michael grabbed his belt and left the target booth, his footsteps growing faint as he walked back down the length of the building.

Vienna turned back to the target, her breathing still a bit labored. She ran her hands down the front of her leather dress to smooth it out, tossed the lace thong in the trash along with the spent bullet casings and headed out.

Maybe she shouldn't give in to him. Maybe she was supposed to be making all of this harder. Supposed to. The *supposed to* in all of this was that she wasn't supposed to like it this much.

It *or* him.

∾

Michael was reeling. He didn't walk back to the mansion so much as stumble his way back. Where had the damn line gone? The one he wasn't supposed to cross. Where was the line? Had he gone too far with Vienna? Was she just a better actress than he'd given her credit for?

This wasn't what he wanted, these emotions. Not at all.

There was something else at work here, something he had to stop denying before he made a mess of the mission and a mess of himself. What was responsible for the chemistry between two people? Chemistry was a separate component from lust. A much rarer thing. Lust was easy to conjure up between two attractive people. Chemistry was an issue of personality. Of connection.

Vienna's looks would have fired up any man, but that spark inside of her . . . some sort of strange chemistry drew him to her, made him want to make love to her, hold her . . . be around her. *Remember . . . she's just part of the job. She's an accessory of the mission.* God, what he would give to take her out one evening and have it just be for the two of them, with nothing to do with ulterior motives and pretense.

The last thing he wanted to do right now was turn her over to the arms of Pierce Mackey.

"Michael!"

Michael stood fast in the middle of the hallway, just past the open doorway to Devlin's office.

Michael knew exactly what he must look like. And he knew exactly what scent lingered around him. He knew he should keep going, head straight for his rooms and clean himself up before Devlin had any clue what was happening.

Instead, he made a choice. He turned and walked into Devlin's office and presented himself in all of his freshly sexed-up glory, spoiling for a fight.

His brother stood with a highball glass in his hand, plenty full. "There are only two kinds of mistakes in life a man can make."

Michael combed his fingers through his messed up hair. "I haven't forgotten."

"Maybe it bears repeating. One involves money. The other, women. You know the requirements of this job. You identify what they want, what they need, and you use it to shape them, to train them. Don't forget your purpose here. You train them, and then you let go."

"I realize that, Dev. I'm thinking about that all the time."

"Are you?" Devlin asked coldly. "I suppose it's helpful to have complete confidence that she's willing to fuck on demand."

"God," Michael said, bewildered, disgusted by his brother.

Devlin narrowed his eyes. "Don't you dare look at me like that."

"I think you owe me an apology," Michael said.

"What?" Devlin looked pissed, but he couldn't have been more pissed than Michael.

"What's happened to you, Dev?"

"You know exactly what happened to me," he said. "You were there."

Michael rubbed his eyes and forced himself to de-escalate the situation. "Are we going to let Pierce win? He sets us against each other, he wins."

"He's not going to win," Devlin said through his teeth, his knuckles white around the crystal.

"Listen, we're in this together. I want revenge as much as you do. So point your anger outside this compound, not inside."

Devlin suddenly seemed to deflate. He downed the rest of his drink and crossed the room to pour himself another one. God only knew how many he'd had that day.

Michael took a good, long look at his brother. Finally, he shook his head a little. "I don't think I've been able to see it until now. I must have been too close."

Devlin took a swig of liquor. "See what?"

"Just how much this has destroyed you. If I think back . . . you were a completely different person."

He took a drink and looked at Michael. "I'm sorry if you feel I'm taking this out on you."

"You want to take it out on me. That's how it's been. And I've let you do it because I still feel guilty. And the thing is, you *want* me to feel guilty."

"You don't want to go there," Devlin warned.

"Actually I do want to go there."

"I don't blame you."

"Yes, you do. And you make sure that it's always between us. You seem intent on making me pay for what happened for the rest of my life . . ." Michael's voice cracked, but he went on. "I admit that I shot Julia. But, god, Dev, you know that was an accident. How many times do I have to say it? You were there. I was grappling with Pierce and it went off. I was trying to stop you two from killing each other."

"I don't need to relive it, thanks very much," Devlin said.

"I've always been on your side. I've always been loyal to you. I deserve better than to have you hold this over my head for the rest of my life. Just remember that it was Julia and Pierce who were disloyal to you, who were disloyal to our family. I may have pulled the trigger, but by rights Julia should have already been dead to you."

Devlin winced, but Michael held his ground. After a weighty silence Devlin finally said, "I want to let you off the hook, Mick. I swear I do. But I just can't get past it until this thing is done. And that brings us back to Vienna. You're going to have to give her to him eventually."

Michael looked away.

"Better do it before you get too attached. Get her out on the mission and then maybe we can get on with the rest of our lives."

Devlin left the room without waiting for an answer and

Michael just stood there staring at the crystal decanter still open on the bar. Deep inside, maybe his brother wasn't that much different than he was—they just expressed it differently.

You both want too much. You both care too much. And in the end, the woman will make love to the man only to turn around and betray his trust. On call. On request. Just like you tell her to. Just like Julia.

Five

O pening night at the theater was always a major event on the Center City social calendar. Pierce would be there. Which meant that Michael and Vienna would be there. They'd rented a box for the night, one close to center for maximum visibility. The objective for the evening: see, be seen, and this time, make contact.

The arrangement was to have Michael fawning over her in the box during the entertainment. It went off without a hitch, Michael touching her, pulling her chair closer to him, kissing her neck. And Vienna was supposed to look like she wasn't quite enjoying it. The irony, of course, was that she was. And when she looked over at Pierce Mackey's box even as Michael pressed his mouth hot against her hair and slipped his hand into her bodice to brush over her nipple, she had to work hard at looking bored. Not easy to do while fantasizing about Michael pulling her onto his lap, moving the folds of her ball gown over his legs and working his cock into her from behind.

Intermission came too soon. Vienna fanned herself with the program, sitting almost chastely by Michael's side while she exchanged glances full of innuendo and curiosity with his nemesis.

She turned and whispered in Michael's ear, "I suppose now is the time?"

He nodded, and Vienna slipped out of the box and into the intermission crowd. She found a spot by the windows overlooking the boulevard below and pressed her cheek against the cool glass.

"What's your name?" a voice said from behind.

She knew who it was. She turned to face Pierce Mackey, the sight of him this close sending a jolt of adrenaline through her system. She smiled. "I'm Vienna."

"Well, Vienna," he said. "What can I do to get you in my box for the second half. Will you join me?"

Vienna blurted out a laugh of disbelief. "Of course not. You know who I'm with. People will see."

He raised an eyebrow. "That's your primary objection? 'People will see'?"

"You know what I mean. I know who you are," she said. "I asked about you after that big fund-raiser."

"I'm flattered."

She leaned back on the window. "Of course, I asked about everyone after that party. This is pretty much new for me."

"You're not from around here," he said, more a question, really.

"I'm not even in the same social strata," Vienna said, tugging awkwardly at the shimmering baby blue fabric of her heavy ballskirt.

Pierce's gaze followed her hand before moving slowly up to her face. "You're very beautiful," he said.

The sadness in his eyes stunned her. If he was thinking what the Kingstons thought, that she was a dead ringer for Julia, then whatever he'd done to take her away from Devlin, perhaps he'd done it for love. Not that it mattered.

He seemed to collect himself, smiling again with a cocky arch in the set of his lips. "Where are you from?"

"Bordertown."

His eyebrow flew up. "Interesting."

"*I* think so. You know it well. So do Michael and his brother."

Pierce studied her face, and she knew he was making his analysis, trying to divine whether she was a plant for some kind of setup or if she were really nothing more than a Kingston prize for the stealing. She watched as his hand went absently up to the sparkling blue ring swinging from the thin chain around his neck.

She turned and stared out the window, knowing her apparent indifference would pique his curiosity that much more.

"How long have you been in Center City?" he asked.

"A month or so."

"What brings you here?"

"Michael," she said, lowering her lashes. "I'm just here with him."

"He's an old friend."

Vienna turned back to him, rolling her eyes. "You're not friends," she said. "I know all about you."

"Then why are you talking to me?" he asked softly.

She raised her chin. "I can talk to anyone I want."

"Michael will be pissed."

"Michael doesn't own me!"

"Ah. Is all not well in paradise? So soon? Did you think you'd hit the jackpot, the poor beautiful girl plucked from the squalor of Bordertown? Except money doesn't buy everything, does it?" He leaned his arm against the glass and moved in close, blowing a breath of hot air slowly into her ear. "I don't keep my leash as tight as the Kingston boys do. Life . . . and love . . . they don't have to be a *prison*, Vienna. You can debate the point with Devlin some time."

Does he know who I really am? Vienna took a step back. "You stole Julia from him. I've heard."

"She came to me," he said, the expression on his face going dark. "And I didn't have to steal her. There are always two sides to any story."

"Tell me, then."

"What?"

"Tell me your side."

He actually looked taken aback at the prospect that she'd be willing to hear him out.

"Michael and Dev. Their parents were like my parents. They adopted me, for all intents and purposes. They took me in. I was a third son, a second brother. We were inseparable. We took over the family business, a slip of a thing, really, when compared to the operations we're both running now. We had these big plans. We dreamed of building something that would make us ridiculously wealthy. But somewhere along the line things changed."

Vienna felt a strange pang of sympathy for Pierce; he was like her in a way, an orphan. They looked at each other in silence and then suddenly Pierce cocked his head. "You're different, aren't you?"

"I don't know what you mean."

"I'd like you to come to my box with me."

She looked nervously over her shoulder, experiencing a small pang when she couldn't find Michael's face. He was watching, though. She was sure of it. "I hardly think that's possible."

"I'm attracted to you, you're attracted to me. I'd like to see you again."

"See me again?" She laughed and shook her head. "I'm with Michael."

Pierce pulled back. "Don't want to take a gamble? Hedge your bets? You think he's a sure thing?"

Vienna looked at him defiantly. "What if I do?"

"Then you'd be wrong. He goes through women like Devlin goes through wine."

The theater bell rang for the next act. He held out his hand, almost gallant in his movement.

"He'll come looking for me," she said, her heart suddenly pounding in her chest.

"And he won't find you." His eyes grew wide, teasing almost, and with a dramatic glance he ducked down and whispered in her ear, "Escape for a moment."

Escape.

Vienna slipped her palm into his and let him steer her away from the crowds in the lobby to an alcove mostly hidden by emerald green velvet drapery where he backed her up against the wall.

Pierce Mackey was a very sexual man. The way he looked at a woman with pure lust in his eyes was almost mesmerizing. Watching him from afar was one thing, being this close something else entirely. She could imagine how Devlin's Julia might have found herself in over her head.

"You think I'm going to let you touch me?" Vienna asked.

"I think you might," he said, slowly pulling at one side of the satin bow that held her bodice together. "Just because I'm an enemy of the Kingston's doesn't necessarily make me a bad guy."

His finger hooked under the loose front of her bodice; Vienna caught his hand in hers. "Doesn't *necessarily*."

"The boys didn't see me as an equal. I had some big ideas; they didn't see what I saw, and it all went downhill from there. The Kingstons, they told me I was like a son to them. They told me I would inherit a share. But they didn't write it down. Michael and Devlin said they didn't want to dilute the shares—they could have given me an equal share. Sounds like they betrayed me, don't you think?"

"So you built a competing business and took Devlin's girl?"

"She chose me," he said, ducking his mouth down towards hers, the implication of a kiss without so much as a touch.

"The way you'd like Michael's girl to choose you?" she murmured, then pulled back sharply as the house lights flickered. "We have to go back. It's starting."

"Let it start," he replied, slipping his hand inside the bodice of her gown to caress her breast, surprisingly gentle as his thumb circled her nipple. Her body reacted to common lust. Part of her didn't care. Michael deserved it. He wanted a good performance; she could make it a great one.

But part of her cared too much. That Michael would let another man, his greatest enemy touch her like this and not be bothered a bit.

"Even if I wanted to, it wouldn't be smart," she said. "Michael cares about me."

"You don't sound convinced of that." Pierce moved his pelvis against the luxurious fabric of her gown and shuddered; she could feel how hard he was as if she'd been wearing nothing at all.

She moaned softly. "I need to go back. He's probably looking for me."

"I'm sure he is," Pierce muttered.

"I can't do this," she said, even as she pressed back against him.

"Tell me you want to," Pierce said.

"It's wrong," she said.

"Tell me you want to," Pierce repeated, something tormented in his voice.

Vienna gasped and threw her head back, closing her eyes as his hot, greedy mouth came down on her neck. "I want to," she whispered, a little terrified that this would escalate to something more right here.

She tried to wrench free from out under him, but he stopped her, his fingers wrapped tight around her wrist. To her surprise he tightened the front of her gown and retied the bow. "I want to see you again," he said.

"I don't know," she said, breathing so hard, her breasts strained the fabric at her bodice.

He held her by both wrists. "Let me treat you as Michael never can and never will."

She craned her neck to look over his shoulder, trying to pull her hands away. "I don't know."

"I have a yacht out at the pier. *The Julia*. Be there tomorrow night, eight o'clock . . . say you will be there."

She stared at him, her heart pounding.

"Say you will be there. It will be your every fantasy. You know you want to."

"I'll be there," she whispered. He let his hand drop away and Vienna dashed out into the empty hall.

Yes, I want to. But not with you.

Michael was standing there, alone, on a bright crimson swath of carpeting. She dashed at him, and blurted out, "I'm so sorry; I'm not feeling well." He kissed her forehead and she just pulled away from him and ran out of the building to wait for the limousine. As she waited outside, her bare shoulders shivering in the cold air, she didn't have to fake her distress.

⁝

Michael watched Vienna just standing at the top of the steps as she waited for the limousine to pull up. Just standing there, not trying to escape, not looking around to gauge their location or gather landmarks. He joined her on the landing and pulled her close. "Did he do something to you? Did he hurt you?"

"He did what you expected him to do. He came on to me," she said blandly.

The limousine pulled up, and Michael helped Vienna inside. Once in, she turned away to the opposite window, her arms hugging her chest.

A hot fury shot through his body. "If he forced himself on you—"

"He didn't have to force himself," she pointed out. "I played it just the way you would have wanted me to."

"Did you . . . ?"

She looked at him like he was insane. "No! Of course not." She added bitterly, "Why go there until I have to?"

"Are you upset because you're being asked to do it, or upset because you like it?" Michael asked.

Vienna turned her face very slowly to his. "Are you upset because I'm turned on by him? Or upset I didn't go further?"

Michael looked out the window, his fists clenching and unclenching as they rested on his thighs. And then he realized that he'd forgotten to blindfold her. He was getting sloppy over her. He glanced at Vienna and saw that she'd just realized the same.

"Go ahead," she said. "I don't care."

Michael pulled the wide black ribbon from a drawer under the bar, scooted over, and tied it carefully over her eyes. He paused for a moment, then found a second ribbon and pulled her hands onto his lap.

Vienna flinched as he began to wind the fabric around her wrists. "Give the training a rest."

"It's not about the damn training!" Michael burst out.

He pushed her gently back down on the long seat, sweeping the fabric of her gown aside to expose her long legs, creamy thighs, and the tease of satin cord around her ankles from her party shoes. Vienna's teeth pulled nervously at her lower lip. "Michael?"

He shushed her and pushed the fabric higher up her thighs, smiling to himself as his fingers ran over the rough lace and clips of her garter belt.

No panties. Just as he preferred. He bent down and ran a finger softly down the center of her cunt. Vienna gasped, her mouth opening in an O.

"Did he turn you on?" Michael asked.

She stiffened. "Is that what this is about? Jealousy."

If he were honest with himself he'd admit that part of him was horribly jealous. And part of him just wanted to please her. He came up over her, leaning his weight on his elbow and whispered in her ear, "This is about . . . you." Vienna arched her back in anticipation. He teased her, moving his hand downward as he caressed her flushed skin before simply trailing his fingertips off her thigh.

"What do you want me to do?" she gasped.

"Come for me," he said urgently.

She parted her legs until she was completely exposed to him, unbelievably wet already. Dizzy with desire, Michael leaned down and ran his tongue along the inside of her leg, from knee to thigh, slowing as he reached her center. He licked her cunt, a slow, languorous movement that had her crying out, arching her back . . . bringing her body even closer to him.

He entered her with his tongue, gently drawing himself in and out. Vienna tossed her head from side-to-side, pulling and twisting her velvet-wrapped wrists in an attempt to free herself that only made them tighter. "Michael, let me—"

"Stop thinking. Just feel."

"Why . . ." She trailed off, her words lost as she sucked in a quick breath.

Michael's heart pounded in his chest as he worked his mouth and tongue against her hot, sweet center.

He lifted one of her legs and let it rest on his shoulder, the satin ankle cords fluttering against the side of his face.

Open even wider for him now, she begged him not to stop. Michael drove her even higher, wanting nothing more than to drive himself into her.

His mind swam with the champagne he'd downed while waiting for her to tantalize Pierce, the thought of her being touched by him, driving him a little mad. He had drunk and drunk, his cock hardening in the shadows of a side room as he thought about where he'd like to touch Vienna, how he'd like to touch her, what it would take to erase those images.

And as he put all of his thwarted passion into bringing her to climax, Vienna cried out in ecstasy, her body rising off the seat.

After a moment, Michael pulled her dress down, released her wrists from their bonds, and lay down alongside her, holding her in his arms until they arrived back at the training compound.

At the gates of the compound, he removed her blindfold. And when the driver opened the door, Michael saw Devlin. *Not now, Dev. Give it a rest.*

"How did it go?" Devlin asked.

"Can't it wait until tomorrow?"

Devlin's eyes narrowed. "No. This is supposed to be about business, Michael."

"I'm fully aware of that," he replied through gritted teeth.

"Are you?"

"I am," Michael said, pushing by his brother and practically leaping up the mansion steps.

And that's exactly why I don't want to talk to you right now.

Six

Vienna entered Devlin Kingston's office in the morning per a hastily scrawled correction to her day's schedule. A secretary ushered her in, announced her, and left. She stared at the back of a large, leather executive chair and waited.

The occupant faced the far end of a 360-degree panoramic window that jutted out from the side of the building. For the first time, she could actually see the big picture of where she was located—that she didn't recognize any landmarks was a different problem.

One arm reached out—black suit, white French cuffs, plain cufflinks, platinum no doubt, the kind of understated ostentation only the truly wealthy would bother wearing. Fingernails buffed, simple signet ring—present and accounted for. And a palm curling in abruptly to beckon her forward.

The chair slowly turned. Devlin Kingston didn't waste any time. "Don't think you're the first. Or that you'll be the last."

"I don't know what you mean," Vienna said.

Devlin pressed his index finger over her lips, signaling her to keep her mouth shut. "He has a soft spot for damsels in distress. It's his biggest weakness."

"I thought you were the one who lost the girl. Why aren't *you* training me to fuck your nemesis?"

Devlin bristled at that.

"You were the one who lost the girl," Vienna repeated harshly.

"Yes, I was," he said, his voice dripping ice. "And it must be the reason that women aren't a weakness of *mine* anymore. Listen to me. Keep your focus on your mission. Just on your mission, or somebody will pay. Somebody always pays."

"What's this about?" Michael asked from behind.

Vienna looked over her shoulder to find him hovering in the doorway. He glanced between the two of them, stepping into the room with a stormy look on his face.

She turned back to Devlin.

He shrugged with an elegant roll of his shoulders. "Leave."

As she left the room, Michael gave her a look that seemed to say, "Don't worry, I'm on your side." Men could say all kinds of things out loud. What they supposedly felt, what they supposedly meant . . . but it was the emotion behind the look and the touch that spoke the truth. She took a last look behind her as Michael prepared for battle with his brother and felt a strange little twinge in her heart. *He cares. But does he care enough?*

❦

Michael waited for the sound of Vienna's heels to fade out before he turned back to his brother. "Well?"

"You know what it's about," Devlin said. "I'm reminding her to retain her objectivity."

"You think she needs a reminder? This is a life-and-death mission."

"Do you think she really understands that?"

"You had no right to interfere. She's my responsibility."

"This is our mission. Or have you forgotten?"

"The mission. The goddamn mission. I'm not you, Devlin. I'm not you, am I? You might have no place for love anymore, but I still do."

"Who said anything about love? You can't be in love with this girl." Devlin looked genuinely horrified.

"I'm not . . . I mean, I feel . . . I . . . there's something about her. It's hard to explain."

"It's not hard to explain." Devlin glowered at his brother. "You're this close to breaking the rule."

"Fuck the damn rule!"

Devlin turned white.

Michael shook his fists. "There is a happy medium out there somewhere."

"That's what I would have said a long time ago, before any of this happened. But women come and go, and we've always said blood was thicker. It's what got us in this mess in the first place, and it's what will get us out." Devlin rose from his desk and moved to the bar where an open bottle of champagne sat on melting ice.

Michael watched Devlin pour himself another glass. "I don't know which brother I like better," he whispered, surprised at the menace in his own voice. "The one who has feelings and who scares *you* or the one who has *no* feelings and scares *me*. Dev, you've got to let all this anger go."

Devlin laughed darkly.

"What's so funny?" Michael asked.

No answer at first. His brother guzzled more champagne, some of it slipping down his neck, soaking into an otherwise perfectly crisp collar. "He's winning again. It took only one beautiful woman to break apart three lifelong friends. And it will take only one to drive a dagger between the remaining two." Devlin's lips twisted. "We had an understanding. A rule. Never let a woman cloud your judgment and come between us. We were going to get revenge. We were going to show him up." He put down his champagne flute and took Michael by the shoulders. "I want revenge, Michael. Don't mess it up by falling for that girl. You've got to be willing to lose her completely."

It's too late. I've already fallen for her. "I can work it out."

"There isn't anything to work out. Give Vienna to Pierce and let her do the job we bought her for. Otherwise, Pierce wins."

Michael paled. "Devlin, the mission is still on. It's just that—"

Devlin put up his palm and shook his head. Grasping the crystal in one hand and the nearly empty bottle in the other, he walked out of his office.

Devlin was a strong man, a strong-minded one at that. But as Michael came to the door and watched him staggering half-drunk down the Persian hall runner, it would have been obvious to anyone that while Julia was long gone, the heart she'd broken still lay in pieces all over the mansion.

As far as Michael was concerned, Pierce already *had* won, several times over. Devlin's obsession and Michael's guilt were victory in and of itself.

Seven

Pierce Mackey's bodyguards spent a long time searching Vienna's high-end shopping bag and evening purse. But even if they'd missed something, there was nothing special about her lipstick, mints, cash, and keys. And certainly nothing they could object to about the brand-new lingerie. They'd finally escorted her up the ramp to the yacht and down into his personal quarters below.

Pierce's yacht was textbook. All glossy wood paneling and crystal decanters. Large enough to impress and small enough to create the illusion of intimacy in spite of the armed bodyguards on the deck above.

Her time with Michael out on the party circuit had done her some good, actually; the trappings of wealth didn't seem so foreign and any discomfort she might reveal could be attributed to guilt over cheating on the guy who'd given her so much.

Pierce Mackey was undeniably a good-looking man, but in Vienna's opinion he lacked something the Kingston brothers possessed—flair. His choices for the game of seduction revealed a lack of originality that made the arrangement seem even more like a job and less like a date.

Red roses. Champagne. A small, slim black velvet box and a larger gold one with a white satin ribbon. Pierce wore loose linen pants and a white shirt open at the collar with the sleeves rolled up, every bit the man of leisure. "Welcome, Vienna," he said standing up to take her hand and help her across the unsteady floor. She took in the size of his living quarters, dominated by an enormous bed and lit by the moon coming through a wide glass window covering most of one side of the room. He kissed her softly on the lips and then more deeply, his tongue sweeping inside her mouth.

When he pulled away, Vienna released a breathy sigh, about two shades more lustful-sounding than she was actually feeling. *Get with it, Vienna. Don't give yourself away.* She was hoping she'd be able to enjoy what she could of the experience, but it had become obvious to her over the course of her training that whatever had made her capable of seducing Michael in their first moments together, it wasn't solely about the end goal of escape. Whatever she was, whatever she'd done with Michael, it was because of Michael himself.

With something akin to growing horror, she realized that whatever fantasy she'd have to conjure up to get through a night with Pierce, it would be Michael on her mind. This would take "faking it" to the level of an art form.

Pierce didn't seem to notice anything amiss. He brought her to his bed, piled high with soft, luxurious pillows, and pressed her gently back on it. "I've asked my men to take us out immediately."

As Vienna listened to the thumping and scraping of rope and anchor being brought on board, it occurred to her that while she'd been counting on an opportunity to escape during this mission, she'd actually walked herself into something more like a trap. A yacht in the middle of the ocean didn't exactly provide one with the easiest route to freedom.

"You seem nervous," he said softly. "Maybe a glass of champagne would help?"

"I'd love one."

He pulled one of two champagne bottles from a silver ice bucket and started on the cork, his eyes focused more on her than on the bottle.

"If you don't stop staring at me, you're going to catch one in the eye," she said with a smirk.

He just smiled, popped the cork with expert finesse and poured out two glasses. Vienna tapped the rim of his champagne flute with hers and took a sip. Then, with the taste of the sparkling wine still on her lips, she kissed him. He slid his mouth from her lips to her neck and as she tilted her head back even more, Pierce grabbed the bottle of champagne and splashed the bubbly over her skin.

Vienna gasped, moaning as he put their flutes away and focused on her body, running his tongue over her wet neck and cleavage. "The Kingstons have good taste," he murmured, his touch becoming more heated, frenzied, his cock hard against her thigh.

The thin wet fabric of her dress pressed against her body, translucent and teasing. She felt Pierce's hand move between their bodies as he loosened the drawstrings on his pants. "Wait," she said.

"Why?"

"Because I brought something to wear for you."

"I can come more than once," he said, his hands pulling at the tiny side string of her panties. "And so can you."

"I thought you said this was my fantasy," she said with a seductive smile. "I want to wear it for you."

He stilled and sat back, the muscled planes of his abdomen taut, his body more than ready to go. He ran his hand under her chin and said, "Then go. It must be a damn hot outfit."

She pressed her mouth to his chest, moving down toward his cock, then pulled away despite his groan of protest and took her shopping bag into the bathroom.

After closing the door, Vienna just sat down on the toilet seat and put her head in her hands. *Dammit*. The Kingstons wanted the ring, and, more important, they wanted Pierce to feel the sting of betrayal at the hands of a woman. But Michael and Devlin had read him wrong. Pierce Mackey had no intention of even pretending he wanted a relationship; all he wanted was to fuck Michael's girl a couple of times. How was she supposed to even try and engage his emotions when he was already trying to have sex with her before they were even out of the marina?

They'd read their old pal wrong. Pushing her quickly into his arms, creating an opportunity for seduction wasn't the way to Pierce's heart. How ironic—the guy probably did love Julia, after all.

Vienna looked up at the door. If she actually had sex with him tonight, there was no way Pierce didn't win in this scenario. The best she could hope for was getting the ring away from him without having to give him her body.

Vienna looked over at her reflection in the mirror. *Oh, Michael. If only you'd told me you wouldn't let me do this. That you wanted to be with me.*

Quickly stripping off her champagne-soaked clothes, she tried to push him away from her thoughts. But every strap she smoothed flat on her shoulder, each stocking she rolled up, every ribbon she tied made her think of the look she would have seen in Michael's eyes if she had been dressing for him.

Fully decked out in an outfit that would have made a perfect illustration for Seduction 101, Vienna turned her attention back to the job at hand. *Here goes nothing*. She crouched down and carefully opened the cabinet doors under the sink. She'd better hope the Kingstons had paid off the right people. Sponges, brushes, cleaning powder . . . and a box of tissue.

She pulled out the box, noting with relief that it was abnormally heavy. Lifting a wad of tissue off the top, she found it, as promised. The gun. Use as needed.

"Vienna?"

Vienna froze, adrenaline pumping through her veins. "Almost ready!" She quickly pulled the plastic from around the gun, checked that it was loaded, and then tucked it into the folds of her discarded dress.

She threw the door open and struck a bombshell pose in the doorway. "I feel more like myself now," she purred.

Pierce dropped to his knees on the bed with dramatic flair. "You slay me."

"Just wait." She dropped the carefully wrapped bundle of clothes on the bedside table and was just barely on the bed before he came up over her and pushed her down underneath him.

He pulled deftly at the laces on the front of her glittering white bustier until the silk ribbon came out in his hand. Vienna pulled his mouth to her breast and as he ran circles with his tongue around her nipple, the ring swung out from the chain around his neck. Vienna realized with horror that he'd switched chains, this one shorter and heavier.

She ran her hands up into his hair—and then down behind his neck where she could feel the clasp. As he kissed her, she moaned softly, still trying to process the fact that this was a much more complex chain. And in fact, she could feel with her fingers that this one had an actual lock. One that required a key.

"What do you like?" he whispered in her ear.

"I like to be on top," she said, pushing herself out from under him and playfully rolling on top.

Pierce smiled. "Nice." He reached out to touch her between her legs.

"Nice," Vienna repeated. Then she hauled back and punched him hard in the face.

Pierce's arm flailed out and hit the wall with a sickening thud. Vienna froze. With her arm still raised, she looked over her shoulder at the door. The light under the door flickered.

Vienna lowered her arm. "Oh, yeah," she said loudly, then fake giggled, and added an ecstatic moan for extra credit. The light changed again and the footsteps faded away.

Pierce lay sprawled out underneath her. She looked wildly around, but there was no key within sight. Not that she would have expected to find one. Instead, she pulled the jeweled pin from her updo, letting her hair fall to her shoulders. Jamming it all behind her ears, Vienna went to work on the padlock. *Maybe we should have had less sex and more McGyver training. I'm not a damn locksmith.*

Vienna wiggled the pin in the lock, her skill becoming even less precise as panic set in. A light sheen of sweat matted the lingerie to her back. No go. *Shit!* She wiggled it more frantically. Pierce stirred, reminding her to make some more orgasmic moans and groans for the benefit of the guards. Only a matter of time before they noticed their boss wasn't moaning and groaning back.

The hairpin snapped off in her hand. Vienna tossed it aside and looked around the room for inspiration, nearly losing it when one of the guards knocked on the door.

"Boss? Sorry to bug you. You missed your check-in."

He missed his check in? Since when do you check in with your bodyguard during a seduction? Vienna managed another boisterous giggle, then said, "He's a little occupied right now, but I can remove the gag if you really want to talk to him."

There was a moment's hesitation. "Uh, yeah. Remove it."

Fuck. He wasn't supposed to say *yes*. Who bugged someone in the middle of bondage sex?

Unless he knew all along.

"Okay, give me a second," she said in her huffiest voice. A little desperate now, she reached behind her and pulled the gun from her clothing, pressing the muzzle up to the lock on the chain. There wasn't enough slack to guarantee she wouldn't blow his head off trying to break the links. *Shit, shit, shit.*

You really going to add murder to your rap sheet, Vienna?

She cocked the trigger, her breath coming out in fits and starts.

Pierce's eyes flew open.

Vienna screamed, igniting a stampede on the other side of the door.

She stuck the muzzle up to his temple. "Tell them everything's fine, or I'll blow your head off. I have nothing to lose."

"Everything's fine!" he yelled and then had the audacity to smile. "I was hoping to fuck you before it came to something like this. That would have really pissed Michael off."

Vienna froze at his feet, using her peripheral vision to scan her exit choices.

"Open the boxes."

She frowned in confusion. "What?"

"The presents," Pierce said. "Open the presents."

Never taking her eyes off him, she leaned over to the table and pulled down the little velvet black box and the larger white one, tossing them at him. "You open them."

Pierce shrugged. He opened the boxes and turned them so she could see inside.

They were empty. "I knew. I was just having a little fun with you. Unfortunately for both of us, the gig's up. But I'm a sporting kind of guy. Did Michael and Devlin tell you that? So, here's what I'm going to do. I'm going to unlock the chain and just give you the ring. Just hand it to you. What do you think about that?"

Vienna's mouth felt like sandpaper. She adjusted her body to put more distance between them, the gun still pointed at his head. "I think there's a catch."

Pierce shrugged, then rolled over on his side and rested his head in one hand. "Well, yeah. There's always a catch. Because I'm going to give it to you, and then I'm going to alert my bodyguards who will go about trying to kill you. And you're going to try and get out of this mess alive."

"You give me the ring and I end up at the bottom of the ocean, that's not a really great place to store your investments," Vienna pointed out. "And you can't go around taunting Devlin and Michael with it."

"You don't understand, do you? I don't care about owning the ring. I can buy all the rings I want. I care about them *not* owning the ring. The bottom of the ocean works by me. I still win." A wide smile spread across his face.

Vienna judged the distance between her hand and her weapon and the bodyguards outside the room. "If you're serious about giving the ring to me, let's have it," she said, switching her gun to her left hand. With it trained on him the entire time, Pierce slowly reached into his pocket and pulled out a key. He twisted the chain and with a flick of the wrist, undid the lock, the chain slithering to the ground as he caught the ring in the palm of his hand.

He held it out in a closed fist, pointing down. "Here. I give it to you, and you leave."

The two of them stood there looking at each other.

"I was wrong about you," Vienna whispered. "You do have an ounce of originality in you. If only an ounce."

Pierce's eyebrow arched up.

She licked her lips, her glance jumping between his eyes and his outstretched hand.

"Ready?"

"Yes."

"Oh, and be sure to tell the boys that the game is still on. Here we go. Three." Pierce turned his fist over.

"Two." Pierce opened his palm; the ring lay there, gleaming.

"One. Guards!"

Vienna grabbed the ring with her right hand, and with her left, she blasted as many rounds as she could get out into the horizontal glass window, leaping at it even as the large pane cracked.

Shattered glass and sea water rained down on her as she smashed through it, and fell, limbs akimbo into the ocean, her hands still gripping both the ring and the gun.

She pushed up through the water and broke to the surface, locking her sights on the lighthouse where she was supposed to head for her rendezvous once the job was done. Freestyling as fast as she could, the beacon of light was welcome navigation. Unfortunately, it also made the guards' job easier.

The bullets came zinging all around her almost immediately. Sputtering and splashing as she treaded water, she heard the sound of someone diving into the water behind her.

Vienna took a huge gulp of air and dived down, more bullets jetting through the water on all sides of her, white bubbling lines coming off the wake.

She finally thought to let go of her own waterlogged gun, and let it drift away behind her as she swam as fast as she could.

The light beacon formed a wide swath in the water; Vienna veered out of the triangle of light and headed for the surface, so low on air that she was blowing the last out of her lungs in a mass of bubbles as she hit the surface.

She heard voices, took another huge gulp of air and dived down, staying in the dark patch and using the edge of the light on her right side as a guide.

The depth-charge sound of a different sort of gun—bigger, louder—echoed above her in the water.

Lungs burning, eyes stinging, Vienna swam for her life. And just when she thought she was safe, a hand came through the water and wrapped around her arm. She struggled against it, but couldn't stay down any longer. Bursting through to the surface she sucked in the oxygen and flailed out with her empty fist.

An odd little *oomph* hit her ears as she made contact, but she didn't have enough juice left to do any more than that. But something in the sound, something she felt sent pure relief coursing through her veins. *Michael*. Vienna relaxed, allowing him to haul her into a motorboat without further struggle.

She was unceremoniously left in the waterlogged bottom of the boat as the engine revved and the boat raced at top speed across the surface of the water.

Vienna looked up to find Devlin manning the motor with Michael running the guns off the back. Clad in a black-armored wetsuit and night vision goggles, he was all business.

But then, it had really been all business all along.

Blood was thicker than water. Loyalty did trump all else. Curling her legs under her, she opened her fist and stared at the ring. Michael had what he wanted. And it appeared that it wasn't her.

Eight

S oft. Very, very soft.

Too soft.

Vienna's eyes flew open to discover that the softness in question was a cashmere blanket covering her naked body on somebody's bed.

She sat straight up, pulling the blanket to her chin, and found Michael Kingston sitting in a club chair in the far corner. Still dressed in the casual layer he'd worn under his wetsuit, he looked like he hadn't slept all night, but he still looked more than wonderful to her.

"Good morning," he said quietly.

She just stared at him, then looked around the room until her gaze stopped at the bedside table to her right. On a small silver tray sat Julia's engagement ring.

"I wish I knew how you like your eggs," he said. "I would have had something ready . . ." Suddenly, Michael ruffled his hair with his hand, all impatience. "Look, tell me to go to hell, if you like. But saying nothing is not an option."

"What *are* my options?" Vienna asked, enjoying the sight of him all torqued up over her.

Michael got up and moved to the foot of the bed. "I suppose that depends on how you feel about me. I owe you an apology, Vienna. I'm sorry. I'm sorry I sent you to him. I'm sorry you were used the way you were."

"Well, on the plus side, I got the ring." She picked it up off the table and held it out to him. "I'll tell you all about it. But in the meantime, Pierce said to tell you that the game is still on."

Michael took the ring and tossed it roughly back on the night-stand. "I'm done with games. Devlin will have to play alone. Don't change the subject or joke about this. The minute the yacht pulled away, I wished that I'd just called the whole thing off. And that I'd told you how I really feel."

Vienna looked down. He'd taken both of her hands in his, almost unconsciously holding them to his heart as he spoke with passion beyond the mere physical.

She couldn't have spoken in that moment even if she'd wanted to, so she leaned forward and Michael met her halfway, taking her mouth with his, a warm, sensual touch of his lips. The cashmere slipped down, and he pulled her toward him, wrapping his arms around her bare body. "You're probably still exhausted."

"Not really," Vienna said with a grin, tugging at his T-shirt.

He pulled his shirt over his head and dropped it on the floor, sending the rest of his clothing quickly after it. "We'll take it easy."

"Don't start going easy on me, Michael Kingston. You'll take all the fun out it."

"I don't think that's possible," he said, slipping under the blanket and covering her with his body.

They had all the time in the world, and Michael took it slow, using the opportunity to explore every inch of her. Every time his fingers swept across her skin, every time his mouth came down on hers, it was as if he was laying down a trail of fire that would consume her.

He rocked his erection against her, gently sucking and biting at her lips, the strain in his taut, muscular body matching the intensity in his eyes. Vienna smiled seductively up at him, goading him on even as he worked hard to hold out.

She didn't want either of them to hold out. She moved her hips and his cock brushed against her very core, an electric sensation that had her begging him to take her.

But Michael was intent on paying her body every possible attention. Touching, tasting, teasing, he moved down her body, pressing his mouth against her breasts, her stomach, flicking his tongue against the slit of her wet cunt.

Vienna gasped. Then, cupping her breasts and writhing beneath him while she played with her nipples, she drove Michael to the edge along with her.

It was all he could take. Rising up, he slid his cock inside her. Vienna closed her eyes, reveling in the sensation of being filled by him.

Michael began to move again, his mouth hot against hers, his tongue mimicking the rhythm of their bodies. Vienna arched into his thrusts. She shifted her hand down to where their bodies joined, sliding her fingers up and down the top of his shaft as he moved in and out of her in a slick, sensual haze.

Whispering his desire into her ear, Vienna's body tightened around his cock. They both reacted with a cry of ecstasy, and any sense of control began spiraling away.

He slowed his rhythm, pulled back slightly, and then thrust hard. Vienna moaned, expecting more, but he'd stilled and the anticipation was almost as delicious as the sensation itself.

"Again," she whispered. He thrust hard once more.

"And again!"

A sound of pure rapture escaped from his mouth as he thrust roughly into her for a third time.

Gripping his shoulders, Vienna nearly came off the bed at climax as the waves of sheer pleasure moved through her. She cried out Michael's name and he just reared up, emptying himself into her with a long, shuddering release.

For a while as they lay there together, all she knew was the sound and sensation of his heartbeat dancing with hers.

"Vienna?"

"Mmm?"

"So . . . in case you're still wondering, *that's* how I really feel."

"Well, I've felt *that* from you before," she teased.

"You know what I mean. I'm in love with you." He sat up, pulling Vienna with him and cradling her against his chest. "Look, there's a passport in the top drawer of the bedside table. You're good to go if you like. You're free. The choice is yours."

She stared at him. "You're letting me go? Officially?"

He nodded. "Of course."

"Does Devlin know?"

Michael burst out laughing. "Let's just say that I paid him the courtesy of telling him what I was doing."

Vienna sat back against the headboard and smiled. "You're letting me go. You're really letting me go."

He kissed her neck, trailing his finger in a circle over her stomach. "Of course, going alone is just one option. I think two men moping around a mansion over broken hearts is a bit much, don't you? You could . . . always take me with you."

Vienna turned and pushed him down on the bed beneath her. "You're an idiot, Michael." She lay her body over his and tucked her head under his chin. "You've got to know I've been dying over you. I think it's possible that I actually started to love you the first time we ever kissed. And here I thought it was just raw talent that got me through it."

"Nobody should be discounting your raw talent." Michael put his arms around her and pressed his lips to her hair. "Let's go together, then. The two of us. We can take as much time as we like, leave the business behind for a while."

Vienna closed her eyes and smiled to herself as Michael pulled her in even closer. "The two of us . . . as much time as we like. Perfect."

Just like she always said, in the end it all came down to two things: Numbers. And time.

Liz Maverick

Award-winning, bestselling author Liz Maverick is an odd jobs specialist whose contract assignments have taken her from driving trucks in Antarctica to working behind the scenes on reality TV shows in Hollywood. She holds a BS in business administration from UC Berkeley and an MBA in marketing and entrepreneurship from UCLA. Be sure to stop by Liz's website at www.lizmaverick.com for the latest information about her work.

Kimberly Dean

UNREQUITED

One

This was a mistake.

Trista gripped her purse more tightly where it sat in her lap. No matter how hard she tried, she just couldn't relax. The air conditioning in the car was too cold, and the seat belt bit uncomfortably into her shoulder. Inside, she felt nearly nauseous.

What had she been thinking? A date?

She wasn't ready for this.

She looked over to the driver's seat and saw Cliff smiling as he drove through the evening traffic. He'd had a grin on his face ever since he'd knocked on her front door. Unfortunately, his happiness made her feel even worse.

"I'm glad we're finally getting to spend some time together," he said, glancing in her direction. "Waving at each other as we come and go from work hasn't been enough."

She smiled weakly. She just couldn't work up a response to that right now. "Are you doing some remodeling at your pharmacy?" she asked instead. "I've noticed you've had workmen there this week."

He nodded. "We're replacing some of the older shelving. Got to keep up with the times, you know. How are things with your catering business? Every time I wander out back, you and Kelly seem to be loading that van of yours."

Trista shifted in her seat, trying to find some relief from the seat belt. "Summer is our busiest time of the year."

"Ah, yes. I suppose that would be the case. Graduations, picnics, family reunions—that type of thing."

"Yes, that type of thing."

The chitchat wasn't working. The longer she sat there, the more Trista regretted her decision. She shouldn't have gotten Cliff's hopes up. He was a nice man, but she never should have said yes when he'd asked her to dinner. And she wouldn't have— if not for all the people poking her in the side and insisting that she needed to "get back out there." She'd been single for eight months now. It was time, they said. She knew her friends had good intentions, but at the moment, she felt like wringing their well-meaning necks.

"I hope you're hungry," Cliff was saying. "I've heard that the Blue Muse's food is fantastic."

Trista gave herself a quick mental shake. "It's very good," she agreed.

Unfortunately, she didn't think the heavy French food would sit well in her stomach tonight.

Enough, she told herself sternly. *It's just one date*.

She forced her grip on her purse to ease up. She could do this. Cliff wasn't asking for anything more than friendly companionship. If she was going to get back into the dating scene, this was the best way to ease into it. The man was perfectly harmless.

"Their dance floor is supposedly the most romantic in town."

Her already uneasy stomach dipped. Dancing? Oh, God. She definitely wasn't ready for that. "Cliff, I—"

She broke off suddenly when he veered right and pulled into a gravel parking lot.

"Here we are," he said. The car's tires crunched loudly as he slowly looked for a place to park. He chose a spot next to a huge Ford truck and turned off the engine.

Trista's brow pulled together, and she looked around the parking lot in confusion. She'd been so immersed in her own thoughts, she hadn't paid attention to where they were going. "Cliff, are you sure . . ."

Her date never heard her. He was already out of the car and moving around to get the door for her. She fumbled with her seat belt, and the safety harness finally gave up its vicelike grip. She accepted his helpful hand, but shook her head as she stepped out of the car.

"Cliff," she said gently. "I think there's been a mistake. This isn't the Blue Muse."

He blinked at her. "Excuse me?"

She gestured towards the sign. "It's the Blue Moon. It's a bar and grill. The Blue Muse is on the north side of town near the Galleria shopping center."

Her date's head snapped so hard to the side, it was a wonder he didn't give himself whiplash. He squinted at the sign and when he read it clearly, his face went as white as his starched shirt. "But I have reservations for seven o'clock," he said dumbly.

She glanced at her watch. "We'll never make it across town in time."

The picture of discomfort, he ran a finger under his collar. "They'll give up our table."

The poor man. She'd never seen someone look so distressed. Feeling bad for him, she glanced again at the bar. Her teeth worried her lower lip as she considered it. The Blue Moon was rough

around the edges, but it was a popular place. She'd been here for
lunch specials before. It served the best New York strip in town,
and the thought of their grilled shrimp actually made her hungry.
"This is fine," she declared.

"But the dancing," he mumbled.

Yes, the dancing. She looped her arm through his. "Let's eat
here."

They approached the bar slowly—Cliff because his carefully laid plans had just fallen apart and Trista because the
gravel made walking in high heels difficult. She had to hang
onto her date a bit more needily than she would have liked, but
she managed somehow not to sprain an ankle. Cliff was still
looking uncertain when he opened the heavy wooden door to
the bar. The sound of raucous Southern rock poured out into
the warm evening air, and his pale coloring took on a distinctly
green cast.

Trista smiled at him reassuringly. She was out of her ele-
ment, too.

One date, she reminded herself. She didn't relish the idea of
being at the Blue Moon after the sun went down, but she'd be
more comfortable here than in the forced romantic atmosphere
of the French restaurant. Besides, the music could fill in the gaps
of what would surely be a stilted conversation.

Already, she could tell that this was going to be a long night.

"Sounds like someone is having fun," she said with more en-
thusiasm than she felt. Before he could change his mind, she
turned on her heel and entered.

It took a moment for her eyes to adjust to the lighting, but the
moment she stepped inside, Trista could feel that the Moon was
thick with Friday night atmosphere. The early crowd was alive
and jumping. People were ready to relax after putting in forty

hours of hard work, and the weekend was just getting kicked off. Rounds of beer had already been served and more than a few peanut shells had hit the floor. The dartboards and pool tables were all taken but, unlike the Blue Muse, there wasn't a romantic dance floor. The bar didn't need one.

Hormones were flaring from every corner of the room.

Apparently Friday night was hookup time—and this crowd wasn't shy about its intentions. The bawdy environment disconcerted Trista. She searched through the smoky room until she spotted an open booth near the back. She pointed towards it, and Cliff nodded anxiously.

Taking a deep breath, she started towards the table. She hadn't made it three steps before a waitress with a serving tray full of beer mugs appeared in front of her. "Oh, excuse me," she called as she stopped short.

"Sorry, hon."

They circled around each other as best they could. Another opening in the crowd appeared, and Trista was about to take it when a wolf whistle cut through the air. The age-old signal of masculine appreciation was long and piercing, overriding the rest of the background noise. It surprised her so much, she actually stutter-stepped. She came to a complete stop, though, when she realized it was meant for her.

"Oh!" she gasped on a swift inhale.

An unexpected, hot shiver had just run through her. Somehow—even with the place as busy as it was—she knew she'd been singled out. Her woman's intuition told her why.

She was overdressed—or underdressed.

It all depended on how one looked at it.

Her classy little black dress stood out in the casual atmosphere of the bar like a sore thumb. She could feel people staring.

Openly. Unabashedly. One gaze, in particular, left a trail of fire as it skimmed down her back.

"Ooo, baby."

Her self-consciousness ratcheted higher as, one by one, heads turned her way. A howl drowned out the whistle, and she felt her cheeks heat. The dress would have been perfectly acceptable at the French restaurant, but here her skirt seemed about two inches too short . . . the sleeveless style too daring . . . the scooped neckline too revealing . . .

The overt masculine appreciation threw her off balance, but even more surprising was her reaction to it.

It aroused her.

Within the space of a breath, she'd become acutely aware of her own body. It was almost as if everything was somehow enhanced. She felt the brush of the short skirt against her thighs. Her breasts were heavier within the confines of her lace bra. And her high heels . . . They seemed not only to emphasize her legs, but lift her bottom in the most inappropriate way.

She wasn't the only one who noticed.

That one incendiary gaze slid over her curved backside, and she shuddered.

It had been so long since she'd felt anything close to sexual that the effect was almost overwhelming. Instinctively, she turned back towards Cliff and the door. To her surprise, her date no longer seemed ready to leave. To the contrary, he appeared half-pleased. With a somewhat cocky look on his face, he put his hand on the small of her back and ushered her the rest of the way to their table.

"You do look beautiful," he said, trying to temper the crassness of what had just happened.

He didn't fool her. His night had been made. People thought his date was hot.

Trista was too flummoxed to be offended. All she wanted was to get out of the spotlight. Away from that hot stare. With relief, she sat down and scooted away from the outer edge of the booth. Cliff settled down across from her and loosened his tie as he looked around with increasing interest.

"You certainly give the joint some class." He grinned across the table at her as his gaze swept down her figure. It was the same once-over he'd given her on her front doorstep when he'd picked her up earlier this evening, but much more bold. He stared openly at her distended nipples, and Trista was affronted.

Greatly.

She opened her mouth to tell him to quit, but stopped short.

She couldn't be a hypocrite. Her body's reaction betrayed just how much she'd liked the sexual interest of a roomful of strangers.

One stranger, in particular. The remnants of that hot gaze lingered.

Shifting uneasily on the vinyl seat, she crossed her arms over her chest. What was going on? Her date's interest left her cold. So why—in God's name—had she felt such a full-blooded jolt out there in the middle of the barroom floor? That male attention couldn't have been more blatant, more base, yet it had evoked a response within her. She could still feel a fire smoldering deep down in her core, and her nipples were poking through both layers of her bra and dress.

"I thought it was rude," she said, unsure whom she was trying to convince.

"Of course, it was," Cliff said, his brow lowering with concern. "I'm sorry. Do you want to leave?"

And walk through the bar again? She didn't think so!

"No," she said quickly. "I'm all right."

Unsettled by the whole situation, she pulled the menu out from behind the napkin holder at the end of the table. She held it up in front of her and pretended to give it her attention.

Only her real attention was still focused somewhere out there in the bar.

Her admirer was still watching her.

She could feel it.

The heat in her belly began to spread. *Downward*. Nervously, she crossed her legs. Her garter belt gave a tug, and she bit back a gasp.

"Are you feeling okay?" Cliff asked. He leaned forward on his elbows. "You look a bit flushed."

A bit? She felt like she was ready to combust. "Don't you think it's warm in here?" she asked as she fanned herself with her menu.

He wasn't going to be dissuaded that easily. Reaching out, he took her free hand. "Don't be embarrassed."

With his touch, Trista felt another jolt—only this one had the temperature of pure ice. Needles prickled at the back of her neck. The vibes weren't coming from Cliff. That *someone* wasn't happy.

Instinctively, she snatched her hand away from her date's touch. Uneasiness settled over her as she looked away from Cliff and slowly scanned the bar. She wasn't usually so intuitive, but she could feel a connection with this unseen man.

The silent seduction was beginning to unnerve her.

Her gaze flicked over the rowdy crowd. Most of them had gone back to whatever they were doing before she and Cliff had shown up. She didn't see anyone still staring.

Except . . .

Her heart jumped when a dark brown gaze suddenly captured hers. It caught and held, refusing to let her go. The will behind those deep soulful eyes was hot and possessive. Strong and sexual. Unable to resist, she felt herself begin to melt . . .

Right until recognition hit.

With all the force of a two-ton brick.

"Oh, my God," she breathed.

It was Ty.

Ty!

The implications froze her in her seat, but she couldn't reign in her body as quickly. The ache between her legs intensified, and she squeezed her thighs together hard to try to make it stop. Oh . . . Oh, *God*.

She'd been reacting to *him*? The idea was so wrong—so inappropriate—she was horrified.

"What?" Concerned, Cliff turned in his seat. His legs swung out over the end of the booth, and the movement effectively broke their stare.

Like a rag doll, Trista sagged back in her seat.

Cliff's head swiveled back and forth. "What is it? What did I miss? You look as if you've seen a ghost."

"No ghost."

Although he was most certainly from her past.

Her eyelids drifted shut as mortification set in all over again. She couldn't believe she'd gotten aroused. She couldn't believe her breasts still ached! Ty wasn't some secret admirer. He hadn't been watching her because he was interested. He'd just been plain, flat-out surprised.

Feeling blindsided, Trista ran a shaky hand through her hair. Oh, this was just perfect. Her first date in eight months and not only had she brought along her baggage, she'd just made it even messier. "My brother-in-law is here."

Cliff's eyebrows jumped. "You mean *former* brother-in-law."

He let out a nervous laugh and tugged at his collar again. "Or I'm in big trouble."

She rubbed her suddenly aching temple. "No, you're right," she said quietly. "Former."

Although Ty was around so much, she tended to forget that.

Cliff craned his neck to take another look. "You're not talking about that muscle-bound behemoth, are you?"

Trista felt her body begin to melt again, but this time she fought it. She knew all-too-well what Ty looked like.

"He's in construction." She caught her date's arm and drew him back around to face her. He wasn't making matters any better by being so obvious.

"I don't understand," Cliff said. "What's the problem?"

She bit her lower lip. The night was quickly going from bad to worse. "Well, this is somewhat embarrassing, but you're my first date since the divorce."

His jaw dropped. "I am?"

She shrugged helplessly.

"But you were married to a professional baseball player."

She looked at him blankly. What did that have to do with anything?

"I'm the first man you've agreed to go out with since Denny Christiansen? The All-Star catcher? The man who batted .328 last year until he blew out his knee and had to go to Japan to play?"

There was so much glee in his tone, it made her grit her teeth. "It's taken me a while to work through things."

Pushing his luck, Cliff ventured another peek. A very quick peek. He was swallowing hard as he turned back around. "I don't think your ex-brother-in-law has gotten there yet. He looks like he wants to pummel me."

Trista couldn't help it. Something inside her chest softened. She didn't doubt that. Ty Christiansen was the most loyal person she knew. Throughout the divorce, he'd been as protective of her as he'd been of his own brother. Looking back, though, she might have leaned on him more than she should have.

Guilt unfurled inside her. Seeing her here must have come as a shock to him. She should have told him her plans for tonight— although, on second thought, that probably wouldn't have been such a good idea either.

She glanced at him again. The look on his rugged, handsome face cut her to the quick. Unable to bear it, she let her gaze drop to her lap.

"He's just surprised to see me with somebody other than Denny," she said quietly.

That had to be it. That had to be why he looked so betrayed.

{❂}

It had been a hot, sweaty, bitch of a week. Ty took a long pull on his beer and savored the cool breeze coming from the air conditioning vent overhead. The shower he'd taken to get rid of the dust and the grime hadn't cooled his internal body temperature. Working outside in this heat wave had been like working in the fires of hell. By the time he and his men had knocked off earlier tonight, they'd all been more than ready for the weekend.

Kicking back in his chair, he grabbed a few peanuts from the bowl in the center of the table. He could use that steak he'd ordered right about now.

"You're up," Frank said. He handed him the darts and reached for his own half-finished beer.

Ty dropped his peanut shells onto the table and wiped his

hands. A Lynyrd Skynyrd song started ripping through the air-waves as he found the spot marked on the floor. He eyed the board carefully. He needed seventeens.

He was taking aim when the door to the bar opened and new customers walked in. Out of the corner of his eye, he saw the flash of a figure. And by that, he meant a *figure*. Long, dark hair. Sleek curves in high heels.

In a word—his type.

For a moment, his concentration was distracted. It was blown to bits, though, when he saw the way she moved. There was something about the tilt of her head . . . the sway of her hips . . . The dart flew out of his hand and embedded itself firmly in the pockmarked wall behind the board.

Frank let out a snort. "That's a first," he laughed.

Ty looked straight over his friend's head and felt the air get knocked right out of his lungs. The woman wasn't just his type.

It was The One.

Trista.

And she was with someone.

Frank swiveled around in his chair. When he saw the beauti-ful brunette, he did what came naturally to construction workers. He let out a whistle. Ty's free hand whipped out and clapped his buddy across the back of the head.

"Ow," Frank said, reaching up to rub the spot. "What's up with you? Just because you saw her first doesn't mean I can't look, too."

"Put your eyes back in your head," Ty growled.

He felt his fingers curl into a fist around the remaining two darts. Men around the bar were eyeing her like fresh meat. Just because he couldn't stop staring didn't mean that they shouldn't. The fucking cavemen.

"Ooo, baby!" A howl erupted from the table of bricklayers beside him, and he'd had enough. Turning, he jabbed his darts halfway up their tips into the men's table. The laughing stopped pretty damn quickly.

"Give the lady some respect," he ordered.

"Sorry, Ty," one of the guys mumbled. He held up his hands defensively. "We didn't hear you call dibs."

"Just back off."

Frank was eyeing him carefully when he turned back around, ready for whomever he had to take on next. "I take it you know her?" his friend said.

Ty's teeth ground together. "Yeah."

He knew her. Hell, he'd been silently obsessed with her for nearly three years.

"She was married to Denny."

Frank perked up in surprise, and he looked over his shoulder again. "That's your sister-in-law?"

She wasn't his sister.

Not even close.

"Not anymore."

Trista was a free woman. She and Denny's divorce had gone through eight months ago. Eight months and ten days, to be precise. She was single now, but this was the first time he'd ever seen her out with another man.

He found he didn't much like it.

He watched in disbelief as her "date" ushered her to a booth at the back. He used the term loosely. After the way she'd been disrespected, a real date would have turned her around and walked her right out of this dive. Instead this . . . this *weenie* had his hand at the small of her back. He was pushing her out in front of him almost as if he liked putting her on display. Or, more likely, because he got off on the attention it was bringing him.

Ty's eyes narrowed as he watched that hand at her lower back. If it dropped so much as a quarter of an inch, the guy was going to lose it.

Serena finally showed up with the food. She strode through the swinging doors to the kitchen with a huge platter lifted to shoulder level. "Here are your steaks, boys," she said as she propped the tray on the back of a free chair.

Frank eagerly reached out to help her. The steaks, baked potatoes, and corn-on-the cob took up most of the table. Their waitress set the bottles of ketchup and steak sauce in the two open spots she could find and let the tray drop to her side. "Anything else I can get you?"

"A gun," Ty bit out.

Both Frank and Serena jumped. Frank was the first to recover. A smile slipped onto his face as he looked at the barmaid. "Why don't you just start with another beer?"

Serena caught on quickly. She followed Ty's gaze and her blond eyebrows lifted. "She's gorgeous. I'll bring you a pitcher."

Ty had a feeling he was going to need something more than that.

Trista was gorgeous—and that dress. God damn! She looked like sex. He felt his gut tighten. What was she trying to do? Bring him to his knees? It wasn't as if she was showing a lot of skin. The dress just . . . clung. He didn't blame it. With that body she had, he'd want to cling, too.

He always had.

He reached for his beer. Unable to stop himself, he let his gaze slide down her back to her tight little ass. Watching it sway was his favorite pastime, and tonight was no different. As always, his cock went on alert.

She was sending out vibes she shouldn't, not here in the bar. His gaze drifted lower to her long legs. He'd had dreams about those legs. Fascinating dreams where they'd been wrapped around his waist . . . draped across his shoulders . . .

His beer mug hit the table with a thump when her dress hitched up as she sat down. Was that a thigh-high he'd just seen?

Shit. How much was a guy supposed to stand?

His pulse began to pound as he looked at her face. The lighting in the bar wasn't the best, but he could swear that dots of pink were coloring her cheeks. The flutter at the base of her throat told him her heart was beating as fast as his was. And her lips . . . He felt his groin get heavy. She'd chewed off half her lipstick.

She was acting edgy. Adrenalized.

Her gaze suddenly swung up and locked with his.

Horny.

His dick nearly jumped out of his pants.

She was aroused. He could see it from halfway across the room. She'd felt his stare, and she was responding to him. As a woman. A freight train started rumbling inside his chest.

Her mouth parted halfway when she recognized him and all he could think about was kissing her. Touching her. Lying down with her the way he'd always wanted. He took a step forward, ready to throw tables aside and knock people out of his way in order to get to her. Her so-called date suddenly turned in his seat, though, and he was stopped cold.

She was here with someone else.

"Easy, Ty," Frank said softly.

He'd forgotten there was anyone else left in the room.

"What the hell is she doing here?" he growled.

"Having dinner," Serena said as she swooped in on them again. The beer in the pitcher swished dangerously close to the spout as she set it on the table. "Like you are. Come on. Sit down. Your steak's getting cold."

He wasn't hungry anymore.

At least not that way.

The waitress turned and placed a hand against his chest. It made him realize how tightly his muscles were clenched.

"Now's not the time," she said calmly. She glanced at the couple at the back booth. "She's interested. Get her name and number and call her later."

Oh, he'd do more than call her.

Still, he drilled the waitress with a look. "How do you know she's interested?"

Serena let out a snort. "Honey, if you could feel the look cutting into my back right now, you wouldn't even have to ask."

Ty looked at Trista again, but she was doing her best to ignore him. Slowly, he sat down.

If she was so interested, why was she out on a date with someone else? And who the fuck was that guy anyway? He knew her friends, or at least he'd thought he had. Ty felt himself start a slow burn. What did she see in the little wimp? His hair was thinning, and he could use another twenty pounds on his skinny frame. She was so far out of that guy's league, he shouldn't have stood a chance.

Well, the pip-squeak still won't.

Ty made up his mind so quickly, it really wasn't a decision at all. Once made, determination settled inside his chest. Mr. "Date" better make the most of dinner, because that was the only shot he was going to get.

౸

The meal seemed endless. Trista poked tensely at her food, wishing that she could snap her fingers and make the clock turn faster.

It wasn't that her meal was bad. The shrimp was delicious; she just didn't have an appetite tonight.

Ty was doing everything he could to make sure she wasn't comfortable.

And that was putting it mildly. He was watching her every move, seemingly listening to every breath. The focused attention made her self-conscious. Worse, it had her confused body still raging. She didn't know whom she was more upset with—him or herself for letting him get to her. Trying to find a way to cool down, she took a long drink of ice water. Goose bumps popped up on her skin when she felt his hot gaze slide down her throat.

Damn you, she mentally cursed. *If you have something to say, why don't you just come over here and say it?*

Her hand shook as she lowered the glass. Water dribbled onto the table, and she let out a breath of frustration. She plucked a napkin out of the metal holder and mopped up the puddle.

Cliff, meanwhile, was oblivious to the nervous energy pulsing around them. He'd tucked into his steak the moment the friendly blond waitress had set it on the table in front of him. The only time he'd come up for air was to ask questions.

Unfortunately, they were tactless. Finding out he was her first date since Denny had given him too much confidence.

"So why did you divorce a guy like that?" "Was it messy?" "How much did you get out of him?" "Is that brother-in-law of yours as dangerous as he looks?"

Honestly, she'd had enough. All she wanted to do was go home, lock the door, take a nice cool shower, crawl into bed, and pretend this night had never happened. Cliff, unfortunately, was blind to body signals. He kept up until her head was pounding.

"Do you want a doggy bag for that shrimp, hon?"

Trista blinked and looked at the waitress who'd appeared from out of nowhere. Their gazes connected, and she could have hugged the woman for coming to her rescue. Cliff had about a quarter of his steak to go, but the sooner she could coax him out of here, the better.

"That would be great," she said.

The waitress winked at her. "I'll be right back."

And she was. A sister-in-arms, she made a beeline for the kitchen. She was back with a Styrofoam container before Cliff could get out yet another question about alimony. "Here, I'll do that for you," she said as she leaned in to take Trista's plate.

"Bad date?" she whispered so Cliff couldn't hear.

"The worst," Trista said under her breath.

The name badge on the woman's curvy chest said SERENA. Casually, she nodded towards Ty's table. "There is something better, if you're interested."

Trista's head jerked back. Oh, God. Had their silent battle been that obvious?

"He's a great guy," Serena whispered as Cliff reached for his drink. "I could say something to him if you'd like."

Trista's stomach plunged. "Oh please, don't. It's not like that." It wasn't like that *at all*!

Cliff set down his empty glass and happily patted his stomach. "That was fantastic. Pass on my compliments to the chef."

Serena let out a sound that sounded suspiciously like a snort. "I'll be sure to let Skeeter know."

It took everything inside Trista not to grab the woman's arm and repeat that she'd misinterpreted things.

Serena must have felt her impatience, though. Efficiently, she reached into her apron and pulled out her order pad. She ripped off the top ticket and set it in front of Cliff. As he was reaching for his wallet, she slipped another piece of paper under the take-out. The smooth move surprised Trista. Trying to be as secretive, she pulled the paper into her lap and peeked at it.

It had Ty's name and phone number listed.

The irony should have made her laugh.

But she couldn't.

Even this stranger had noticed the tension between her and her ex-brother-in-law. Serena just didn't know the reason for it. She'd made a logical leap in assumptions, but hooking up with Ty . . . Trista shivered. The idea was unfathomable. Wild. Forbidden.

And it sent a hot flush running through her body. One that left her nipples hard and her pussy tingling.

She was still fighting the effects when the waitress brought back Cliff's credit card receipt for signature. Suddenly, it all became too much. The bar's heavy atmosphere, the insinuations, the anticipation . . . Her fist closed around the slip of paper, crumpling it into a tight ball. Forgetting her take-out, she slid out of the booth and headed towards the door.

She felt the stares again, only this time she knew where they were coming from. It only made matters worse. She hit the door at almost a run, and Cliff struggled to catch up with her in the parking lot.

He caught her arm as they neared his car. "Do you want to see if we can still go dancing at the Blue Muse?"

She let out a breath of disbelief. He hadn't caught a whiff of what had happened in that bar. "Thank you, Cliff, but I think we'd better cut the night short."

His brow furrowed. "How about a walk on the waterfront? It's cooled down a bit."

Could a person really be so unaware? Trying to contain her impatience, Trista took a deep breath of the heavy air. The heat might have abated, but the humidity was still there. She could feel it pressing on her. "Maybe another time. Please, take me home."

He stood there for a moment, staring at her. "All right," he finally agreed. "Here. Let me get your door for you."

She nearly sagged in relief.

The drive back to her house was made in silence. Trista did her best not to think of Ty. When she considered Cliff, though, she felt badly for the way the night had turned out. It *had* been mostly her fault. She'd entered into this date with less than good intentions. She hadn't really given him a chance, and she'd paid virtually no attention to him over dinner. She'd been too caught up in her own personal world.

Mainly, her ex-brother-in-law.

"I'm sorry, Cliff," she said, once again holding onto her purse as if it were a lifeline. "I haven't been good company tonight."

He glanced at her and the dejected look on his face lightened. "That's okay," he said, reaching out to pat her thigh.

She crossed her legs uneasily when his hand touched more bare flesh than she was comfortable with.

"I made a terrible mistake with the restaurants," he admitted, "although that was the best steak I've had in years."

Trista couldn't help a small smile. "Thanks to Skeeter."

Cliff shared her grin. "We'll just have to try it again."

Her momentary amusement withered. She hated to tell him, but there wasn't going to be a second date. She'd accept responsibility for tonight, but she wasn't willing to put herself into this kind of a situation again. They simply weren't compatible. Somehow, though, breaking the news to him tonight seemed cruel.

Besides, she just didn't have the energy. The tension at the bar had left her exhausted.

"Take a right here," she said quickly, seeing he was about to miss the turn onto her street. "It's the one with the porch light on."

"Oh, yes. Here we are."

He pulled into her driveway and stopped. Her hopes for a clean getaway died, though, when he turned off the engine and the lights. He hopped out of the car and hurried around to get her door again. Trista's patience was wearing thin, but she forced a gracious smile on her face as he helped her out of the car and escorted her to the house.

She had her keys in hand before they even hit the first step of her porch. "Thank you for the evening out," she said, strategically opening the glass screen door and holding it between them.

"It was my pleasure," Cliff said. "Let me help you."

Showing more moves than she gave him credit for, he pulled the screen door open wider and slipped in beside her. Trista took a deep breath of surprise at his closeness, and her breasts accidentally brushed against his chest. Startled by the sensation, she took a step backward. The porch railing stopped her from getting far.

Cliff smiled as if he didn't have a clue as to what he'd done. Instead, he reached for her keys. She relaxed. He really was going to unlock her door for her. She waited as he dealt with the lock, swung the door inward, and dropped the keys back into her uplifted palm.

Finally, the date was over. "Thank you, Cl—"

She'd let down her guard too soon. Seeing his chance, her date leaned forward and boldly kissed her. For a moment, she was too dumbfounded to react. When she finally did, the sensation of his dry lips against hers made her lurch up onto her tiptoes. Unfortunately, he took that as a sign of encouragement. He wrapped his arm around her waist and pulled her closer.

As sensitive as her body had become over the course of the night, Trista found herself responding. But she knew it wasn't to him. Automatically, she reached for the hand that was dangerously low on her back. Too late, she remembered her keys.

"Ah!" Cliff hissed, flinching sharply when she jabbed him.

She used the opportunity to slip into her house through the open door. She was suddenly glad she'd left the lights on. "Good night," she said as calmly as she could.

"But—"

"Good night." Firmly, she closed the door and threw the deadbolt into place. *Now*, the date was over. Shoulders sagging, she let her head drop forward. Her forehead rested against the doorjamb, and she counted to ten.

What a disaster.

She let out a shaky sigh. The only good thing about tonight had been the shrimp—and she hadn't even been able to enjoy that.

Men.

Turning, she tossed her purse onto the overstuffed living room chair. Still tense, she rubbed her hands up and down her arms. That shower was sounding better and better. She just wanted to rinse the evening off of her. Forget it forever. Turning on her heel, she headed for the hallway.

The knock on her door came just as she was unzipping her dress.

At once, her anger flared. She didn't like conflict, and it took a lot to get her riled. Unfortunately, tonight had burned most of her long fuse.

Pivoting, she glared at the door. She'd been as pleasant to that man as she could through all his rude questions at dinner. She'd thanked him for taking her out. She'd offered him a friendly good night and had even let him get away with kissing her, for God's sake.

No more. She was nipping this in the bud.

Her footsteps were crisp as she marched across the room. Her hand wrapped tightly around the handle and she whipped open the door. "Cliff, I don't want to see you again."

"That's good." Ty stood on her doorstep. He hovered over her with a hand propped against each side of the doorframe. "Because I just sent that loser packing."

Two

"Ty!" Trista gasped.

Almost simultaneously, a car peeled out on the street in front of her house. The screech of tires against asphalt was jarring, and she winced. Poor Cliff sounded as if he were running from the hounds of hell.

Or one very pissed off brother-in-law.

Irritated, she looked at Ty with accusations ready to fly. The words died on her lips. He *was* wound up. She could see it in the way his jaw clenched and his muscles flexed.

His uncharacteristic irritability made her hesitate. She'd known he'd been upset at seeing her on a date with a strange man. She'd even known that he'd want to talk about it. She'd just expected that discussion to take place tomorrow or next week—and on the phone. Not here on her doorstep with him looking like he was ready to pop.

"What are you doing here?" she asked. "Did you follow me?"

"Yeah. I did. You got a problem with that?"

His voice sounded tight, almost rough. It made her stomach drop. She'd been expecting to find a meek, balding man on her doorstep. Instead, she got the exact opposite. With the way Ty stood over her, he looked big, impatient . . . and sexy as hell.

All the feelings she'd experienced at the Blue Moon came rushing back—the arousal, the excitement, the *panic*.

"Yes, I have a problem with that!" she sputtered, even as she felt her belly sizzle. "You've . . . You've got no right."

His dark gaze centered on her face. "We'll see about that."

They stared at each other until the air practically hummed. Trista gripped the door handle a bit tighter. What was wrong with her? Why was she reacting to him like this? He was her friend. For all intense purposes, he was still family.

"Who was that guy?" he asked in a deceptively soft voice. "And what were you doing with him?"

"Oh, for heaven's sake," she snapped. This was stupid. This was Ty! "His name is Cliff Nealon. He's a perfectly nice man, and you know what I was doing with him. We were having dinner."

The look on Ty's face darkened. Pushing himself away from the doorjamb, he stepped into the house. Trista automatically took a step back to avoid contact. It wasn't that she was afraid of him. She knew he'd never hurt her. With her senses on overdrive, though, everything was taking on a different hue.

"What did you say to scare him away like that?" she demanded, trying to keep her thoughts focused.

He shrugged off the question, but with the snug black T-shirt he wore, she could see the bunching of his muscles.

"Tell me."

Those muscles flexed again when he crossed his arms over his chest. "I asked him to leave—*politely*—although I might have thrown something in there about not coming back."

"Oh, Ty," she groaned. "You should have let me handle it."

"Like you handled that kiss?"

Her gaze whipped up to his face. He'd seen that? Embarrassed, she ran a hand through her hair. With the movement, though, she suddenly realized that her dress was still halfway unzipped. Her fingers stopped, tangled in her curls. With the back of her dress gaping as it was, she felt exposed.

"It was just a peck," she said nervously.

"He's lucky he can still walk."

She swallowed hard.

She'd never seen Ty like this. He was so edgy. So primal. Lowering her hand, she tugged at the wide shoulder strap that threatened to slide down her arm. Her state of undress was making her feel distinctly uncomfortable. *Vulnerable.*

The action only drew his attention to the problem. His gaze heated, almost scorching her as it raked over her bare skin. "Forget him," he said flatly. "He's not the right guy for you."

"How would you know?" The dress was killing her. She couldn't think straight with the way it kept sliding and dipping. With the rapt way he watched, she'd never been more painfully aware of a man in her life. "You hardly met him."

"I know," he growled.

He reached out to help her, and she flinched. A muscle ticked along his jawline when he saw her instinctive reaction. Slowly, he lowered his hands to his sides. His fingers opened and closed, though, as he stared at her. "What were you doing out with him anyway?" he finally asked. "Where did you meet him?"

Her patience had been rubbed raw—along with fifty other emotions. "What is this? An inquisition? If you must know, he's a pharmacist at the drugstore down the street from my shop."

At her tone, Ty took another step forward. It put him too close, inside her personal space. "Why did you go out with him? What made you say yes?"

Electricity began to prickle along her skin. What had gotten into him? Why was he pushing her like this, challenging her?

A thought came at her from left field. Oh, God. Was he still hoping she'd get back together with his brother? Because that was never going to happen. She looked at him dead-on and refused to take another step back. "The divorce has been final for over half a year now, Ty."

"I know that."

"I can date whomever I want, whenever I want."

The muscle in his jaw ticked a little faster. "I know that, too."

"Then why are you acting this way?"

Something hot and wild flared behind his eyes. "Because you didn't let me know you were back on the market!"

Trista jerked.

He couldn't mean . . .

But he did.

Alternating heat and cold rushed through her already sensitized body. She could see it in his dark eyes. Feel it in the waves of energy buffeting her. Oh, God. Her instincts in the bar had been right. "You want—"

"Yeah, I want."

He came at her fast, giving her no time to back away. When his hand slid under the curtain of her hair and wrapped around the nape of her neck, she was stunned motionless. It was a sexual touch. Intimate and possessive.

It was nothing compared to his kiss.

His mouth came down hard on hers, and arousal swept through her like a flash fire. Caught off guard, she clutched at his T-shirt. She'd had no time to prepare. No time to build up any defenses. His lips stroked and nipped at her until her brain couldn't suppress what her body was feeling.

"Damn," he said hoarsely. "I waited too long for this."

The fingers at the back of her neck tightened and his other

arm wrapped around her low on her hips. Trista shuddered as he pulled her flush against him, lifting her right onto her tiptoes. She felt overpowered and feminine as he fit her against him. His body was big and tough, and the bulge behind his zipper was impossible to ignore.

"That's right, baby. Feel me."

Shocked, she looked up at him. She didn't know what to say. She didn't know if she *could* say anything.

His dark eyes watched her closely. Then, purposely, he kissed her again. This time, though, he came at her stronger, harder. Opening her mouth wide, he pressed his tongue deep. She moaned when it tangled aggressively with hers and lapped up her taste.

It was her moan that set him off.

With sudden intent, he wrapped his foot around the open door. Putting his heel into it, he kicked it shut. The loud bang finally managed to register in her brain. Disoriented, she tried to pull back. "Wait. What are you doing?"

"What do you think?"

"We can't!"

"The hell we can't."

Her pulse took off as he started backing her towards the nearest wall.

"I saw how you reacted to me at the bar," he growled. "You felt me looking at you, and you got horny."

She clutched at him as she stumbled backwards. "But I didn't know—"

"You knew your nipples itched."

"Ty!" she gasped. He'd never said anything remotely like that to her before. The effect was devastating. She felt the tingle at the tips of her breasts as starkly as if he'd reached out and pinched her.

"You knew your pussy ached."

She let out a cry as she felt the wall press into her back. He kept coming until she was tight against it—her heels, her butt, the back of her head . . .

She was breathing so hard, she couldn't catch her breath. Things were moving too fast. They didn't know what they were doing. "We should think about this—"

"This is all I think about."

She bucked when he fisted his hand in her dress's bodice and pulled straight down. With it unzipped as it was, the material slid right down over her breasts. The skirt hitched up at the back and the scooped neckline tucked naturally under her breasts. He let go, and it snuggled right into place, framing her bust like a sexy smile.

"Ah!" she cried.

Breathing heavily, he stopped and stared.

Trista was never more surprised in her life than when she felt herself cream.

The dampness in her panties was unavoidable, but the sharp arousal brought with it a tinge of fear. Things were spiraling out of control too fast. She'd never thought of Ty like this before. She'd never considered—

Her hands flew to cover her bra cups when she saw the intent in his eyes. "Wait!"

He was having none of it. Catching her, he pulled her hands away. He pressed her wrists above her head against the wall and locked them in place with one hand. "I'm tired of waiting. It's time you thought of me as more than your friend. You want to get back in the dating game? Fine, but you're doing it with me."

He leaned into her, letting her take his weight. Her breasts cushioned his hard chest, and she let out a whimper when he began to grind against her in slow circles. "I'm not ready for this," she panted, trying to get him to slow down.

"Baby, you're raring to go. Just stop thinking so hard."

Her entire body rocked when his other hand slid intimately up the back of her thigh. With the way her dress was contorted, her bottom was nearly exposed. His fingers paused when he found her garter belt, and his brow creased. "Stockings?"

Trista was shaking so hard, she couldn't stop. His fingers were brushing against curves that the Brazilian cut of her panties didn't quite cover.

This was *Ty* feeling up her ass!

She let out a guttural cry when he grabbed the elastic band and let it snap against her tender thigh and cheek. The sting put her arousal right on the edge. "I put a run in my nylons," she said quickly. "They weren't for him."

"Good answer," he growled.

His fingers slid around to the front of her thigh, right to the crease at the top of her leg. Trista fought for air, her breasts pressing hard against his chest. He knew. He knew what he was doing to her.

Slowly, his fingers traced her panties right down between her legs.

He found her sopping wet. His shuddering breath hit the side of her neck. "Is this for me?" he asked, his fingers investigating more intimately.

"Yesssss!" she groaned.

With that one tortured word, she surrendered.

Her concerns were many, but she pushed them away. She just wanted to feel again. She knew Ty better than she knew any other man—or she thought she had. It didn't matter. He'd seduced her at that bar without saying a word. She trusted him and, at the moment, she wanted him more than anything in the world.

He felt it, and he moved on her fast. The hand that had captured her wrists let go and reached for the zipper of his jeans.

Impatiently, he kneed her legs open and stretched the crotch of her panties to the side.

She squirmed in discomfort as the material bit into her hip and tugged uncomfortably over her mound. He tucked the wet panel in the tight notch between her leg and her swollen pussy. The brush of his fingers against her, skin-to-skin, was too much. She felt her body begin to tighten.

"Not yet," he said, almost desperate. Roughly, he freed himself from the front placket of his briefs and stepped back up to her. His thick cock stood fully erect, pointing at her.

Trista's eyes widened at seeing that private part of him, but she shook in anticipation. She wanted that big rod. She wanted to feel it spreading her, feeding her . . .

"Hold on, baby," Ty said as he caught her again. "I'm coming."

His hands slid under her bottom to the backs of her thighs. With a quick hitch, he lifted her up and adjusted her against the wall. Her eyes drifted shut at the display of raw strength, and she wrapped her legs around his waist. She was so far gone. So intoxicated.

Her eyes flew back open, though, when he began to penetrate her.

She was slick and ready, but it had been a long time. "Ty?" she said anxiously.

He didn't back off. Instead, he groaned and adjusted his angle. Her breath caught when the pressure intensified. She was tight, and he felt huge. He pushed deeper and deeper until he was sliding right over her G-spot.

Trista went almost light-headed. Her hands clapped onto his shoulders, and her fingers bit down hard. "Oh! Oh, God! Right there!"

"Fuck!" Rocking his hips, he gave her what she needed.

The pleasure was blistering hot and all-consuming. Her nails clawed at him as she flew over the edge.

The orgasm came sharp and fast, but it wasn't over.

When she regained her senses, she found Ty pumping into her fiercely. He seated himself as far as he could go with every thrust, and the sensations were even more intense. She clung to him as her hips rocked in tempo with his, taking his thrusts as well as she could. Mindlessly, she stared over his shoulder.

Too late, she realized that the door had bounced open.

Her ravaged pussy spasmed, and Ty let out a groan. His knees buckled before he caught them both. Leaning her back into the wall, he used it for leverage as he shafted her.

With the porch light on her doorstep and the lamps on inside her home, any of her neighbors could see their frantic coupling. The Downeys. Mrs. Frances. Dirty old man White.

Trista went off like a firecracker.

Ty blew with her.

Muscles tensed. Breaths caught. Sensation peaked. The moment stretched out in time. Frantic with need, they held onto each other until slowly, gradually their bodies relaxed.

{⊱⊰}

When Ty's brain began to function again, concern for Trista overrode everything else. He couldn't believe how things had spun out of control. He'd just come over to make sure her squirrelly date hadn't gotten fresh, but then he'd seen the bastard kiss her . . .

All bets had been off then.

Things had swirled up in a frenzy—but she hadn't been ready. She hadn't even seen it coming. Hell, *he* hadn't been ready for *that*!

The thought that he might have scared her or—God forbid—hurt her left him momentarily paralyzed. Was she all right?

He found her surrounding him and, for a moment, the physical sucked him back in. Her arms were circled around his neck, her legs were wrapped about his waist, and her warm, snug pussy held his cock like she didn't want to let it go. Just the feel of her made his breath shudder hard in his lungs.

Damn. He'd dreamt about being with her this way for so long, it was hard to believe it was real. Yet it was real—devastatingly real. If he'd known how good it would be between them, he wouldn't have been able to keep his hands off her for this long.

His greedy paws.

Uneasiness took another sharp nip out of his ass. He'd pushed her too far and too fast. Seeing her at the Moon with another guy had driven him a little crazy. The urge to put his stamp on her, to make her his, had taken precedence over everything else.

It still did.

Involuntarily, his grip on her tightened. This hadn't been a mistake. He wouldn't let it be.

Slowly, he pulled his head back from the crook of her shoulder to look at her. Perspiration sat like dew on her forehead. Her eyes were closed, but the lines of her face still showed her pleasure. Her cheeks were pink, and her lips were parted.

Desire reared back to life inside him, but he tamped it down. He needed to play this right.

Moving as well as he could with his jeans halfway down his legs, he carried her to the couch. He let his knees finally give out as he dropped onto it. She stirred, but he kept her close, straddled over his lap.

His cock was still buried balls deep—and he intended to stay that way.

Moving fast did have one benefit. He'd gotten past her barriers. There was no way he was pulling back now.

"Easy, baby," he murmured. He pulled her close so she lay with her head on his shoulder. Comfortingly, he ran his hand over her long, dark hair. Her breaths were still coming hard and fast. "Easy."

He wasn't in much better shape. She'd ridden him ragged.

Talk about fire. Once she'd given in, her heat had nearly singed him. The sweet thing. How had she kept all that passion bottled up for so long? Turning his head, he placed a gentle kiss at her temple.

He braced himself when she stiffened.

Oh, shit, he thought. *Here it comes.*

She was starting to think instead of feel.

He rubbed her back as she tried to orient herself. It took a moment. When she finally pulled back to look at him, her eyes were wide. Confusion had darkened the lavender in them to almost purple. "Ty?" she said, no louder than a breath.

Tension suddenly made it hard to breathe. "It's all right," he said.

She looked down sharply, but her gaze went right past his hands, past her rumpled dress, to the spot where they were still intimately connected. Her cheeks flared red and her body tensed. "Oh, my God!"

Her muscles jumped, but he settled his hands on the fronts of her thighs when she tried to lurch upright.

"Don't," he said, holding her in place. He swallowed hard and did his damnedest to make his voice soothing. "Stay."

Distress radiated from her beautiful eyes. The intimacy was too much. She squirmed atop him, only making matters worse.

"Stop," he said hoarsely.

She went still like he'd known she would, but that didn't make the situation *or the position* any easier for her to bear. She froze as if scared to move, but her gaze skittered around the room. It bounced from the wall where they'd just been to the front door and back again. "What did we just do?" she said, scandalized.

Her embarrassment was hard to watch.

Had she never thought about the two of them together? Never given in to a little harmless curiosity?

"I think you know," he said as calmly as he could. "Or do I have to explain the birds and the bees to you?"

That light teasing brought her gaze back to him, but she wasn't amused. Her hands opened and closed before she clumsily wrapped her arms about herself. When she realized just how little her twisted dress covered, her entire face flushed.

Ty wasn't liking this at all. She'd enjoyed it; he knew she had. He'd held her as she'd come. Determinedly, he stroked his hands up and down her thighs. "Relax."

"We shouldn't have done that!" she said, her voice tight.

He let out a quick breath. Anything but remorse. He'd take anything she threw at him, but he wasn't going to regret what had happened between them. "We didn't do anything wrong."

"You're my brother-in-law!"

The flash of anger was immediate. "Not anymore. As you just so helpfully reminded me, you're divorced."

Reaching up, he cupped her face and made her look at him. He knew they could bypass all this nonsense if he just started screwing her again. He could fuck her all night if he wanted; she was that receptive to his touch.

But he wanted her to be fully aware of whom she was with.

And he wanted her willing.

"I'm sorry that I pounced, but we didn't do anything wrong," he repeated, talking slowly so he made himself clear. Watching her closely, he swiveled his hips. Whether she knew it or not, her body was responding. Her bottom was relaxed against his legs and, inside, she offered no resistance more than her natural tightness. "In fact, it feels pretty damn right to me."

Her mouth dropped open in a surprised O. Reflexively, she clutched at his forearms.

He wasn't above playing dirty—not when so much was at stake—so he deliberately did it again.

"Ty!"

"I want you, Trista."

"But . . ."

"But nothing," he said firmly.

Trista felt as if she were about to come out of her skin. She couldn't believe what they'd just done—what they were still doing! The feel of him within her was overwhelming, and in so many different ways. The way he was growing and stiffening was just . . . Oooh . . . She struggled not to respond, to grind down on him as she so badly wanted, because despite what he said, they shouldn't be connected this way. It was wicked. Taboo.

She knew that.

But her body didn't much care.

No matter how loud the screaming in her head, she couldn't make herself pull away. It felt so good to be touched. To be wanted.

He still watched her with those dark eyes. Just like at the Blue Moon, she felt captured. *Turned on*. When he slowly reached for her, she couldn't move away.

He caught her dress where it was tangled about her waist. She felt herself tense, but when he started to lift the material, she let him. Embarrassingly, it caught around her breasts. With a soft word, he reached around her and undid the zipper the rest of the way. Her eyelids became heavy at the near embrace. She wanted to rub her cheek against the softness of his hair, to pull him close and ease the ache in her breasts . . .

"Lift your arms, honey."

Her arms felt heavy as she obeyed. He pulled the dress off her; it dropped to the floor, forgotten, as he stared at her.

"God, Trista. You're perfect."

Emotion built up inside her chest. He didn't know how much she'd needed to hear that. Her arms fell limp at her sides, and she sat immobile in front of him as he studied her.

Sensuality hung heavy in the air. His face softened, but inside her, she felt his cock harden. It made her abruptly aware of the way she looked. Planned or not, she was dressed for sex. High heels, sheer hose, lace garter belt, black bra and panties . . .

Oh, God. Her panties.

She'd forgotten the discomfort, but the way they were pulled and stretched suddenly became unbearable. Her gaze flashed downward. The black lace cut into her hip on one side and stretched wide to accommodate him. Without her dress, everything was visible. The tightly pulled fabric, her dark curls, his heavy, drawn-up balls . . .

The panic returned.

"Relax," he said softly.

"I can't!" The need to get away was fierce. This was too intimate. She needed time to think about this.

She tried to climb off him, but this time he caught her around the waist. With a slight flex of his chiseled muscles, he kept her seated. *Impaled*.

His brow furrowed. "Are you afraid of me?"

Her reaction was instinctive. "No!"

"I won't hurt you, Trista."

"I know that."

His head tilted slightly. "Don't you like me? Just a little bit?"

"Like you? I lo—" She broke off in embarrassment. "You're one of my best friends."

"Then let me be more."

Ty had had enough. This wasn't what he'd planned, but she wanted him. Her body couldn't lie. She was letting unimportant things get in their way.

He reached for her hands, surprising her. Good, he needed to keep her off balance so that rapid-fire brain of hers couldn't function. Besides, if he didn't feel her touch on him again soon, he'd go stark raving mad.

He placed her hands palm down on his chest. Pleasure tore through him, and he groaned. Arousal flared in her eyes.

It was the only sign he needed.

She gasped when he began tugging on his T-shirt, taking it off, but then she was helping. His heart was pumping hard when he yanked it over his head and threw it aside.

He caught her staring at him. Engrossed. Unbelievably, he was happy for that week of backbreaking work. It had left his body strong and honed. Sexy, from the look in her eyes.

"Go ahead," he said, his voice like gravel. "Touch me."

He needed to remember to be careful what he asked for.

Her fingers stroked tentatively, and his reaction was instinctive. His hips swung upward, and she let out a cry as they shifted on the couch.

Ty was too far gone to slow down. He'd wanted her for too long, and the little taste he'd gotten wasn't nearly enough. Reaching around behind her, he found the clasp of her bra. He dispensed of it within record time. Before the bra cups had even slipped off her, he was pushing his hands under them and taking possession of her full breasts.

She moaned at the way he squeezed, and her head dropped back.

His thumbs flicked roughly over her already stiff nipples. "We've been working toward this for months now, baby."

"No," she said, rolling her head and looking at him. "I didn't see it."

"You felt it. Nobody's closer to you, Trista. The only thing that was missing was the sex."

"No." Even as she disagreed with him, she couldn't stop touching him. Her fingers were tracing the lines of his muscles all the way down to his abs. She inhaled sharply, though, when she got a little too low and he bucked.

"Yes," he said firmly. With a firm pinch of his thumbs and forefingers, he emphasized his point.

Her groan emanated from deep in her chest but, still, she fought him. "This can't go anywhere. You're Denny's brother."

"But I'm not an idiot. I know a good thing when I've got it." It was time to get serious. Letting go of her breasts, he caught her by the waist. She let out a cry when he pulled her up and off him. The reluctance with which her body gave him up made him smile grimly. If that didn't prove things, nothing did.

"What are you doing?" she gasped when he lifted her in his arms.

He kissed her hard. "Taking you to bed. Get ready, baby. Your ex-brother-in-law is spending the night."

Three

Trista's heart gave a somersault. He planned to spend the night in her bed—and they wouldn't be sleeping.

The idea made her body quicken.

Right or wrong, she wanted him there. Her sexual nature had been ignored for too long. As fast as that romp against the wall had been, the aftereffects were still rippling through her. He'd tapped into that private part of her and, now, it refused to be repressed.

But that little voice inside her head . . . It kept yelling that she should say no.

She shivered when his nose brushed against her temple. "Don't overthink it," he whispered into her ear. "Just let it happen."

She had to overthink it. Somebody needed to. "This is crazy," she warned.

"Crazy right."

Her whole body went hot when he adjusted her easily in his arms. His rock hard physique was the thing of women's dreams, and she wasn't immune. He had her so revved up that even the brush of his warm skin against the side of her breast made her want to cry out. Trying not to give in, she braced her hand against his chest.

She found his heart thudding like a big, bass drum.

Warning signs flashed inside her head. They were rushing down a wild path. He didn't want to acknowledge it, but there were other things to consider. Their friends. His family. *Their friendship*. There was no way to change what had already happened, but they could still be smart about this. If she told him she wanted to stop, she knew he would.

She just couldn't make herself do it.

She wanted him too badly, and he was holding her too closely.

His steps slowed. "Look at me like that much longer, and we'll never make it to the bedroom."

With the way he'd pulled out of her so abruptly, he'd left her aching. It made everything else superfluous.

She wanted this night with him. For once, she wanted to just immerse herself in feelings. To give pleasure and to receive it. Giving in to the impulse, she turned and wrapped her arms around his neck.

The contact made her groan in delight.

"Trista!"

She felt his knees buckle as she deliberately ground her breasts against him. His reaction made the feminine side of her preen. She did it again, and her excitement soared when he cursed and began to lower her to the floor.

Their skin clung as humid heat poured in around them. The scent of lilacs filled the room, and she heard the air conditioner kick on high. Lilacs? She struggled to open her eyes. When she did, she found herself watching a moth flutter haphazardly around the light on her front porch.

They were right in front of the open door. Again!

"No, no," she said, kicking her legs. "Not here."

"Shit!" he said hoarsely, struggling to keep his grip. "Where?"

The lights in her house stood out like beacons against the darkening night. "Close the front door!"

"Hell." He hitched her higher and strode towards it. "Don't do that again unless you're willing to follow through."

Trista ducked her head into the crook of his neck. She'd never been more embarrassed in her life. He was carrying her, practically buck naked, right where everyone could see. "Ty!" she gasped. "The neighbors."

"Hey, if you haven't noticed, my dick's hanging out there for the world to see, too."

"It's not hanging."

His head snapped towards her, a wicked smile on his face. "What did you say?"

She felt her cheeks heat. She'd meant that nobody could see him, because she could feel it bumping up against her hip. "Just close the door!"

He laughed. "Chicken."

Using his foot, he once again nudged the door shut. This time, though, she reached out and turned the lock, making sure it wouldn't pop open again. She didn't need any more surprises tonight.

He'd already given her a big one.

The lascivious thought made her eyes widen. Groaning, she covered her face. "The Downeys have kids!"

"And they were probably putting them down for the night." He shrugged as he started to carry her down the hallway. "On the other hand, Old Man White probably got his first boner in twenty years. Poor guy. By tomorrow, he'll have forgotten all about it."

She refused to touch that scandalous comment with a ten-foot pole. Besides, those weren't the neighbors that she was worried about. "Mrs. Frances knows your mother," she hissed.

His brow furrowed. "That, she does. Well, I guess it's time Mom found out. It will be a shock, but she'll have to come to terms with the fact that I have sex."

"Not with me, you don't!"

His eyebrows lifted.

"Didn't." She shook her head. This teasing side of him was too familiar. It made the intimacy between them all that much more sexy. "Ty, she can't find out."

"Don't worry about her." He turned into the first room to the left. "Worry about me."

All playfulness left when he stopped in the middle of the bedroom. The guest bedroom, Trista saw with relief. If he'd taken her into the bedroom that she'd shared with his brother . . . She put a stop on those thoughts the moment they started. She wouldn't think about that.

She couldn't.

Slowly, he set her on her feet. She braced her hands against his bare chest, but suddenly caught movement out of the corner of her eye. She looked sharply to the side, but froze when she found their reflection in the mirror.

It made the breath rush out of her lungs.

They looked incredibly sensual together—like some couple in the centerfold of an erotic magazine.

Ty was watching them, too. They were both naked from the waist up. His skin was darkly tanned from hours of outdoor work, and hers looked pale by comparison. All he wore were old jeans and work boots. She couldn't have contrasted more starkly in her high heels and sexy lingerie. As they both watched, his hand slid over the curve of her hip. Trista felt a thrill go through her when it disappeared into her severely abused panties. Gliding through the stretched-out leg opening, it settled onto her bottom.

"Ahhhh!" she gasped when he cupped her cheek possessively. One finger. Then two . . . Then all four dipped into her tight crease. She caught his biceps for support as his fingertips stroked her. Squeezing with his thumb for leverage, he parted her cheeks, only to stroke more deeply in the crevice of her ass.

"Ty!"

"I think it's time we got these off of you," he said gruffly.

She felt his muscles bunch. The next thing she knew, she was flat on her back on the bed. He'd left her parted legs hanging over the side, but he stepped up to the mattress before she could close them.

Trista breathed hard as she stared up at him. She felt like a sacrifice as he stood over her with his cock raring. Earlier, she'd worried that she was in for a long night. She found herself thinking the same thing—only this time she was concerned about her stamina.

"What . . . What do you want me to do?" she asked, unable to hide her nervousness.

This was still so new to her. So shocking.

"Do whatever feels good, baby." He was staring hard at her garter belt. Reaching out, he traced the line of it low along her abdomen. Her belly shook. She could feel little zaps of electricity shooting from his fingers. They met down deep in her core, and her arousal flared.

His hand trembled, but then it was sliding down the front of her hip. He traced the elastic to the clasp that held the top of her hose. With a flick, it turned loose. He went through the same meticulous process with the other.

"Do you have any idea what you do to me?" he whispered.

She melted back against the mattress. She knew what he was doing to her. The desire and the need were clouding her head.

How could she not have seen this in him? In herself?

Kneeling down in front of her, he gently gripped her ankle. He placed a hot kiss on her inner thigh as he slipped off her shoe. She groaned and reached down to hold him there. He wasn't through. His damp breath heated the crotch of her panties as he turned his attention to her other leg. Her fingers raked through his hair, and he rewarded her with a sharp nip that had her nearly vaulting off the bed.

Standing up quickly, he rolled her onto her stomach.

Trista's hands came up to her shoulders. Anticipation had her nerves singing, but she'd been a good girl for too long. The picture they painted had to be lurid. Her in such a submissive position. Him so dominant.

She felt him stand upright again and resume his position far up between her parted legs. Shyness made her grind her forehead into the mattress.

His hands came down on her again. "So smooth. So tight," he said under his breath.

The back catches on her garter belt turned loose. The left one, though, gave way with a snap. Her back arched, and she let out a cry.

"So reactive," he muttered. "Like TNT."

When he spread his hands wide across her bottom and squeezed hard, the comparison wasn't far off. Trista surged upright into his hands, pressing herself into his touch. She knew that being with him like this was somehow forbidden, but that made it all the hotter.

"Ty," she panted. "I can't take much more."

His voice sounded even more constricted. "Neither can I."

His fingers fisted in her panties and tugged down. Her breath caught at the idea of him seeing her this way. Still, she shimmied her hips as he worked the restricting material down her legs. She gave a hurried kick and sent her underwear flying.

Flipping her hair, she looked over her shoulder at him. His concentration was total as he rolled down her hose.

Trista knew she should be scared. At the very least, uneasy. She hadn't planned to take a new lover tonight. *Certainly not her former brother-in-law.* As much as she'd resisted, though, she was suddenly happy it was Ty seducing her.

She trusted him.

And his relentless pursuit had proven to her how badly she wanted him. "Please," she begged, losing all sense of shame.

He raked a hand through his mussed hair as she lay before him, naked and vulnerable. "I've got to warn you, baby. This isn't going to take long."

"I don't care."

The world spun as he caught her hips and rolled her again. She moaned as he yanked her to the very edge of the bed. The friction against her back was like fire.

So was the heat between her legs.

His cock bobbed as he caught the backs of her thighs.

"Hurry," she said.

"Help me."

She knew what he wanted. Lifting her legs, she started to wrap them around his waist. She only managed to loop one before he caught the other in the crook of his arm.

Uncertain, her gaze flashed up to meet his. The lines of his face were rigid. Gradually, he lifted her right leg up to his shoulder.

The position was unfamiliar, but the strangeness sent Trista's heart to beating. It about slammed through her rib cage when he positioned himself at her opening and began to slide in.

"Oh!" she gasped. "That's . . . That's . . . Ahhhhh!"

"Good?" he grunted, straining to go slow.

She didn't want to go slow. Not like this. Closing her eyes, she grabbed the coverlet beneath her and lifted her hips. Her thigh muscles clenched greedily, and he slammed home. Her cry of satisfaction filled the small room.

"Fuck!" Ty exclaimed.

It was too late to stop. His control had been shattered. Catching her by the bottom, he lifted her until only her shoulders were braced against the bed. His hips swung in a wide arc as he fucked her hard.

Trista writhed as the pressure inside her grew. Their bodies heated, and the back of her leg became slippery against his chest. The denim and zipper of his jeans bit into her other leg, but the minor irritant only added to the sensations swirling inside her. Her climax was coming fast, and it was coming like a dragon.

Ty swore as their coupling became even more insistent. His hands bit into her hips and he watched intently as his hungry cock disappeared into her again and again.

It seemed like forever, but it was over fast. Trista arched like a bow as ecstasy overtook her. Ty lasted for a few more thrusts, but then he was grinding into her and throwing his head back.

Soon the only sound in the room was that of harsh breathing.

Trista felt limp. Wrung out. When Ty eased her back on the bed and fell down beside her, she couldn't move. Breathing had suddenly become the most taxing thing in the world. "Is it always like that?" she panted.

"We'll just have to . . ." he said, stopping to inhale deeply, "keep trying and see."

At last, they worked around until her head was on a pillow and her body was fully on the bed. Ty still hadn't recuperated. He lay exhausted with his head on her breasts.

"Damn," he said. "I meant to get my pants off that time."

It was such classic Ty, she almost giggled. It just took too much energy. She smiled instead and brushed his hair back from his forehead. The familiarity was becoming easier and easier. "We're not going to make it all night."

The challenge made his head snap up. "Want to bet?"

He still wasn't moving quickly, but he managed to sit up. Leaning over, he got rid of his work boots. She did giggle when he had to stop and sit with his forearms braced against his knees. Teasingly, she poked her toe into his muscled side.

He looked at her with one eyebrow lifted.

It was amazing how fast the man could move once motivated. He stood up and his jeans and white briefs came off in one fell swoop. The look that settled onto his face when he slowly crawled up over her, though, wiped the smile right off her lips.

He looked like a predator—and she was his prey.

"You're dangerous," she whispered.

"So are you."

Watching her with his eyes sparking, he lowered his weight onto her. Trista's awareness jumped. He was heavier than he looked. There wasn't an ounce of fat on his toned body. He was all muscle.

And heat.

It seeped into her, and she shifted. He let her get comfortable until he settled on her for real. The feel of him made her bite her lip. She was so close to coming again, it was unbelievable.

"It feels good, doesn't it?" he said softly. He was so attuned to her, he could read her with a glance.

She looked up at him shyly. Their legs were entwined. His sex was tucked against hers. Their stomachs were sealed together, and her breasts cushioned his muscular chest. It didn't just feel good.

It felt right.

And that scared the hell out of her.

͜͡

Ty found himself in unfamiliar territory. He worked in a danger-ous profession. He lived hard, had rowdy friends, and liked to push the limits. As tough as he was, though, he could feel fear breathing down his neck.

Everything was on the line tonight.

Everything.

He'd been infatuated with Trista for what seemed like for-ever, but he'd made a move before he'd been ready. Before *she'd* been ready. That little dweeb Cliff Nealon had pushed up his schedule, but there was no turning back now.

He had this one chance to let her know how he felt.

One chance to give her so much pleasure, it bound her to him in a way words couldn't reach.

He looked down at her as she lay beneath him. The way her silky body cushioned his made it hard to think. Moonlight shone through the window, softly lighting her delicate features. She was watching him with a mixture of surprise and uncertainty—yet her pleasure was impossible to hide.

Those lavender eyes of hers killed him . . . Always had.

Carefully, he raked his fingers through her hair. It was spread like a dark curtain on the pillow beneath her head. Damn. He'd never been jealous of a pillow before. He suddenly wanted to feel those velvety strands stroking across his skin.

He needed to slow down.

Everything had been like gunfire tonight, rapid-fire and explosive. He needed to take his time. *To enjoy her.*

"What do you like, baby?"

Her hands paused, low on his spine. "What?"

His concentration was momentarily broken. An inch lower and she'd be cupping his ass. Taking a steadying breath, he looked into her wide eyes. She'd heard him. "What do you like?" he repeated. "Sexually?"

Her color darkened in the cool light and, beneath him, he felt her squirm. It made his cock jump. She wasn't the only one who was responsive. All he had to do was look at her, and he got hard. Touching her? It was a wonder he could remember his own name.

"I want to satisfy you," he said quietly. Rolling slightly to the side, he worked his hand between their tightly pressed bodies. Watching her closely, he cupped her breast. "Tell me what feels good. What turns you on?"

For a moment she looked dumbfounded, but that surprise rapidly turned to embarrassment. Ty felt himself stiffen with anger—but not at her. Had Denny never asked her that? Had he never put her first? He knew his little brother could be self-involved, but was he really that big of an ass?

He booted the thought right out of his head. Even if he was, Denny didn't deserve to be in this room. He'd let her get away, and he wasn't getting a second chance. Tonight, it was all about Ty and Trista. One-on-one.

"Tell me," he whispered.

"I can't," she said, clearly horrified.

"There's nothing to be embarrassed about." He forced his body to relax when he felt hers grow tense. He wanted her to be comfortable with him, to trust him in this area like she did others. Looking down, he watched as his thumb worked her nipple. "Your breasts seem sensitive. Do you like to have them sucked?"

A soft sound left the back of her throat. It made him look up at her sharply, but she hastily turned her head away. His determination strengthened. If there was one thing he couldn't resist, it was a challenge—and he wasn't going to let her shyness spoil this. He kept fondling her, tickling and pinching the already stiff bud. He didn't let up until she gave him a jerky nod, confirming what he already knew.

"Licked?"

Another quick nod.

"Squeezed? Tell me," he insisted. "I want to hear it."

He watched as she swallowed hard. It made him want to ease up, to let her off the hook. Something inside of him, though, wouldn't let him. He needed her to take this step. It was important for both of them.

At last, she hesitantly turned back to face him. "I ache there," she whispered. "Whenever I get . . . aroused."

His thumb and forefinger tightened automatically. Knowing it and hearing it were two different things entirely.

"And not just the nipples," she stressed, wanting so much that she forgot her embarrassment.

His cock got hard so fast, his balls throbbed. It took everything inside him to keep from thrusting into her right then and there.

"That's right, baby," he said through clenched teeth. "Tell me what you need."

Giving her what she wanted, he flattened his palm over her. Slowly, he ground her breast in a tight circle. She moaned and lowered her hands to his backside.

Ty swore when she massaged him there. Uncontrolled, his head dipped onto the pillow beside hers. He'd had some pretty vivid dreams about her, but nothing had prepared him for her touch. He felt like he'd died and gone to heaven.

Sinners' heaven, for sure.

His persistent boner nudged against her wet pussy—but she didn't pull away. It didn't escape his attention.

"What about you?" she whispered.

That wasn't hard. "All you have to do is breathe, Trista, and I'm turned on."

Sliding down her body, he took position over her breasts. He felt his mouth water as he looked at her. When he'd told her she was perfect, he hadn't been lying. She was full and firm, with a shape tailor-made for bikinis and wet T-shirts. In all his fantasies, though, he'd had to wonder about her nipples.

They didn't disappoint.

Red and perky, they begged for his attention. Carefully, he rubbed his whisker-covered cheek against her. The prickly contact made them spear straight up at him. For a moment, he forgot his head.

"Did you ever think of me like this?"

The moment the question slipped out, Ty wanted to pull it back. Damn! There was no good answer to that. Either she admitted to what she'd consider adulterous thoughts or he'd just set himself up for a massive hurt. She went quiet for too long, and his stomach dipped.

"I was married, but I wasn't dead," she finally said. Her voice was so soft he could barely hear her. "I didn't consider you for myself. I couldn't. But I did think about setting you up with Kelly."

His head snapped up. "Your business partner?"

She bit her lip. "I thought you two would make a cute couple."

The idea of it was so ludicrous, he found himself actually

laughing. Of all the words that had ever been used to describe him, *cute* had never been one. "Cute is for teddy bears," he said, deliberately lowering himself over her again. "But I'm the big, bad wolf."

Bracing himself on his elbows, he caught a breast in each hand. They plumped as he pressed them together. She let out a soft cry that sounded like an invitation to him. Determinedly, he dropped his head.

"Oh!" she gasped when he blew against one stiff nipple.

He gave her no time to prepare before his tongue snuck out and raked across the distended tip. The sensation was so good, they both shuddered. He felt her hands slide up his back and tangle in his hair. Giving in to a need he'd had too long, he opened his mouth and started suckling.

"Tyyyyy!"

The room heated as he feasted on her. Bedsheets crumpled. Moans blended with sighs. He licked and nipped until his cock was straining for her. Beneath him, Trista was a molten mass of need.

The pressure was suddenly on to make things perfect.

He wanted to give her everything she wanted. Inside and out of the bedroom.

With effort, he lifted his head. "What position, baby? What's your favorite?"

Her body undulated as she tried to bring his attention back to her breasts. "I don't care!"

The possibilities made his head spin, but this time was for her. "Trista, tell me how you want me."

Her eyelids drifted closed, but she was too far gone to be timid anymore. "From behind," she whispered. "I like it from behind. Deep and slow . . ."

Ty felt himself grow tight. A woman after his own heart. "On all fours?" he asked, nearly choking on the words.

She shook her head.

"Ass lifted?" He'd already begun to roll her. "On your belly?"

The protracted sigh gave him his answer.

Desire reared up inside him, but he tamped it down. He was going to ride her long and slow, just like she'd asked.

And he'd keep going until she was his.

Reaching out, he grabbed a pillow that had been bumped from its spot along the headboard. Circling his arm underneath her hips, he lifted her. Deliberately, he slid the pillow underneath her. It propped her up at just the right angle to drive him crazy.

Ty felt his heart lodge in his throat as he brushed her hair to the side. She'd put so much trust in him, it was humbling. Wanting to keep her at that fever pitch, he settled his mouth at the base of her neck. She trembled.

"Spread your legs wider, honey."

He took his position as her legs hesitantly slid open to accommodate him. Then he was directing himself at her notch. She was so hot and slick, he almost forgot himself. Only her sigh of pleasure kept him in check. Bracing himself with a hand on each side of her on the mattress, he began to slowly fill her.

Her neck arched as her head came off the pillow. "Oh, Ty."

"Feel good?" he grunted.

"Yes," she groaned, relaxing back down.

He felt the pulse pounding in his temples as he slid into her to the hilt. She stretched so tightly around him, he worried that he was hurting her. The way her body shifted to take him eased his concerns.

Almost leisurely, he began thrusting in and pulling out. He

kept the strokes elongated so she felt every centimeter of him—and he felt every centimeter of her around him.

God, there was so much he wanted to give her. So much he wanted to share with her. He let his body lower until she took more of his weight. Her bottom cushioned his heaviness and accepted the brush of his balls almost eagerly.

"That's right, baby. Let it take you."

He felt the protective side of him surge. The small bedroom cocooned them, increasing the privacy of their connection, but he wasn't stupid. He knew what problems they faced outside that door. It was going to take other people time to adjust to the change in their relationship. He didn't want anyone else's prejudices affecting her, though. He'd protect her from as much of it as he could.

Moving slightly to the side, he stroked his fingers down the arch of her spine and into the crevice of her bottom. Using his hips, he spread her cheeks. She tensed when he caressed the small, pursed opening of her anus.

"Easy," he murmured. He knew she liked it. She'd nearly come apart when she'd watched him touch her there in the mirror.

He rubbed her bud again and again until she became comfortable with the touch. Only then did he slide it lower. He tickled her swollen pussy lips, making her even more aware of him. Then, gently, he stroked her opening where it was stretched so widely around him.

She let out a cry as her control shattered.

Easing his hand underneath her, he wrapped his palm around her pubic bone. His fingers tangled in her curls and began searching for her clit as his thrusts from behind became more aggressive. With each inward stroke, their bodies slapped together.

"Ty!" she cried out mindlessly.

The feel of her so uninhibited gave him hope. In this, he finally had her.

He rubbed her clit relentlessly as she quivered and swayed. Finally, he felt her body tense. He was coming when her climax hit. She arched beneath him, and he spurted into her for what seemed like an eternity.

At last, he lowered his weight onto her. Their skin clung. He felt her ragged breaths . . . heard her thudding heartbeat . . .

It felt good.

It felt right.

Giving in to the feeling, he rested his head on the pillow beside hers. His lips brushed her ear as the truth finally came out. "I love you, Trista."

Four

When he woke up later that night, Ty found himself alone in the bed. Instinctively, he reached out to Trista's spot next to him. It was cool. Uneasiness pricked at the back of his neck, and it brought him fully awake.

Shit! What had he done?

Pushing back the covers, he went in search of her. She wasn't in the master bedroom, and she wasn't on the couch. Her car was in the garage, but the house was dark. Where had she gone? He was in a near panic when he found her sitting on the steps of the back deck. Bracing his arm against the wall, he waited for his heart rate to slow down.

Damn, why did he have to be such a bull in a china shop?

He hadn't meant to pressure her. It had just slipped out.

He watched her uncertainly through the sliding glass doors. She looked so small and alone out there. Everything inside him pressed him to go to her, but what the hell was he supposed to do? Hadn't he said enough already?

Fuck.

Just standing here wasn't going to fix things. Reaching out, he caught the handle and rolled the door along its track. He saw her spine stiffen at the sound, but otherwise she didn't move. He approached her carefully.

"Can't sleep?" he asked as he sat down on the step behind her. He stretched his legs out on either side of her. She was wearing one of those slippery satin robes. Hot pink if he guessed right. The moonlight didn't do the color justice, but he had a feeling it would be a knockout in full sunlight. It looked pretty good as is—even if she did have the belt tied around her waist so tightly it was almost knotted. The material only came to midthigh and it left most of her legs bare. He gritted his teeth when their skin brushed.

Now was not the time.

She shifted her legs, trying not to let him see. "I'm not used to having someone take up all the space," she said noncommittally.

"Sorry."

The night was quiet around them, but Ty had never felt more edgy in his life. Trying to be as relaxed with her as he could, he reached for the glass in her hand. The plastic tumbler was sweating. The temperature had gone down with the sun, but the humidity still hung heavy in the air. He tried to tell himself that was why he was finding it hard to breathe. Casually, he took a drink of her lemonade. He could have used a shot of whiskey, but the tartness hit the spot.

Needing to break the tension, he gestured to the backyard. The shadows couldn't hide that the grass was starting to get long and ragged. In this weather, it was impossible to keep up. "Your lawn boy needs to get to work."

He thought he saw a ghost of a smile cross her lips. "He's a slacker that one."

Playfully, he nudged her shoulder. He was her lawn boy. "Maybe he just needs more incentive."

It was the wrong thing to say. Her smile disappeared, and his shoulders slumped. Tact had never been his forte. He was more of a straightforward type of guy. Going with his strength—and his gut—he wrapped an arm about her from behind. He cupped his hand over the ball of her shoulder and gently pulled her back against him.

"You don't have to say it back," he told her softly.

She stiffened and tried to pull away. "But I . . ."

"Relax. It's all right."

Those three words cost him more than he'd like to admit. He might as well have reached into his chest and ripped out his own heart. Nevertheless, he kept her close. She resisted, but eventually her weight eased back against him.

That, at least, made the claws in the back of his neck finally ease up. She still felt safe with him. That was something.

They sat together for a long while, neither of them saying a word. Crickets chirped, and somewhere an early bird started to sing. The cheerful sound rubbed Ty the wrong way. He hoped the damn thing croaked on its stupid worm.

"How long?"

The sound of her voice surprised him. "What?"

She didn't respond, and the silence just about killed him.

"How long have you felt that way about me?" she finally asked.

He took a ragged breath. Oh, now they were getting into dangerous territory. She'd asked, though. For once, he wanted her to know. He'd been hiding it for too long. "Since Denny brought you home for Thanksgiving dinner that first year."

She looked over her shoulder sharply. "That was the first time we met."

"That was all it took."

She became less settled in his arms. He gave her a squeeze and took another drink of lemonade. His throat had just gone dry as sandpaper. "You walked in the door, and I was done for."

"I . . . I never noticed."

"You didn't think that I walked funny?" He tried to laugh it off, but couldn't. With a sigh, he rested his chin on her shoulder. "You were Denny's girl; then his wife. I knew that. That's why I made sure you didn't notice. That nobody did. If you'd been anyone else, though, I would have had you flat on your back before the night was out."

He paused. "Or your stomach, given what I know now."

She made a tight sound and reached for her drink. "Give me that," she said hoarsely.

He passed her the lemonade and pressed a kiss to her temple. He saw the way her hand shook as she lifted the glass. He knew how she felt. He was more than a bit rocky himself.

"It wasn't just physical," he confessed, wanting to make sure she knew that. "You were gorgeous; I wasn't blind. As I got to know you, though, I realized how sweet you were. How smart and resourceful. A roughneck like me never stood a chance."

The lemonade was gone. She set the glass aside and nervously rubbed her hands on her thighs. "The divorce has been final for a long time, though. Why didn't you . . . Not that I expected it, but you never . . ."

"Shh," he whispered into her soft hair. "I know how badly that whole thing hurt you."

When they went quiet this time, not even the crickets made a sound.

The divorce hadn't been contentious. As far as most people knew, it had been almost friendly. Ty knew better. When that marriage had ended, Trista had been shattered. He knew because he'd been the one to pick up the pieces—not because he was trying to take advantage, but because he'd been disappointed, too.

He'd hoped it would last.

Honest to God, he had. Denny was his brother. He'd wanted them both to be happy, even if he was getting the short end of the stick.

But the way it had ended . . .

Just thinking about it got him fired up all over again.

For as long as he could remember, Denny had been the golden boy. The favorite. He couldn't do anything wrong—not with his family, his friends, the media . . . Learning that his All-Star little brother wasn't perfect had been a kick in the gut.

Especially when he thought of all the time he'd wasted standing back in the shadows.

Ty let out a quick curse and ran his hand up and down Trista's arm. She deserved better. They both did. "When I told you we'd been working up to this, I wasn't lying. I'm more than your lawn boy."

"I know that," she said quickly.

"I'm more than your ex-brother-in-law, too, so stop trying to use that as an excuse." He gave her a little jiggle when she started to shake her head. "For the past eight months, we've been dating. We just haven't been having sex."

She might not have admitted as much to herself, but it was true. At first, he'd just started helping her around the house. When he'd seen the rotting board on the front porch, he'd become her fix-it man. Then her mechanic. He hadn't wanted to push her, but slowly and surely, they'd gotten closer. She'd started making dinner for him whenever he came over to mow the lawn. Tuesday night had become movie night—sometimes out and sometimes in—but always with popcorn. Now they talked on the phone daily.

That was why he'd gone ballistic when he'd seen her out with that pharmacist. She hadn't told him about the date but, more to the point, she was *his*.

Her hands were trembling as she folded them in her lap. "I thought we were friends."

Son of a bitch. Anything but the "let's just be friends" line. *Anything*.

His voice went rough. "Did you ever notice how you're shy and quiet with everyone but me?"

She paused. "Yes."

"There's a reason for that." Trying not to let his desperation show through, he wrapped both arms around her. Determinedly, he slipped his hands inside the edges of her robe. "I can't be just your friend anymore, Trista."

She arched when he caught her breasts, but he simply held her. She couldn't deny the physical. He'd already proven that much, and he wasn't above using it to his advantage. Dropping his head, he nuzzled the side of her neck. "I don't think you want that either."

The air seemed to almost shimmer about them. He could feel her resisting, fighting her own response rather than him. Almost at once, though, she gave in. Her head dropped back onto his shoulder, and her hands came up to cover his. He brushed his lips across her neck and felt her pulse pounding.

"Ty, I'm scared."

The words stopped him cold. Suddenly, it was hard to get oxygen past his heart in his throat. "Of me?"

"No . . ." She shifted in his embrace. "Of this."

He didn't understand. "Why?"

"I do love you . . . just not that w—"

He jerked. "Don't say it."

She turned in his arms, finally looking at him. "You don't understand. That's why this is so frightening to me. I care about you, and I don't want to hurt you."

"What did I tell you about overthinking things? Just let it happen. We both want it."

She tilted her head beseechingly. "I've got too much to lose."

"No. Listen," she said when he started to argue. She scooted around on the step, and he spread his legs wider to give her more room. "When I divorced Denny, I lost more than a husband. I lost your parents, too."

"My parents? What the hell do they have to do with this?" His voice carried across the backyard louder than he'd intended, but *damn*. If she was stretching that far for excuses, then he'd read her wrong. He started to get impatient, but the feeling vaporized when she lifted her hand and cupped his cheek.

"I don't have any other family, Ty."

His gut tightened. Her eyes looked big and wounded as she stared at him in the moonlight.

"I was an only child," she said quietly, "and I lost my parents in a car wreck when I was twenty."

"I know that," he said. His voice was as quiet now as it had been loud a moment ago. If she cried, he didn't know what he was going to do.

"Your mother won't hear anything against Denny, and your dad won't even look at me." She swallowed hard and shook her head. "I can't lose you, too."

Lose him? Ty looked at her helplessly. He'd waited for three years already. She couldn't shake him if she tried. "You won't lose me."

"I lost Denny."

Well now, wasn't that the kicker? "That was his fault."

"I have to take some responsibility. A marriage takes two people."

"Right. Two. Not three or four or ten."

Her eyes widened, and her lips parted in surprise. "You know?"

"That black eye he had during the playoffs didn't come from a foul tip."

He saw the embarrassment start to come over her again, but he wouldn't allow it. None of that had been her fault. Denny may be his brother, but if he found out the arrogant snot had made her think she'd deserved to be cheated on, he had another ass-kicking coming. So help him.

Ty felt his anger building, but he pushed it away. He wasn't going to be the one to pay for his brother's mistakes. Lifting his hand, he brushed her hair back from her face. He didn't even care if she felt his hand shake. "Listen, I know how it feels to be left in Denny's shadow, to feel second best. Mom and Dad don't mean to do it. They still love you; I know they do."

She let out a soft sound and turned her head away.

He cupped her face and made her look at him again. His jaw tightened when he saw the shimmering in her eyes. Tears. Damn. "What's happening here between you and me—it's got nothing to do with anybody else," he said gruffly. "I'm not my brother, Trista. I won't hurt you. I swear. Just give me a chance."

She let out a shuddering breath. "This isn't going to be a one-night stand, is it?"

"No," he said firmly. "Not even close."

Finally giving in to the need, he leaned forward and kissed her. Somehow, he managed to keep it light and slow. He let her deepen it, and his hand fisted in the dark tangles of her hair. It was only then that she noticed he was naked.

And aroused.

"Come back to bed, baby."

She stared at him for a moment that seemed to last forever. Ty waited tensely, his muscles feeling like they wanted to jump out of his skin. He watched her steadily, though, letting her see whatever she needed to see. It must have been enough, because slowly, silently, she leaned into his embrace.

For the first time since he'd awakened alone, Ty relaxed.

One way or another, they were going to make this work.

⊱⊰

"Okay, enough already," Kelly said as she took another batch of cream puffs from the oven. She set the cookie sheet on top of the stove and tossed the pot holder onto the counter. Turning, she planted her hand on her hip. "If you won't tell me on your own, I'll just have to ask. How did last night go?"

Trista froze in the middle of what she was doing. Absolutely froze. Her partner knew? Already? But how?

Oh, God! The open front door! She'd known people could see!

Panic flared inside her chest. How was she supposed to explain? How could she? She didn't really know what had happened herself. There'd just been so much heat. Lust. And Ty.

Lots and lots of Ty.

"Last night?" she said, hedging.

"With Cliff. The pharmacist."

Cliff! *Her date.* The first one she'd had in eight months . . . The one Kelly had insisted she go on . . . Trista nearly sagged in relief. She'd forgotten all about it.

"Don't play coy with me," her friend said impatiently. "You know I have ways of making you talk."

"Mmm," Trista murmured. She'd nearly made her confess without even trying.

With a quick breath of relief, she resumed her work on a batch of cream puffs that had already cooled. Without thinking, she sliced open each puff and scooped out the insides. She was grateful for the mindless task, because her mind was definitely elsewhere. "The date was . . . unusual. Things didn't go quite as Cliff had planned."

"How was that?"

"He took me to the wrong restaurant."

"Wrong? What do you mean by that? Wasn't the food good?"

Trista glanced at her friend, amusement finally shining in her eyes. "He took me to the Blue Moon."

"The Moon!" The oven door closed with a *whump* as Kelly set a new batch inside. "Why would he take you on a date there?"

"He thought it was the Blue Muse." Trista pressed her lips together. It wasn't polite to laugh, but it was so funny now. The look that had settled on Cliff's face when she'd told him about the mix-up had been absolutely priceless. "He had reservations and everything."

Kelly let out a hoot of laughter. "But you were going to wear your flirty little cocktail dress."

"I did," Trista said, her color heightening at the reference. That was where her trouble had all started. "And he was wearing a suit. We fit in like British royalty at a monster truck rally."

"Oh, no. Didn't the gravel parking lot give him a clue that he might be in the wrong place?"

Trista shook her head. "He didn't know until I pointed out the neon sign."

Kelly broke out in new gales of laughter. As always, it was contagious. Soon, they were both bent over laughing.

"Crap," her friend said, wiping the tears from her cheeks. "I had such hopes for him."

"It was an honest mistake," Trista said, trying to sober up. "He's a nice man—except for the fact that he's a fan of Denny's."

Kelly groaned. She'd never been a fan of her ex's. "No way."

"He couldn't stop with the questions about him." Trista gave a halfhearted shrug. "I think that's why he wanted to go out with me."

"Right. And that face and those legs of yours have nothing to do with it."

Trista felt a thrill rush through her. Ty had had more than one compliment for her legs last night. She felt the heat start to rise in her cheeks.

"Denny," Kelly scoffed, rolling her eyes. "Unbelievable. Well, scratch him off the list. We'll have to find you somebody else. Somebody yummy."

Yummy. Now that was a word that described Ty to a tee. Trista kept her head down as she plucked a deflated cream puff off the sheet and set it aside.

Kelly began dropping spoonfuls of the raw pastry onto another cookie sheet. "Somebody who'll be more interested in tearing off your clothes than talking about baseball."

Cream puffs, Trista reminded herself. *Concentrate on the cream puffs.*

"What time is that going-away reception this afternoon?" she asked, trying to steer the conversation in a less dangerous direction.

Kelly's head slowly turned. "Two," she said, her eyes narrowing. "You know that. You're the one who scheduled it."

"Yes, well . . . We'd better speed up or we'll be late." Trying to keep moving, Trista opened the refrigerator and pulled out the vanilla pudding. She could feel her friend's stare drilling her in the middle of the back.

"What's up with you?"

"What do you mean?" Trista said, her voice jumping.

Kelly started to slowly approach. "You're all flush."

"It's hot in here."

"I'm the one working the oven." Her friend propped her hip against the counter and folded her arms over her chest. "And you didn't get red until I said 'yummy.'"

Trista tried to keep her face placid as she started filling the little pastry bowls. "Isn't it about time for that batch to come out of the oven?"

Kelly drummed her fingers against her arm. She looked like a military strategist debating her next move. "And you've been absentminded all day."

"Yes, well. I've had a lot—"

"Sex."

The one, blunt word surprised Trista so much, she jerked. Vanilla pudding plopped onto the counter.

"I knew it. *You had sex!*" Kelly declared. Triumphantly, she reached out and poked her in the shoulder. "I knew it the moment your knees buckled when I mentioned someone tearing off your clothes!"

Trista was too tongue-tied to deny it.

"So . . . How was he?" Kelly asked, the question rolling off her tongue like a delicious secret.

"Ooo!" she squealed before Trista could choke out a response. "Hotter than that oven from the looks of you."

Reaching out, she grabbed her by the shoulders and turned her to face her. "Come on. Spill! I never pictured that in Cliff, but I guess it's like they say. It's always the quiet ones. I bet he was trying to make up for that dinner."

Trista felt like a little rowboat being tossed about by the tide. She couldn't stop her friend's momentum, until she realized what

Kelly had just assumed. "Cliff?" she squawked, her eyebrows lifting to nearly her hairline.

Her friend's face froze almost comically. "No?"

Trista used the time to get away. She shrugged off Kelly's grip and determinedly turned back towards the counter. With a spurt of frustration, she flung her spoon back into the pudding bowl and reached for a paper towel. Why couldn't she have a better poker face? She wasn't ready for people to know what had happened. She still needed to figure things out for herself.

Kelly wasn't about to be dissuaded. "But you did have sex. If it wasn't Cliff, who was it?" she demanded.

Trista wiped up the spilled pudding and tossed the paper towel into the trash. Stiffly, she moved to the sink to wash her hands. She didn't look at her friend as she returned to her cream puffs. Concentrating as if it were dynamite she was handling, she began replacing the tops one by one.

"Tell me," Kelly said.

"No."

"No? But . . . But . . . You have to!"

"No, I don't."

Her friend looked as if she might burst. When the bell over the front door of the shop jingled, she did. "Shit!"

Throwing her hands into the air, she stomped over to look at who was interrupting her inquisition. "It's Ty," she said, going still. "And he has *flowers*."

Her head snapped to the side, and Trista was pinned where she stood. Shit!

Kelly's eyes bugged out and her jaw dropped. It took a moment, but she finally managed to silently mouth, "Oh, my God!"

Trista slowly closed her eyes. She wasn't ready to deal with him. She wasn't ready to deal with this. She couldn't handle being the center of another scandal. The public divorce had been bad enough.

When Kelly finally got her voice back, it came out as an excited squeal. *"OH. MY. GOD!"*

Trista began to shake. One catastrophe at a time. Right now, she'd rather deal with Ty. "Can you watch things?"

"Are you kidding? Get out there!"

Trista wiped her hands down her front and realized she was wearing her apron. Quickly, she tugged it off.

"Hairnet," Kelly hissed, pointing at her head.

Trista straightened herself as well as she could. Before she walked through the doorway into the front room, though, she took a quick peek at the stainless steel toaster to see how she looked. For as excited as Kelly was, Trista was just as nervous.

She'd hurried out of the house this morning. Snuck out, actually.

Ty didn't have to work on weekends, but she did. Admittedly, her job had been a convenient excuse. Waking up in the bright morning light and finding herself tucked up against his big, naked body had been disconcerting.

Delicious, but disconcerting.

Daylight just illuminated things more starkly. Things that she'd managed to ignore in the darkness were now bright, bold, and demanding attention.

Everything had changed. Everything.

Nervously, she rubbed her hand over her stomach. She still wasn't sure how she felt about that. Her emotions had been on a roller-coaster ride ever since she'd first made eye contact with him at the bar. When she thought about the two of them together, she alternated between excitement, fear, desire, and dismay.

Last night, he'd made her feel things she hadn't felt for a long time.

Today, though, there was no getting around the fact that he was Denny's brother.

"Hurry up!" Kelly said.

Trista took a shaky breath. There was no point in dragging this out. She summoned her courage and stepped into the front room. One emotion immediately jumped to the forefront and shoved the rest behind.

Desire.

It hit her hot and hard.

Ty seemed to take up most of the room. He looked so big and *yummy*, her knees went weak. Reaching out, she grabbed the glass display case. They made a decent income on the local snack crowd, and her ex-brother-in-law definitely looked interested in something sweet.

He just wasn't looking at the cookies.

"Hi, gorgeous," he said in a low, rumbling voice.

His gaze swept leisurely down her figure. Cooking in the summertime was hot business, so Trista did what she could to stay cool. Suddenly, though, her tank top seemed too skimpy. Her shorts too short. It was the bar all over again. Her nipples peaked hard, tenting the fabric of her top, and the tingling sensation in her stomach plunged lower.

"Hi," she whispered.

He headed towards her with that walk that construction workers seemed to have patented, and she swallowed hard. What was she going to do about him?

"Busy?" he asked.

She glanced over her shoulder. Kelly was back there listening! "Yes," she said, telling the truth.

"I won't take much of your time." His look was smoky as he leaned against the counter and held out the flowers. "You just ran out so fast this morning. I wanted to see if you were okay."

"I'm fine." She shuffled her feet uncomfortably and concentrated on the flowers. "Thank you. They're beautiful."

She took the bouquet, but glanced at him in surprise when she smelled a familiar scent. "Lilacs."

Unbelievably, his look became even more intimate. "I've suddenly developed an affinity for them."

A dangerous sense of weakening came over her. "Ty," she sighed.

"Have dinner with me."

She looked at him mutely. This wasn't fair. Yesterday, dinner would have been no big deal. Today, it was huge. Today, it carried so much more with it—and she still wasn't sure what her answer was supposed to be.

"*Are you crazy?*" came a stage whisper from the back room. "*Say yes!*"

Trista looked at Ty helplessly.

"Listen to her," he said in that low, rough voice that sent shivers down her spine. "Don't worry so much, baby."

"I can't handle this pressure," she whispered.

"No pressure. We'll keep it casual—go back to the Blue Moon, if you want. You can wear jeans, and I'll teach you how to play darts." He reached across the counter and slid his hand around the back of her neck. "I just want to spend time with you, Trista."

He was nearly impossible to refuse. Still . . . "You won't expect . . ."

"The night will end up wherever it ends up." He tugged her closer until her lips almost brushed against his. "I'll be honest, though. I'm voting on the bed."

He kissed her then, long and slow. She didn't fight. She couldn't. He'd broken down all her barriers last night.

Besides, the warmth building inside her was comforting. Drawn to it, she stepped closer until her toes bumped up against the base of the display case. He tilted his head to a different angle, and the kiss suddenly became seductive. Carnal. Trista felt her breasts start to ache, but then he was slowly pulling away.

"Tonight," he said, breathing hard.

"Tonight," she agreed, sagging against the countertop.

"I'll be at your place," he said as walked backward to the front door. He winked at her as the bell overhead jingled. "I've got a lawn to mow."

Trista was still frozen in place when Kelly came out from the back room. They stood side by side, watching as Ty's truck pulled away from the curb and headed down the street.

"My God, is that man beautiful."

As much as Kelly despised his brother, Ty was at the top of her A-list. "There's more to a man than looks," Trista said quietly.

"And that one's got everything a woman could want," her friend said, shooting her a look. "But don't stand there sagging against the cookie case and tell me that he doesn't make you melt."

Trista blushed. "He does have that big, tough, construction worker thing going for him."

"Yeah," Kelly said. For a moment, they both paused to stare sightlessly midair. "And to think that you were going to give him to me."

The twinge of possessiveness was fiery and pure—so much so that it surprised Trista with its intensity. "He had other ideas on the matter," she said tightly.

"Obviously." Curious, Kelly propped her hip against the counter. "So what happened?"

Trista bit her lip. There was no hiding it now. Besides, she could use a friendly ear. "He was at the bar last night."

"And he saw you with Cliff?" Kelly's face became animated. "Oh, Lordy. I would have paid to be a fly on that wall. I take it that jealousy finally pushed him over the edge?"

Trista could feel the tips of her ears burning. That was the understatement of the year, considering the way he'd come barreling through her front door. One word, though, caught her attention more than anything else. "Finally?"

"I've seen the way he looks at you when he thinks nobody is watching." Kelly nodded to the bouquet of flowers and sighed with envy. "Wow. Romance and great sex. You are one lucky gal."

Trista glanced shyly again at the lilacs. They called to that soft spot inside her, but she'd built armor around her heart for a reason. "Am I?"

"Hmm?" Kelly said absently.

"Lucky?"

Her friend went still. "What are you saying?"

Trista cautiously traced the edge of the plastic wrap that surrounded the flowers. Did she need to point out the obvious? "He's Denny's brother."

"So?"

She looked steadily at her friend. "So am I a fool to get involved with another Christiansen man all over again?"

Kelly took a step backward. "Oh, my God. Did Denny do a number on you."

"I'm serious," Trista said. "What are people going to think? What are they going to say?"

"Uh . . . That the two of you are great together? That you should have gone for him before you went for that baseball lothario?"

"Kelly!"

"Who cares what they say?" Her friend's eyes narrowed. "Denny Christiansen cheated on you in every National League city across the country, Trista. He's probably making his way through Japan as we speak. He's a loser with a capital L. Ty's the real catch, and you know it!"

She slapped her hand down on the counter, making Trista jump.

"Don't be a fool. Follow your heart and grab that man."

The plastic wrap crinkled as Trista's grip tightened convulsively. "But what if I don't know what my heart's saying?"

"Then figure it out. And fast!" Kelly let one eyebrow rise. "Or I guarantee you'll regret it."

Five

Trista woke up to the smell of breakfast drifting in from the kitchen. A bed had never felt more comfortable, but the enticing scent was enough to pull her out of a sound sleep. For a moment she lay on her side with her legs tucked up to her chest. It was still early. Too early, really. She loved waking up this way, though, feeling all light inside. Happy.

Her lips curled into a smile. She and Ty had been together for nearly three weeks. She'd done well to heed Kelly's advice—although she still didn't have all the answers she needed. At the moment, she didn't care.

Slowly, she rolled onto her back. She tried to stretch, but her legs caught in a twisted sheet. Lifting her head, she saw how disheveled the room was. The morning sun highlighted the rumpled bed, scattered pillows, and even the cockeyed bed stand. Her body ached in all the right places, and she blushed at the memory of how little they'd actually slept last night. Despite the discomfort, though, she felt energized and ready to face the day.

Other than the fact that she was starving.

"Food," she murmured.

The lure of bacon and eggs became too much. Knowing Ty

would soon be in to get her, she kicked the sheet aside and sat up. Every time he did that, their breakfast got cold. Or burned. Her robe was lying in a hot pink heap on the floor. Reaching down, she swiped it up and hurried to the shower.

The quick rinse washed the last of the sleep from her eyes. Feeling excited but still a bit timid, she dried off and pulled on her robe. Things were still new between them. The intimacy was shocking at times, but it made her feel good. *Wanted*. After Denny, she hadn't known if she'd ever get her self-confidence back.

Well, she didn't have that problem anymore, she thought with a smile.

She tied her robe around her naked body as she trod down the hallway on bare feet. When she came to the kitchen, though, she came to a complete stop.

"Wow," she mouthed silently.

There wasn't much that looked better than Ty Christiansen in the morning.

Her knees went weak, and she leaned her shoulder against the kitchen archway. His hair was damp. He must have showered in the master bathroom, because she hadn't heard him at all. He'd pulled his jeans on, but his feet and his chest were bare.

She couldn't help but stare. Just looking at that chiseled back made her fingers itch.

He glanced over his shoulder, spatula in hand. He caught her staring and their gazes locked. Heat unfurled in her belly. He looked like he wanted to devour her.

"I knew that hot pink number would give me a hard-on in the daylight."

She blushed. Without a word, though, she walked over to him. It felt so natural the way his arm wrapped around her waist.

He held the spatula away from her as she went up on tiptoes and kissed him. The moment their lips touched, the heat in her stomach dropped lower. She'd never been big on morning sex, but he was quickly helping her change her mind. She could feel her body revving.

Giving in to temptation, she caressed his chest. The muscles felt like hot marble. His tight nipples perked up under her touch, and she boldly leaned forward to lick one. A growl of satisfaction left his lips.

Unfortunately, it was answered by one from her stomach.

One of his eyebrows lifted. "I'll try not to take that as an insult."

"Sorry." She smiled weakly and backed away. Her stomach didn't let up.

He chuckled and ran a hand over the top of her head. "How about sustenance and then sex?"

Her face flared. "You do that on purpose, don't you?"

He grinned. "You look so sexy when you get shy, I just have to."

He was too devilish for his own good. She pushed him away, but his offer of food couldn't be ignored. She looked into the pan with a critical eye. "What are you making?"

Seeing he'd teased her enough, he backed off. "Omelets."

Her mouth watered. "That sounds good."

She was impressed with his handiwork. The bacon was draining on a plate covered with a paper towel. Beside the stove was a package of shredded cheese, a bowl with chopped green peppers, and another with . . . *onions*.

She stared. "You didn't put any of those in there, did you?"

"What? These?" Reaching out with his spatula, he gave the onions a little stir. "They're good."

"But you know I don't like them."

"Oh, come on. They're good for you."

She was still looking at the spatula. He was using it to push the omelet around in the pan. "Ew. You're getting onion juice on my eggs. Stop!"

A wicked look entered his eyes. Watching her closely, he pinched some onion out of the bowl and took a bite. "Mmm."

She winced. "Gross!"

He leaned towards her. "Gimme a kiss, baby."

She shrieked and scurried away. "Stay away from me, onion breath!"

He caught her anyway. She pressed her lips together tightly and tried to turn her head. He was impossible to resist—even with the taint of onions. His tongue rasped into her mouth, and she forgot all about her aversion to Vidalias.

He was grinning when he pulled back. "Your omelet is on the table. No onion juice, I promise."

She swatted at him. "That wasn't funny."

"Sure it was."

She rolled her eyes. The brute. She only kept the icky things around the house because he liked them on his hamburgers. See how funny he thought it was next time they grilled out and there weren't any in the crisper drawer.

She made a face at him and grabbed the plate with the bacon. He scooped up his omelet, put it on a plate, and followed her to the table. Humor was still in his eyes, but so was intimacy when he sat down next to her. "Feeling okay this morning? We got kind of crazy last night."

She shifted on her chair. The shower had made her aware that her body was more sensitive than sore—especially when her sudsy hands had drifted down low. With the sunlight spilling into the room, there was no hiding her reactions from him. "I feel good."

He caught her hand and quickly kissed her palm. "Me, too."

The look they shared was private, but he pulled back. "Go ahead. Eat before it gets cold."

He'd put the lid from the frying pan over her plate. She set it aside and found a golden omelet with cheese melting temptingly out of both ends. Tentatively, she used her fork to open it so she could peek inside.

He was already digging into his food hungrily. "What is it with you and onions?" he asked between bites. "You're a caterer. You must use them all the time."

"That doesn't mean I have to eat them." Satisfied that he'd told the truth, she tried a bite. She groaned in delight. It was perfect.

At ease with each other, they ate in silence. That wasn't to say they weren't communicating. The way his bare foot kept brushing against hers was distracting, and the looks that crossed the table were positively scorching.

She was starting to suspect that when he'd said "sustenance and then sex," he hadn't been joking.

Finally, there was nothing left to eat. Trista looked under the paper towel with one last ray of hope. She saw a tiny piece of bacon that had broken off from the others, and she pounced. She felt Ty's hot gaze watching her as she lifted it to her lips.

"I should feed you more often," he said huskily.

She brushed her napkin over her lips self-consciously. "You have a one-track mind."

"Honey, I've got three years to make up for."

And there it was, the thousand-pound gorilla that they'd been tiptoeing around for weeks.

Slowly, Trista folded her napkin and tucked it under the side of her plate. As intimate as they'd become, she still hadn't been able to say back those three little words he'd confessed on her deck steps.

She wished she could. They just wouldn't come.

Ty went quiet. He hadn't pressured her. Not even once. Spreading his legs wide, he sat back in his chair, nearly draping himself across it. As casual as the pose was, though, he was tense. "I think it's time we had the folks over for dinner."

Surprised, her gaze flickered up to meet his. He'd just jumped from the gorilla to its big, ugly mate. When she saw the determination in his eyes, the bottom dropped out of her stomach. "Can't we wait a little longer?"

He shrugged a shoulder and the muscles of his chest moved sinuously. "It's time, Trista. We can't keep sneaking around."

Why not? Things were going so well. She didn't want to stir up all those old wounds and hurts. "They won't approve, Ty."

"You don't know that."

She didn't, but she wasn't strong enough yet to find out for sure. "Please?" she whispered, looking at him pleadingly.

He stared at her, the fight stirring behind his eyes. After a moment, though, he wavered.

"Shit," he grumbled. In one smooth move, he sat upright and caught her. He had her on his lap before she could react. "All right. We'll wait, but you've got to stop using those big, lavender eyes to get what you want."

"Ty!" she gasped. She was straddling his lap, and he'd somehow worked her robe down to her waist. Her arms caught in the sleeves when she tried to grab onto him for balance. He took advantage of her vulnerability and caught a breast in each hand.

He began to massage her deeply. "What time do you have to be at work?"

"Soon," she groaned. He squeezed harder, and a shiver shot straight to her core. "Ty, we don't have time for this."

His teeth nipped at her earlobe. "Consider yourself lucky I let you have breakfast first."

She shuddered when he reached between her legs to deal with the zipper of his jeans. Before she could manage to wrestle her arms free, he was lifting and positioning her.

"Ah!" she moaned as his thick cock slowly pushed up into her. She grabbed his shoulders, and her head fell back.

He suckled hard at her breast, taking as much of her warm flesh into his mouth as he could.

"I do own my own business," she said on a high note.

He was lifting her on his lap with each deep thrust. "And I'm the foreman of my crew," he growled as he turned to her other red nipple. "I think we can be late just this once."

"Mmm, really late," she groaned. Enthralled, she scraped her fingernails down his chest.

"Fuck it!" His hands clamped down hard on her hips. "We'll get there when we get there."

෨

He was late, all right. Ty waited impatiently at the intersection for the light to turn. The guys wouldn't be able to let this one pass. He was going to catch hell for days.

It had been worth it, though.

In some ways . . .

His shoulders clenched.

"Damn it."

He reached up to rub the tense muscles. They were getting worse every day.

He sighed. How was it possible to be so happy and miserable at the same time?

Frustrated, he rubbed his fist around the steering wheel. Something had to give. The past three weeks with Trista had been unbelievable. Except for one thing . . .

She didn't feel about him the way that he felt about her.

Reflexively, his foot tamped down on the gas pedal. The engine revved, raring to get off the starting line.

Hell. That's where he felt like he still was, the starting line.

He didn't know why that surprised him. He'd known the facts when he'd gone into this. That hadn't stopped him from charging in headfirst. He'd wanted her. Fool that he was, he'd thought he could change her mind. That once they got past the Denny thing . . .

"Come on," he growled at the light. He shifted out of first gear and then back into it.

The sex was great. Great? She'd nearly made the top of his head come clean off this morning. Just being around her should have been enough. Her smile, her good humor, her friendship. He needed it all.

But he wanted more.

"Fuck," he cursed under his breath. The stoplight finally turned green, and he stomped on the gas.

His truck went flying into the intersection.

੪੩

Trista was rushing around the kitchen, trying to do too many things at once. The menu was big today. They were doing a retirement party for a furniture store's owner, and apparently that called for gluttony. The cake was in the oven, the meat and cheese tray was done, but stuffed mushrooms and miniature quiche took time.

She never should have let Ty make her late.

Although, looking back, she might have had some part in that. Her smile couldn't be repressed.

Kelly, fortunately, wasn't looking. She was too busy swearing at the phone as she hung it up. "Add little weenies to the list. Apparently, they're the boss's favorite. What does that say about a man?"

"Oh, for heaven's sake!" Trista looked up from the spinach mixture she was stirring for the quiche. "This is ridiculous. Why didn't they order them sooner?"

Kelly shook her finger. "You don't get between a man and his little weenies, hon."

As harassed as she was, Trista had to laugh. "Lucky for them we have some on hand."

"Lucky for us, I negotiated a steep price for the late menu change."

"Hey! Well, okay. Little weenies, it is."

The phone on the wall rang again, and Kelly gave an exaggerated sigh. She was turning to get it when the timer for the oven dinged.

"Get the cake," Trista said, wiping her hands. "I'll handle them this time."

Kelly pulled on an oven mitt. "If they want crackers with Cheez Whiz, tell them no. I don't care how much they offer."

Trista hurried to the phone. "Hello?"

"Trista?"

"Yes," she said, her brow knitting. She plugged her finger into her ear when her partner opened the squeaky oven door. The voice on the other end of the line sounded familiar, but she couldn't place it.

"This is Frank. From Ty's crew. We met last week at the Blue Moon."

"Oh. Hi, Frank." She tucked the cordless phone between her shoulder and her ear and returned to her spinach filling. "What can I do for you?"

"Well, I hate to bother you at work, but I thought you should know there's been a little accident."

Her spoon stopped midstir. "An accident?"

"Now, don't panic. Ty just—"

At once, her knees wobbled. "*Ty?*"

Ty had been in an accident? But she'd just seen him. She'd just talked to him. They'd just made love!

"What happened?" she asked, her throat clenching around the words.

"Whoa, whoa," Frank said awkwardly. "I said *not* to panic."

Trista felt Kelly come over to stand at her side. Her friend's hand settled on the middle of her back, but Trista couldn't stop the shaking that had started inside her.

"Is he okay?"

"He's fine," Frank said quickly. "Fine, I swear."

"What does that mean?" she snapped. She knew men. Denny had once been hit by a pitch on the hand. He'd sworn it was just a bruise until the team doctor had run X-rays and found that his finger had been broken.

"Sprained ankle," Frank provided promptly. He was starting to learn.

"I'll be right there."

"He just can't drive," Frank called loudly, sensing that she was about to hang up on him. "It's his clutch foot, but he won't let any of us take him home."

"I'll be right there!"

"Here," Trista said, shoving the bowl and the phone into Kelly's hands. She reached under the counter and pulled out her purse. "Call Susie in to help you."

She looked around the kitchen. "Laura, too."

"Don't worry about this. I've got it under control," Kelly said, waving her out the door.

Not willing to argue, Trista untied her apron and pulled it over her head. She tossed it at the hanger on the wall, not stopping to see if it caught on a peg. She ran out the back door. She tried to calm down as she stuck the key into the ignition. When she pulled out of the spot, though, the tires squealed.

Her nerves were screaming. What had happened? How badly was Ty really hurt? She knew how dangerous construction sites were.

Oh, God.

Oh, God. Oh, God. Oh, God!

She needed to see him. She needed to touch him. She needed to make sure he was all right!

The drive across town went much too slowly. In truth, she was lucky she didn't get a ticket. The construction site was busy when she got there. Sweaty muscled men were carrying things, climbing things, and driving big pieces of equipment. From what Ty had told her, the downtown parking garage was ahead of schedule.

"Awful thing," she spat. If it had somehow hurt him, it couldn't be finished fast enough for her.

She parked in the only spot she could find. The fact that it was in a restricted zone didn't faze her. She hopped out of her car and squinted as she looked upward. When she saw a man balancing on a steel frame four floors up, she went light-headed.

Oh, she couldn't even think about that.

"Ma'am?" somebody behind her called. "This is a restricted area. You can't be here."

Spinning around, she saw a man in a white hard hat. "Trista Christiansen," she said.

The man's eyebrows lifted. "Oh. That way," he said, pointing towards a makeshift office.

Trista hurried "that way." Once the construction workers caught sight of her, she heard more than one whistle. Her purple tank top and white shorts were like honey to the bees, but she didn't care. There was only one man she wanted to whistle at her right now. She just couldn't find him, and that made her even more nervous.

She did spot Frank, though. She hurried over to him. "Where is he?" she asked without preamble.

Frank's head came up. When he recognized her, he stood up straighter. Immediately, he jerked his thumb over his shoulder towards where the workers had parked their cars. "His truck is over there. Be careful. He's in a touchy mood."

So was she.

Trista felt like she was about to snap as she rushed to the parking area. Her heart was pounding and her hands were sweaty. She knew she was being silly. If it were serious, Frank would have rushed him to the hospital.

Wouldn't he?

Her tennis shoes skidded suddenly in the dry dirt. "Ty?"

He was sitting in the back end of his truck with the tailgate turned down. He looked up sharply when he heard her voice. "Trista."

Relief overcame her so swiftly, she had to reach out and hold onto the side of somebody's SUV. He looked okay—at least from a distance. With unsteady steps, she crossed over to him. When she was within reach, he caught her hand.

"What are you doing here?"

"Frank called me."

The look on Ty's face darkened. "What the hell did he do that for?"

His head swiveled as he looked for his second-in-command. "You didn't have to come all the way down here. I know this is a busy day for you."

"Shush." Worriedly, she looked him over from head to toe. His tanned body looked too healthy to be injured. "Are you okay?"

His gaze rushed back to her face. When he saw how close to tears she was, his mood swiftly changed. "I'm fine," he said, giving her hand a squeeze. "Just a little banged up."

His shirt was off and so was his left sock and boot. His foot was propped up on top of his clothes, and an icepack was draped over his ankle. Already, it was turning bright shades of yellow and purple. Unable to help herself, she ran her hands over him, looking for other wounds.

"Twisted ankle, that's all," he assured her.

She laid her hand over his muscled chest. His skin felt warm, and his heartbeat was reassuring. Her emotions jumbled, and she took a shuddering breath. She was horrified when tears spilled from her eyes.

Ty's face whitened, and he sat up sharply. "Oh, God. Don't do that."

She swallowed hard. "I can't help it."

For such a big, tough guy, he looked unraveled at the sight of a few tears. Almost roughly, he pulled her onto the tailgate with him. Trista sat down in relief, but her hip bumped against his. She winced at the way it jarred his ankle.

"It's fine. I'm fine," he assured her. His hands were shaky as he tried to dry her cheeks.

"What happened?" she asked.

He grimaced as if embarrassed. "My head wasn't on straight when I got here. I accidentally stepped on a piece of rebar and rolled my ankle. But hell, it's not even a decent sprain. I'll be able to walk on it tomorrow."

She closed her eyes. She was overreacting; she knew it. She just couldn't stop.

He'd scared her.

"Please stop crying, baby." His voice was gruff, but his hand was soothing as it slid down her side. He rubbed her leg gently. "You're killing me here."

She tried to pull herself together. "Let's get out of here," she said softly.

He glanced towards his crew. "I can't. I need to—"

"Frank wants you out of his hair," she said firmly. She gave one last sniff and wiped her eyes. She slid off the tailgate and held out her hand to him. "Come home with me. Please, Ty. I want to take care of you."

෫෬

Trista's protective instincts were raging by the time she helped Ty into the house. He was too macho to admit how much that ankle really hurt, but he let her flutter about him anyway. It made her feel somewhat better, although she didn't know how much she was helping. She just wanted to ease his pain—inside and out.

"This way," she said, stopping him when he started to sit down in a kitchen chair. Looking at him steadily, she caught his hand. "To bed."

She slipped her arm around his waist. He felt so solid. Warm and steadfast. Giving in to a moment of weakness, she pressed her face against his chest. When she'd heard he'd been hurt, her entire world had swung upside down. She was still trying to regain her equilibrium.

His fingers tangled in her hair. "It's not that bad," he said, dropping a kiss atop her head. "Just stick me in the easy chair in the living room. I'll prop my foot up on the hassock."

He wasn't going to win on this one. "Come to bed with me, Ty."

At first, he resisted. Then the air snapped, and his eyes turned smoky. All it took was a gentle tug to pull him away from the table. Trista felt her legs start to shake, but she wrapped his arm around her shoulder for support. Silently, slowly, she led him down the hallway.

Bright rectangles of sunlight lit up the floor, but she walked past each of them as she headed to her destination. He hobbled beside her, and she felt him try to turn left when they hit the guest bedroom.

"Not there." She knew his ankle must hurt, but she kept on going. This would make it feel better; she knew it would.

He paused for a moment in confusion, but then she felt his intensity skyrocket. She was leading him to the master bedroom.

"Are you sure?" he asked gruffly.

"I'm positive."

Today had been a huge wake-up call for her. It had shaken her out of her complacency . . . made her realize how unfair she'd been to him by sitting on the proverbial fence. He'd told her once that he knew how it was to feel second best, to be forgotten in the shadows.

Well, he was second best to *nobody*. She needed to show him that.

"This is the room you shared with Denny," he said, refusing to enter. "My little brother."

Turning, she looked up at him. "You're my lover now."

How could she have ever thought to compare the two of them? Besides, after the divorce, she'd wiped every trace of Denny from the room. The furniture had been rearranged, and the brown earth colors were now a cool, soothing blue. The autograph collection on the dresser had been replaced with perfume bottles, and she'd changed the morning alarm from rap to easy listening. It was her bedroom now.

And she wanted to share it with Ty.

She drew him into the room. Lines of stress remained on his face. From pain or worry, she couldn't tell. Gently, she reached up and smoothed them. "I'm sorry you were distracted this morning. I know it was my fault."

His eyes deepened in color, but his characteristic wiseass smile reappeared. "You do do your best work in the kitchen."

She refused to play along. "You weren't distracted by the sex."

She'd hurt him this morning.

And that hurt her almost more than she could stand.

Impulsively, she kissed him. It rocked them both on their feet. Unfortunately, in Ty's condition, that wasn't a good thing. She pulled back immediately at his grunt of pain.

He reached out for her. "Get back here. It's nothing."

"It's something." But it wasn't something they couldn't deal with. Not breaking eye contact, she cupped her hand over his erection. "We need to get these jeans off of you," she whispered.

His face slackened in surprise, but the bulge behind his zipper swelled. She took a deep breath and anticipation fluttered in her chest.

"Trista," he groaned. "I don't know how much I can do."

She smiled seductively. "Don't worry. I'll do all the work."

Leaning forward, she kissed his chest. His six-pack clenched, and he reflexively reached out to the dresser for support. Emboldened, she undid the button of his jeans. The importance of the moment shook her. Her fingers felt clumsy, but before she could lose her nerve, she caught the tab of his zipper.

The walls of the room seemed to close in on them. Ty swore under his breath and his other hand came up to tangle in her hair. Feeling weak and yet powerful at the same time, Trista slid the zipper down its track.

He was harder than she'd ever seen him.

He waited for an excruciating moment as she simply stared. "You don't have to," he finally said.

She pushed his hands away. After the scare she'd had, her arousal seemed even more acute. "Don't you dare," she whispered.

Somewhere in her subconscious, she heard the air conditioning kick on. Cool air blew at her legs, but she'd never felt so hot in her life. She wanted this.

She wanted him to know.

Impatiently, she caught his jeans and tugged them down. Once she got them past his hips, he moved clumsily to sit on the bed. She followed him and dropped into a crouch to pull the denim off his legs. When she glanced up, she found his cock hard and erect. Without thinking, she leaned forward and kissed his broad tip.

"God! Trista!"

His fingers bit into her shoulders—whether to hold her down or pull her up, she couldn't tell. She knew what *she* wanted. She fisted one hand around his big rod and determinedly gave him a pump. His hips jerked, and the sensitivity in her body came roaring back to life.

Before things could spin out of control, she stood up again. He looked at her, his eyes untamed. "Don't tease," he warned. "I'm not in the mood."

"Neither am I," she swore. Arousal gushed through her. She had so much she needed to say to him. So much she needed to show him. She reached for the bottom of her purple tank top, and he went still.

He made a choking sound when she pulled the constricting material off and threw it aside. "You came to the construction site braless?"

"I was in a hurry." Her nipples felt raw and hard. "Besides, it's got a shelf bra."

She toed off her shoes, and her hands went to her shorts. He reached for her convulsively, but she stepped away from the bed. He'd let her take charge so far. She practically begged him with her eyes to let her continue. "You've got a bad ankle. Lie down. Please."

A muscle in his jaw constricted. "You're going to drive me insane."

"Please?"

"Frickin' insane," he groaned as he awkwardly situated himself onto the mattress.

Naked, Trista climbed onto the bed with him. She was nervous, but she wasn't going to let that stop her. She wanted to soothe him, to make him forget how hesitant she'd been with her feelings before. Uncertainly, she scooted up higher on the bed so her knees were near his shoulders.

His hands fisted into the bedspread. "God damn."

He squeezed his eyes shut as she leaned down over him. Full of curiosity, she slid her hands down to his balls. They were already pulled up tight. She licked her lips as she stared at his cock. Looking at him like this, she realized why she always felt so full when he pushed inside her. He was thick, and he was long.

She felt a pang deep in her pussy, and she let out a low murmur.

She flinched when his hand suddenly cupped the back of her neck. His fingers were tight, but he didn't pressure her. He didn't have to.

"I want to," she whispered.

She lowered her mouth and, tentatively, licked the bulbous head. He was hard, yet his skin was soft. She liked the way he felt against her tongue. Opening her mouth wider, she took more of him inside.

"Fuck," he groaned underneath her.

Trista shivered with arousal. Letting her throat relax, she took all of him that she could. He was more than a mouthful, all thick and hot. He shifted uncontrollably and she almost panicked when he went down her throat. Once she realized how it felt, though, she let it happen.

Ty's low curses filled the air as her head bobbed up and down. Her hair brushed against his hips, and the room heated until the air conditioning couldn't keep up. Somewhere outside, a lawn-mower flared up. Knowing what they were doing in secret while a neighbor worked around them made Trista all the hotter. Planting her hands on both sides of his hips, she went down on him more aggressively.

His heels dug into the mattress, and he suddenly swore. "Damn ankle. That's it," he growled. "Get over here."

Her head snapped up in surprise when she felt his hands work under her and catch her by the hipbones. "Oh!" she gasped when he lifted her.

His strength was exciting—especially when he lowered her so her knees were settled on either side of his ears.

"Ty!" she gasped in shock.

She craned her neck around. Helpless to her own desire, she watched as he pulled her down for a taste. Even knowing it was coming, her head still flung back when he gave her that first intimate kiss.

"Ahhh!" she cried.

His tongue was strong and persistent. It began to investigate all her tight niches and swollen ridges. Trista began to quake, but then she felt his hand slide up her spine. He caught her by the nape of the neck again and urged her down.

She groaned as his cock reared up in her face. The intimacy was irresistible. She began to pleasure him as he was pleasuring her.

Soon it became a test of endurance. Bodies rocked, but Ty

kept his arms wrapped around her waist in a tight bear hug. Trista's concentration was split as enjoyment surrounded her. She sucked and licked as she felt Ty do the same. She knew he could taste her. She'd gotten wet when she'd first crawled onto the bed with him. *Her bed*. When his lips moved lower, though, her body arched like a rainbow.

He'd found her clit.

Ecstasy came on hard. Their bodies began to buck and sway as they worked each other into oblivion. For once, she got to him first. She felt him swell impossibly, and she ran a finger down the vein that ran the length of his cock. He slammed upward. She sucked him hard and trembled in satisfaction when he began to come.

Beneath her, his tongue pressed solidly against her clit. Devil that he was, he wouldn't relent until her taut body finally sprang loose. Trista let out a cry and ground herself against his mouth as she came and came.

Breathlessly, they rolled onto their sides. Overcome with emotion, Trista had to blink back the wetness that threatened to fall from her eyes. When Ty caught her and coaxed her around, she cuddled against him. She lay with her hand on his chest and her head on his shoulder. He was still breathing hard. She could feel his heart racing.

Timidly, she glanced up. She was surprised by the fierce look on his face. He looked like a man driven to the edge.

His arm suddenly tightened around her. "Why?"

"Why?" she repeated, lifting her head.

His gaze was hot and intent. "Why all the worry?" he asked gruffly. "Why the tears? *Why this bed?*"

The hopeful, but uncertain look on his face made Trista's breath catch. Suddenly, she knew what he was asking . . .

"Because I love you, you big roughneck."

He flinched, almost as if he'd been bracing himself for another answer. She couldn't blame him. Just this morning, she hadn't been able to tell him what he'd needed to hear.

She peppered kisses across his chest. "I've been so stupid," she confessed. "So scared and selfish."

Propping herself up on her elbows, she looked down into his face. Emotion swelled up inside her again. She hadn't been protecting herself by shutting down her feelings. All she'd done was cheat them both.

"I love you back, Ty."

He let out a shuddering breath.

She smiled. "I love you back!"

Kimberly Dean

Kimberly Dean first began writing erotic romance in 2001. Since then, she's gone on to publish many steamy stories about love, desire, and devotion. When not writing, she enjoys reading, movies, sports, and music. She never knows what will spark an idea for her next work! To learn more, visit www.kimberlydean.com or email Kimberly@kimberlydean.com.

Lynn LaFleur

VICTIM OF
DECEPTION

A special thank-you to Cheryl Scheetz and Jeremy Norton
for letting me use your poetry.

Prologue

North Texas, May 20, 1910

"Harder, Aaron. *Harder!*"

Aaron slipped his hands beneath Mary's plump buttocks and pulled her tighter to him. He felt her fingernails scrape his back as he pounded his shaft into her. He didn't care if her nails scarred him for life. Nothing mattered except fucking her as hard and fast as he could. Nothing mattered except for the two of them to be together like this for as long as possible.

Her breath caught. Her back arched. Aaron knew those were signs she was close to her release. He called on all his inner strength to keep from reaching his climax before she did.

He bit lightly on her earlobe the way he knew made her crazy. "That's it, sweetheart. Let me feel that sweet pussy grab my cock when you come."

"Aaron!"

She shuddered beneath him. A moment later, Aaron followed her over the edge into bliss.

He lay on top of Mary, fighting for breath. They'd been

married for two years. Each time they made love was better than the last.

He'd never believed he could love a woman so much.

The gentle caress of Mary's hands on his back gave Aaron the strength to raise his head and look into her eyes. She smiled. "Hi."

He returned her smile. "Hi."

"That was wonderful."

He kissed the tip of her nose. "It certainly was."

"How can it be better every time we make love?"

"I was just wondering the same thing." He kissed her softly, sweetly. "I love you, Mary."

She smiled tenderly. "I love you, too."

Aaron started to kiss her again, but a mewling sound stopped him. Glancing over his shoulder, he looked at the small bed against the wall. The shuffling of covers indicated they'd woken their daughter.

"I don't think Katie likes all this ruckus."

"If we're quiet, maybe she'll go back to sleep."

Aaron chuckled. "You know better than that. If one of us doesn't hold her for a few minutes, she'll keep right on crying."

Mary bit her bottom lip. "Do you think we've spoiled her?"

"Hopelessly."

Katie's mewling turned into a full cry. Aaron withdrew from the warmth of Mary's body and threw back the covers. "I'll get her."

He padded across the wooden floor to Katie's bed. "Hey there, baby," he crooned as he bent to pick up his daughter. "Did you have a bad dream?"

"Is she wet?"

Aaron checked her diaper. "Nope. You fed her before we made love, so she can't be hungry yet." Lifting her to his shoulder, he walked back toward the bed. "I think she just wants attention."

He laid her on the bed next to Mary, then lay beside her. Katie looked at him with her huge blue eyes . . . the only physical trait she'd inherited from him. She was her mother made over except for having his blue eyes instead of her green ones.

No longer crying, she thumped him on the chin with her small fist. "Hey!" Aaron playfully growled and tickled his daughter's tummy. Katie blessed him with her smile.

A knot of emotion lodged in his throat. He touched the soft blond fuzz on Katie's head as love swelled in his heart. He was so blessed to have these two beautiful ladies in his life.

"She's so pretty, Mary. She looks just like you."

Mary smiled. "I see a lot of her father in her, too." She pulled up the sheet and tucked it around Katie's body. "I cannot believe she'll be five months old in a few days."

"Me either." He picked up Mary's hand and kissed her palm. "Maybe it's time for Katie to have a brother or sister."

"I haven't lost all the weight I gained from having Katie."

"I like the way you look now. You were too skinny before you had Katie."

Mary's mouth dropped open. "Skinny!"

"Yeah, skinny." Aaron loved to tease her. His teasing usually turned into a playful wrestling match, which turned into lovemaking. "I like your body now."

To prove his words, he cradled one heavy breast in his hand and skated his thumb across the nipple. It peaked beneath his caress.

"You like my big breasts."

"I certainly do." He swiped his tongue across her nipple. She tasted of woman and milk. "What do you think about having another baby, Mary?"

A pink blush climbed into Mary's cheeks. "I'd like that very much," she whispered.

"Then maybe I should put Katie back in her own bed so we can start working on that brother or sister."

Once Aaron had Katie tucked into her bed, he turned to look at Mary. She lay with the rumpled sheet at her side, exposing her naked body to him. He gazed at her full breasts, rounded stomach, the blond curls between her thighs. As he watched, she spread her legs so he could see between them. Her lips were pink, swollen, and wet with the combination of her juices and his.

She held out her arms to him. "Give me a baby, Aaron."

He took two steps toward her.

"You cheating bastard!"

Aaron whipped around at the sound of the woman's shriek. Eva stood in the bedroom doorway, a shotgun pointed at his stomach.

"Eva?"

"How could you, Aaron? How could you cheat on me?"

Aaron had no idea what she was saying. Eva worked at the general store. He saw her every now and then when Mary would ask him to pick up supplies for her. Although he always tried to be polite to Eva, he'd never given her any special attention.

He held out one hand toward her. "Eva, put down the gun so we can talk."

She raised the shotgun another inch. "You should be with *me,* not this whore! I can love you so much more than she can."

Fear crawled up Aaron's spine. He'd heard stories of Eva's insanity, but had ignored them. With a shotgun pointed at his belly and the wild look in her eyes, he could no longer ignore the rumors.

"Eva, Mary is my wife. We have a daughter."

"I can give you all the children you want. You don't love *her*. You *can't* love her. You're always so nice to me at the store. You have to care about me. You wouldn't be so nice to me if you didn't care."

"I *do* care about you, Eva, but I love Mary."

"*No!* I won't listen to your lies!" She raised the shotgun to her shoulder. "If I can't have you, neither can she!"

Eva's screaming woke up Katie. Aaron heard her soft whimper. Sweat beaded his forehead and trickled down his temple. He had to get that gun away from Eva before she hurt Mary or Katie.

Out of the corner of his eye, he saw Mary rise from the bed. "Mary, stay there!"

"I have to get to Katie!"

Eva swung the shotgun toward Mary. "You stay where you are, whore!"

Seeing the gun pointed at his love snapped Aaron's control. He lunged toward Eva, hands outstretched to snatch the gun away from her.

A loud blast made his ears ring. He stumbled backward when something burned his skin. Looking down, he saw blood running from the large wound in his stomach.

"*Aaron!*" Mary cried.

She'd shot him. Eva had shot him. Sinking to his knees, he stared at the woman with the crazed eyes. He never would have believed she could do such a thing.

Mary grabbed him and hugged his neck tightly. He could feel her warm tears fall on his shoulders. That's all he felt. It should hurt. He'd always thought a gunshot would hurt. He didn't understand why it didn't.

His vision blurred. He wanted to return Mary's hug, but he couldn't get his arms to work. He blinked and watched Eva pop the two empty shells from the shotgun and reload it.

"N-no, Eva," he said, his voice slurred. "Don't."

"You didn't give me any choice, Aaron. You chose this slut over me. I can't allow that, don't you see?"

Through the buzzing in his ears, he heard Katie crying. His daughter needed him. He had to stop Eva before she hurt anyone else.

"That should be *my* baby, not this slut's! Katie will be mine from now on. I'll take her and raise her. I'll love her so much, she'll never miss either of you."

"*No!*" Mary screamed. "You can't have my baby!"

Mary rose and ran toward Eva. She made it no more than two steps when the shotgun blast sent her backward. Aaron watched his wife fall to the floor, blood pouring from the wound in her chest.

"*Mary!*"

She didn't move, she didn't blink. Aaron sensed Eva's movement, but his gaze focused on Mary. It was getting harder for him to breathe, yet he had to get to her. He had to help her. Sliding through a pool of blood, he made it to Mary's side. He gathered her up in his arms.

"Mary," he whispered. "Please don't die."

He looked up at Eva. She stood over them, the shotgun in one arm and a crying Katie in the other. Now he clearly saw the madness shining in her wide eyes.

"I curse you, Aaron, and your whore. I curse you to walk the floors of this house forever." She shifted Katie to her shoulder and rocked her gently. Leaning forward, she hissed in Aaron's face. "You'll be together, but will never be able to touch each other ever again. You'll suffer from your lust for all eternity!"

Her maniacal laugh vibrated in Aaron's ears as she strode from the room.

With shaking fingers, Aaron closed Mary's unseeing eyes. Tears filled his eyes and clogged his throat as he inched closer to his love and tightened his arms around her. He kissed her lips once more before the darkness settled over him.

One

> *I fear she may be mad.*
> *She is good to me and I believe she loves me. But I*
> *have heard tales of her treachery, her evil, her witchcraft.*
> *I have heard she is not my real mother.*
> *I must find out. Somehow, I must find out the truth.*

A knock on her open office door made Karessa Austin close the tattered diary and look up. She smiled at her assistant, Joy. "Is everything ready?"

"All unpacked and ready for you to inspect."

Excitement surged through Karessa's body. A new display for the museum always gave her goose bumps. It was better than sex.

Well, at least better than the sex she'd experienced lately.

She followed Joy from the executive offices of The Gage-Austin Museum. Walking down the lushly carpeted hallway made her feel closer to her parents. They'd died nine years ago when she was twenty-one, but not before establishing this beautiful museum close to Trinity Park.

"Did you have the chance to read your great-grandmother's diary?" Joy asked.

"Part of it. I'll read more after I've seen the display."

"Have you decided yet what you'll do with the house?"

Karessa shook her head. "No. That's something else I'll have to look at later. I have no idea why my Aunt Grace left me that old Victorian."

"You told me she never married, never had any children. You're the only family she had."

"I know, but I have no use for a house that's over a century old. I run a museum, but I like modern conveniences. My condo works perfectly for me."

Karessa pushed open the heavy metal door that led to the back room of the museum. Deliveries were made and any unpacking done here. This is where she looked at all the items that came into the museum and decided whether they go into an existing display or a new display be created.

She loved her job.

Her warehouse manager, Marco, smiled as she approached him. "You'll love all of these, Karessa."

Karessa returned his smile. Marco was thirty-five, dark from his Italian heritage, and built like Conan the Barbarian. If he didn't work for her, she'd jump his bones in a second.

I can fire him, at least for a weekend. We can have wild monkey sex, then I'll rehire him on Monday. With a body like that, he's got to be incredible in bed.

Karessa sighed as her hormones jumped for joy. They'd love it if she did exactly that. Unfortunately, her conscience would never allow her to take advantage of her employee.

Darn it.

Shifting her attention back to the large crates on the warehouse floor, she watched as her men opened them and carefully removed the paintings by Thomas Abernathy. Her heartbeat sped up at the sight of the beautiful scenes of charming English cottages. The thatched roofs, white walls, cloudy skies, colorful flowers . . . they all combined to create the masterpieces for which he'd been famous.

There were seven in all, donated to the museum by Abernathy's granddaughter. She could've picked any museum in the world to display her grandfather's paintings. But she'd picked The Gage-Austin, a fact that made Karessa so proud of her parents and the museum's sterling reputation.

"I have the letter Ms. Abernathy sent with the paintings," Joy said. She opened the portfolio she always carried with her. "She said she would've donated all eight in the series, but one painting was bought by a private collector for, and I quote, 'an obscene amount of money.'"

"I can believe that." Karessa stood before the painting called *Twilight* and stared at it. How she'd love to have this hanging in her living room. Too bad she couldn't slip it into her purse and take it home with her. "Did she mention the collector's name? Maybe we could make arrangements for him or her to lend it to us for the showing."

"Yes, it's right here. His name is Maxwell Hennessey."

She shivered at the sound of his name, but not from pleasure. Maxwell Hennessey was the lowest form of scum on earth. She hoped she never saw him again for the rest of her life.

"Do you want me to contact him?" Joy asked.

"No," Karessa said quickly. Realizing her voice sounded sharp, she cleared her throat and smiled at Joy. "No, that's fine. We'll have a wonderful showing with the seven paintings."

"Are you sure? I can contact Ms. Abernathy and try to find—"

"That won't be necessary, Joy."

The puzzled look in Joy's eyes didn't surprise Karessa. Normally, she would jump at the chance to have a full collection on display. But she'd rather eat raw liver for a week than have anything to do with Maxwell Hennessey.

It wasn't exactly an uncommon name, yet Karessa had no doubt the Maxwell Hennessey who owned the eighth painting and the one she'd been involved with five years ago were the same man. Max collected things of value and beauty. He liked to possess things . . . including the heart of a naïve twenty-five-year-old who fell in love much too quickly.

"Joy, will you take care of this? I'd like to leave a little early and drive out to my great-aunt's house."

"Of course. The Egyptian display is set to come down from the Red Room Friday. Do you want this collection set up there?"

"That'll be perfect. I'll want the flowers changed, too . . . something with an English garden theme."

"I'll take care of it."

Leaving the details in her capable assistant's hands, Karessa left the room and returned to her office. She began gathering up her things, intending to go home after she drove by her great-aunt's house. She'd have to talk to a real estate agent about selling the house and thirty acres as soon as possible.

She hadn't seen the house since she was a young teenager. Her great-aunt had been quite wealthy and loved to travel; rarely had she stayed at home for longer than a month at a time. When she did come home long enough for a visit, she was the one who always went to Karessa's condo with gifts, mementos, and pictures. There'd been no reason for Karessa to go back to Aunt Grace's house.

Her great-aunt's death from a stroke a month ago had been a shock. She'd always been so healthy, so vivacious—one could have assumed she'd live forever. Now, with Grace's death, Karessa no longer had any family. She was totally alone.

Where did this horrible case of self-pity come from? Straightening her shoulders, Karessa picked up her briefcase and purse from the bookshelf behind her desk. She glanced over her desk to make sure everything had been put in its place. The tattered diary on the corner drew her attention. She'd planned to leave it here, where it could be locked up in the safe. On impulse, she picked it up and placed it in her briefcase so she could finish reading it at home.

⊷⊰

Max Hennessey closed his *Washington Post*, folded it neatly, and laid it next to his plate. The article he'd expected to find wasn't there. That meant his source hadn't lied and nothing had been leaked to the press.

At least, not yet.

Rumors of hidden treasure often brought out the ones looking to make a quick buck. But more often than not, rumors of hidden treasure were forgotten as soon as they were heard. Getting something for nothing would be too easy.

Max had become a multi-millionaire by following those rumors.

He had plenty of time. He'd finish up his business here in Washington, D.C., before heading for Houston. Once in the Lone Star State, he'd contact his source again for exact details on where the bearer bond was hidden.

As long as he stayed away from Fort Worth, he'd be fine. He didn't want there to be the slightest chance that he might run into Karessa.

Thinking of the beautiful blonde still caused a sharp pain in his chest. He'd deceived her and dumped her when the lure of fortune proved too much to resist.

Money in the bank hadn't made him less lonely.

He picked up his cup and sipped the cooling coffee. He'd wondered many times how his life would be now if he'd stayed with her, if he hadn't let greed color his judgment.

There'd been women since Karessa. He was a healthy forty-year-old man who greatly enjoyed sex. He knew women found him attractive. Finding an available bed partner had never been a problem.

Finding someone to love was an entirely different matter.

"May I warm your coffee, Mr. Hennessey?"

Max looked up at the lovely brunette waitress. She'd been especially attentive to him for the three days he'd been at this hotel. He had the feeling it would take very little encouragement for her to warm his bed as well as his coffee.

Smiling, he held up his cup. "Thank you."

"You're very welcome. Is there anything else I can do for you?"

Time to move in for the kill. "As a matter of fact, there is. I'll be leaving town in a few days and haven't had the chance to do much sight-seeing. Business hasn't let me play tourist."

"It would be a shame for you to leave Washington without seeing the sights."

"My thoughts exactly. So . . ." He glanced at her name tag. "Leslie, would you be interested in showing me around town, perhaps have dinner with me tonight?"

She smiled. "I'd love to."

Two

Karessa fell in love with the house at first sight.

Surrounded by huge oak trees, the two-story house made her think of a time long past—a time when people weren't in such a hurry, when there wasn't as much stress in their lives, when every moment wasn't filled with something that had to be done immediately. It made her think of family, love, and romance.

She didn't remember the house ever having such a powerful effect on her.

It'd been at least fifteen years since she'd been inside, perhaps longer. She studied the thick columns supporting the second story, the wide veranda that completely circled the house, the large windows that let in the morning sunshine. Aunt Grace had generally kept up the house over the years, but had never personally taken care of it since she traveled so much. Karessa's trained eye could see bits of decay here, evidence of neglect there.

The house would be so beautiful with a complete refurbishment.

Thanks to a healthy inheritance from her parents, and now from her great-aunt, she had more than enough money to renovate the house. She could even live here during the remodeling.

The house had four bedrooms, perhaps five. She'd have plenty of room to—

Karessa blew out a deep breath. *What are you thinking? You can't live here!*

The thought had no more than formed in her mind when she asked herself, why not. Her ancestors had lived here. The house had been passed down to the women of her family. She knew for a fact that her great-grandparents—Aunt Grace's parents—lived here. Perhaps the line went even further back than that.

She couldn't sell this piece of living history without a lot of thought.

Karessa climbed the steps to the veranda. Her hand shook slightly as she unlocked the front door and stepped into the cool interior.

&&

"She's coming inside! Aaron, she's coming inside."

"I see that." Aaron leaned down next to Mary and looked out the window at the lovely blond woman climbing up the steps. "God, Mary, she looks just like you. Her hair is shorter, but she looks just like you."

"I've seen her. She was here several years ago to visit Grace."

"She's our descendant, Mary. She'd be our . . . what? Great-great-granddaughter?"

"She's Elizabeth's daughter, Karessa. I remember her coming here for holidays." Mary shivered. "It's so hard to believe, Aaron. Our beautiful Katie grew up, married, and had two daughters. We watched her children grow up right here in this house." She straightened and faced Aaron. "Despite Eva's curse, our family continued."

Tears filled Mary's eyes. Aaron reached out to touch her face. His hand met an invisible barrier two inches from her . . . just like it had for almost one hundred years.

"*Damnit!* I wish I could touch you."

"I wish you could, too," Mary whispered.

Aaron began to pace the floor. Years of frustration tore at him. He wanted to hit something, to ram his fist into the wall. He'd tried, several times, but his fist simply passed right through the wood. "There has to be a way to break the curse, a way for us to be together again."

"How? We've tried everything we can think of."

"God damn Eva! I hope she's rotting in hell where she belongs."

Mary stepped closer to him. "Aaron, don't say that. Don't think or say anything bad."

"Why not? It's how I feel."

"I know, but I can't help feeling we need to do something . . . good for someone."

Aaron held out his arms. "How can we do something good for someone when no one can see or hear us? We've stood directly in front of people in this house. They didn't even blink."

"I don't know! I just know we can't give up. We have to keep trying until we can be together again . . . in every way."

Aaron gazed at Mary's long blond hair, huge green eyes, and full figure covered but not hidden by her floor-length white dress. She chose for them to wear clothing while he'd prefer to see her nude at all times. He respected her wishes, knowing she wore the dress to keep his mind off her body.

As if that could ever happen.

"Ah, Mary. How I wish I could make love to you again."

"I wish you could, too," she whispered.

"I don't understand this whole thing. We're dead. I know

we're dead. Eva shot both of us. But we don't feel dead. We breathe, we sleep, we feel emotions. We can pick up and move things, even though we can walk right through a wall." He turned in a circle, his arms outstretched. "We can go anywhere in this house, but we can't take one step off the veranda. We've been trapped here for almost a century! I'm tired of being in limbo."

Mary's tears overflowed and ran down her cheeks. "I know. I'm tired, too, but I don't know what we can do."

He stared at his wife, the woman he loved. He could see her sweet smile and voluptuous body. He could smell her floral scent. He couldn't touch her, but she could touch herself. "I know one thing you can do for me."

"What?"

"Make yourself come."

She bit her bottom lip. "Aaron—"

"Please, Mary. You know how much I love to watch you touch your pussy. I can't touch you, so do it for me." He stepped as close to her as he could until the barrier stopped him. "Think about my lips on yours. Think about my hands touching your back, your bottom, your breasts. Think about my tongue between your legs, lapping up your juices. Think about my cock buried deep inside your sweet pussy."

Her eyes glazed with passion. Her chest rose and fell with her shallow breaths. Her nipples beaded beneath her thin cotton dress. Aaron longed to suck them.

She took two steps back. Aaron's own breathing became unsteady as he watched her gather up the hem of her dress and pull it over her head. She stood before him naked, her ivory skin flushed with desire.

Silently, she walked across the room to the rocking chair. Sitting on the cushioned seat, she draped her legs over the arms.

Aaron had a clear view of her wet pussy. He moved closer and dropped to his knees between her legs. The aroma of her arousal drifted to his nostrils.

"God, Mary, you smell so good. I wish I could taste you again."

Mary slid one hand over her full breast and down her rounded stomach. "So do I."

She touched her labia. Aaron swallowed hard as she picked up the cream from her slit and spread it over the swollen lips. "That's the way. Rub your clit for me. Make yourself come."

She stared into his eyes while caressing herself. Aaron alternated between looking into her eyes and looking at her pussy. The feminine lips turned darker, wetter, with her caressing. How he longed to touch her, taste her!

He damned Eva all over again.

Mary's fingers moved faster over her clit. Aaron unfastened his pants and withdrew his hard cock. He stroked it in time with her fingers, wanting to come at the same time as she.

Her lids slid closed.

"Don't close your eyes, baby," Aaron rasped. "Watch what I'm doing."

Mary looked at his shaft. Aaron tightened his grip and pumped quicker. "Do you want me to come first?"

"Yes," she whispered.

The orgasm built in the base of his spine and tightened his balls. Aaron groaned. He continued to pump his cock as semen shot out the head and ran over his hand. Gazing at her face, he wilted to the floor, totally spent.

His strength quickly returned when he focused his attention on Mary's hand. He loved when she pleasured herself. It was one of the most erotic things he'd ever seen.

"Aaron!"

Her hips bucked, her back arched, her nipples beaded. She moaned loudly. He stared at her pussy, watching the inner lips pulsate with her orgasm. His mouth watered with the desire to drive his tongue deep inside her.

"Ah, Mary," he whispered. "I love you so much."

"I love you, too." Her voice broke on the last word. Tears cascaded down her face again. "It feels good when I do that, but I wish it could be you touching me."

"Soon, Mary. I'll hold you in my arms and make love to you again, soon."

"H-how?"

"I don't know yet, but it will happen. I promise you."

⁂

She heard the soft moan the moment she stepped inside the house.

Karessa froze, her hand still on the doorknob. She waited several moments, but didn't hear the sound again. Certain her ears had been playing tricks on her, she closed the door. That's when she heard a woman weeping.

Okay, this is really weird.

Goose bumps skittered across her skin. She didn't know whether to leave or stay. All her protective instincts screamed at her to get out of the house as quickly as possible.

Karessa pulled the strap of her purse higher on her shoulder. This was *her* house. She wouldn't let some strange noise scare her away.

Even though it gave her the creeps.

The house was stuffy from being closed up for over a month. Karessa walked through the downstairs rooms, opening a window in each one to let in the pleasant seventy-five-degree air. Due to the hot North Texas summers, air conditioning would soon be a necessity. For now, she wanted the gentle breeze to clear out the stale smell.

She laid her purse and briefcase on the dining room table. The large mahogany table would seat eight comfortably. Karessa remembered coming here as a child with her parents and grand-parents for holidays. She smiled. Such pleasant memories of fam-ily and laughter.

Thinking of her family made her remember the diary in her briefcase. It seemed right to read her great-grandmother's words while here in the house where Katie had lived so long ago.

Karessa prepared herself a glass of iced water, then sat at the table. She carefully pulled the antique diary from her briefcase and opened it to the page she was reading at the museum.

I must find out. Somehow, I must find out the truth.

I wish I could ask someone for help, but there is no one I can trust. It is as if she has everyone around us un-der a spell. No one comes to the house. No one speaks to us when we walk on the street.

She works to support us, but does not let me out of her sight. I must go to school, then directly to the store until she is finished for the day. We come home, have sup-per, then I do my homework while she sews or reads in the big book she will not let me see.

I have looked for the book, but have only minutes to myself to hunt for it. I long for friends, for someone to share secrets and desires. She will not allow it.

The loneliness is crushing at times. I fear I will never meet a boy to love and who will love me. I fear I will re-main in this house forever.

Karessa wiped a tear from her cheek. Her great-grandmother had been so young when she'd written these words, barely a teenager. How sad to be full of so much despair at such a young age.

She turned the page and continued to read.

May 29, 1925—I saw him today. He came in the store shortly before my mother and I left. Tall, dark-haired, handsome. My heart started beating funny as soon as I looked up and saw him.

Karessa smiled. She remembered her own first "love" when she was fifteen. Seeing him had made her heart beat funny, too.

I did not find out his name. I tried to wait on him, but my mother pushed me back with a stern look and told me to help Mrs. Chatham. Perhaps he will come back in the store tomorrow and I will see him then.

Whatever I do, I must not let my mother know that I wish to see him. She would forbid me to stay in the store with her, even though Mr. Lewis likes me to be there. He says I am like a ray of sunshine. It is his store and he should make up the rules, yet I fear my mother could convince him I should not be there.

He sometimes gives me money when she is not looking. He says it is payment for working there. Taking money from him does not seem right, but it is nice to have a little money of my own. I have to hide it from my mother, just like I have to hide this diary and anything else I do not wish her to find.

I love her, but she frightens me.

Karessa drained her glass of water and rose to refill it. She stopped halfway to the kitchen when cold air flowed over her. It felt as if she'd stepped beneath an air conditioning vent, yet she hadn't turned on the air conditioning.

Slowly, she turned in a circle. A movement in the air ten feet in front of her made the goose bumps erupt on her skin again. It looked like a heat mirage, one a person sees over a highway on a very hot day.

She hadn't thought it was possible to see something like that inside a house.

The air shifted, became wavy and distorted. Karessa's heartbeat sped up. Her palms grew damp. She blinked, certain she had to be seeing things.

The movement stopped.

Karessa stared at the spot for several moments. When nothing else happened, she blew out a deep breath.

You're letting the house get to you. There's no one here but you.

Feeling calmer once again, she turned and headed for the kitchen to refill her glass.

෩

"Aaron, she saw me!"

"She can't see you, Mary."

"She looked right at me! She knows I'm here!" A huge smile spread over her face. "She's the key, Aaron. Our great-great-granddaughter is going to help us break the curse."

Three

Max tossed his garment bag on the bed. Unzipping the side pocket, he withdrew a white clasp envelope. Frankie had met him at the airport and handed the envelope to him. He'd offered the guest room in his house for a couple of days, but Max had declined and rented a hotel room instead. He wanted to be alone when he looked at the contents.

His friend was a strange guy. Frankie liked the hunt, liked to dig up information about hidden treasure. He searched the Internet, old newspapers, courthouse records. The research turned him on, not the physical search for the pot of gold. He didn't care about actually finding the treasure. Max had never been able to understand that. Frankie had a lot of money, but he could have so much more if he found the riches he helped others to find. Yet he was perfectly happy earning his finder's fee from people like Max before he started the next research project.

Max would be all too happy to give Frankie the twenty percent finder's fee he demanded if the contents of this envelope led to the bearer bond worth millions.

He unfastened the clasp, but hesitated before opening the

envelope. Before he looked inside, Max decided to shower and have a drink.

Anticipation always made the prize sweeter.

The flight from D.C. had been rough thanks to strong thunderstorms. Even a seasoned flyer would feel queasy after the bumpy ride. Max stood beneath the warm spray, letting the water revive him. Only a full body massage would feel better right now . . . followed by a naked, willing woman.

He lowered his head so the water could beat on the back of his neck. Leslie had certainly been willing. She'd been a pleasant diversion for a few hours, even though neither his heart nor his mind had been with her. His mind had been too focused on getting to Texas and looking inside that envelope. His heart . . .

His heart still belonged to Karessa.

Women had come and gone in his life in the five years since he'd fallen so hard for the beautiful blonde. None of them came close to making him forget about Karessa. So many times, he'd thought about calling her, seeing if she'd give him another chance. He'd always hung up before the call had gone through. The way he'd hurt her, she'd never forgive him. And he couldn't blame her for that.

So he remained alone, taking pleasure from women whenever his body's urges became too strong to ignore. The women paraded in and out of his life through a revolving door. With each new one, he hoped for that spark, that connection that might lead to love.

It never happened.

Max turned off the faucets and opened the glass door. After swiping most of the water from his body, he wrapped the oversized towel around his waist and padded back into the bedroom. An investigation of the small refrigerator and bar produced a miniature bottle of bourbon and can of Coke. He'd rather have Scotch, but right now he wouldn't be picky. He mixed the drink and propped himself up on the bed with the pillows behind his back. Once he'd emptied half the glass, he reached for the envelope.

His instant erection made him shift on the bed. Uncovering a new treasure always gave him a hard-on.

Ignoring the randy part of his body, he bent open the clasp and dumped the contents on the bed. One thing about Frankie—he was thorough. He always included the notes he took during his research so Max could be sure of every step Frankie took. After years of working with him, Max trusted Frankie enough to ignore the hand-written notes and scribbles. All he cared about was the bottom line.

He searched through the paperwork until he found the single sheet of neatly typed blue paper, Frankie's trademark.

Fingering his thick mustache, he read from the beginning. Charles and Belinda Blackburn had moved to America from England in 1898. Already a man of means, he'd made a fortune with wise investments. Part of those investments included buying a bearer bond from a small railroad. Over the years, that railroad had been absorbed into a larger one, which was bought out by a national transportation company.

That company had been bought by Tharwood Energy.

"Holy shit," Max muttered. Tharwood Energy was the largest producer of electricity in the United States. If one of those bonds still existed, it could easily be worth millions, Frankie claimed.

Max's erection throbbed.

Scanning farther down the sheet, Max searched for where the Blackburns had lived. They'd settled in a small town outside the city limits of . . .

Fort Worth.

"Hell."

Of all the hundreds of cities in Texas, it had to be the one where Karessa lived.

Max pushed his damp hair off his forehead. It didn't matter. He could get in and out of the area within a few days. He'd find the bond and leave before there was even the slightest chance of running into Karessa.

He continued to read. The house the Blackburns had built—the house where Frankie believed the bond was hidden—still stood. The owner recently passed away and had left it to her grand-niece.

Karessa Austin.

"Aw, *fuck!*"

Max wadded up the paper and threw it across the room. He watched it bounce off the wall and fall silently to the thick carpet. Karessa's house. He couldn't even contemplate the odds of the one thing he wanted being inside her house. There was no way he could get it now.

Max stared at the crumpled piece of paper for several moments before he rose and picked it up from the floor. Smoothing it out, he quickly scanned the words again. The bottom line on the blue sheet drew his attention: the bond's estimated value— $176 million.

Max groaned.

He couldn't possibly give up on such a huge prize. Surely he could find a way to get inside the house, find the bond, and get out before Karessa discovered his presence.

Yeah, and the sun would start coming up in the north tomorrow.

He needed a fool-proof plan. Max began to pace as he thought of his options. The first step would be to catch the next plane to DFW Airport. Once he arrived in the Metroplex, he'd rent a car and . . .

He didn't know yet what he'd do after he rented the car, but the plane ride and drive to Fort Worth would give him time to come up with something.

Flopping back on the bed, Max slipped his hands beneath his head and stared at the ceiling. He'd see Karessa. He knew of no way to get around that. His heartbeat increased at the thought of seeing her again. Gorgeous curly blond hair. Huge green eyes. A luscious figure with full, round breasts. A perfect ass. Long, shapely legs. A sweet, tight pussy.

Max groaned softly. His erection flared back to life, and it had nothing to do with finding the bond.

Her last words to him were, "I hope you rot in hell." Hell couldn't be any worse than the pain he'd felt because he'd hurt her.

He wished he could make it up to her. Knowing that wouldn't be possible, the smartest thing he could do would be to find the bond and get the hell out of her life . . . permanently.

ᚻᚱ

"You're looking at a lot of money, Ms. Austin."

"Karessa, please. And I don't care. I'm not going to say money is no object, but I 'm not opposed to spending it. I want the house to be perfect when it's done."

She studied the handsome contractor as he totaled figures on his calculator. Marco had recommended Grayson Construction, saying Kevin Grayson would do a good job for her and wouldn't screw her over financially. Marco's recommendation was enough for her.

Besides, Kevin was *really* nice to look at.

Inwardly, Karessa sighed. She couldn't help the way she felt. It'd been a while since a man had held her, touched her, made love to her. Maxwell Hennessey had completely spoiled her. He'd been an incredible lover, taking her to heights she'd never been, and likely would never be again. She'd dated since Max and she'd had lovers. No other man had made her body sing.

Kevin appeared to be in his late thirties. Perfect. Maybe she should find another contractor and concentrate on something more personal with Kevin.

A glance at his left hand and the gold wedding band on his fourth finger quickly shot down that notion.

Oh, well, it was a nice dream.

Kevin made a couple of notations and removed a piece of paper from his clipboard. "Here's my estimate. I suggest you get at least two other contractors to give you estimates also."

Handsome and scruples, too. Life simply wasn't fair.

Karessa accepted the piece of paper from him. "Marco recommended you. That's good enough for me. When can you start?"

"My crew is finishing up a job this week. We can start first thing Monday morning."

"That would be perfect."

❦

"What are they going to do?" Mary asked.

"She's going to renovate the house, make it more modern."

"What will that mean for us?"

"Nothing. No one can see us, so we won't be in the way."

Mary rose from the living room loveseat and walked to the window. Crossing her arms over her stomach, she looked outside at the beautiful spring day. The sun shone, a gentle breeze rustled through the oak trees. She could step out on the veranda and feel the breeze. It wouldn't be enough. How she'd love to walk beneath those trees while the wind caressed her face.

She sensed Aaron come up behind her. "What's wrong, Mary?"

She shrugged. "Restless, I guess. I've done the same thing over and over for a century. I'd like to change something. I'd like to take a walk outside."

"I know," he said softly.

"I don't like strangers in our house." Turning to face him, she bit her bottom lip. "Do you think she'll change our bedroom?"

"I don't know. Maybe."

"I don't want our room changed, Aaron."

"There's no way we can stop it, baby."

"People have made changes to the house over the years. No one has ever touched our bedroom. It's almost as if . . . as if Eva put a spell on it so no one would go in there."

"I think she did. Remember the two guys who came and took our bodies away? I don't know how she could've gotten anyone to do that without them telling the sheriff."

"She was a witch, Aaron. We know that now."

"Yeah, we do."

"At least she was good to Katie. I'm grateful for that."

"She smothered her, Mary. Katie barely got the chance to breathe without Eva's permission."

"But she loved her. That's the important thing. She loved her and took care of her."

Aaron smiled tenderly. "You always try to see the good in people."

"I'd rather see the good than the bad." She wandered away from the window toward the television. "Watching this has shown us how the world has changed, even if we haven't been able to see it ourselves. We've seen a lot of good and bad over the years."

"Grace's computer has helped us see the world, too."

Mary smiled. "You do love playing with that thing."

Aaron grinned. "Yeah, and I'm getting good at it."

"You're good at everything you do."

His grin faded. "There's one thing I'm not good at—getting us out of here."

"You don't have to be good at that. She'll get us out of here," Mary said, nodding toward Karessa.

"You can't be sure of that, Mary."

"Yes, I can. I feel it here." She touched her chest, over her heart. "Our great-great-granddaughter will help us. I promise you that."

Four

Max parked beneath an oak tree seventy-five feet from the house. Several vehicles were parked at odd angles on the property, so he doubted if one more would raise any suspicion. He saw a van from a satellite company and one from a plumber. A blue truck held various sizes of glass and windows in its A-frames. Apparently, Karessa had decided to do some remodeling of the old house.

Great. With people coming and going all the time, he'd never get any alone time to search for the bond.

A gray pickup with Grayson Construction stenciled on the side was parked closest to the house. A memory tickled the back of Max's mind. He'd gone to college with a guy named Grayson. They'd played football together. What was the guy's first name? Keith? Kelvin? No, Kevin. Kevin Grayson. He watched the man talking to Karessa on the steps. Right height, right build, if Kevin had kept himself in shape over the years.

Max chuckled. Grayson wasn't exactly an odd name. Besides, he'd gone to college with Kevin in Florida. Running into an old college chum in Texas would be highly unlikely.

The man stood to one side, his back to Max. His position gave

Max an unimpeded view of Karessa's body. She wore faded jeans and a pale green T-shirt. He narrowed his eyes, studying her. She'd put on a few pounds in the last five years.

The extra weight only made her sexier. Her breasts looked fuller, her hips more rounded. He wished she'd turn around so he could see her ass. With her weight gain, he'd bet it was larger, too.

He groaned as blood surged into his cock. He'd love to drive his shaft deep inside Karessa's wet pussy. Or into that sweet ass.

Karessa smiled at the man. A surge of jealousy tore through Max. Those beautiful smiles should be reserved for *him*.

Forget it, man. She'll never have anything to do with you. Get in the house, find the bond, and get on with your life.

Max rubbed his mustache. Guilt gnawed at him. The bond wasn't left to Karessa, but it might be in her house. He didn't like taking something away from her.

He couldn't think of the bond belonging to Karessa. This was a job, just like every other job he'd ever done. As long as he remembered that, as long as he didn't let any leftover feelings for her confuse him, he could pull this off. He *would* pull this off.

The man turned and headed for the gray pickup. Max watched him. It *was* Kevin. Older, yes, but he still looked the same as he had in college. He wondered if Karessa had awarded the remodeling job to Kevin. If so, that would be the perfect way for Max to get inside the house without anyone questioning his presence.

Max smiled. This would be so easy.

⋈

A shiver danced up Karessa's spine. She had the spooky feeling someone was watching her. She looked out across the yard. A midsize car pulled out onto the lane, followed by Kevin's pickup. She couldn't see anyone standing around.

Still, the feeling persisted.

Karessa descended the steps and looked up at the house. She could swear the curtain moved at the window to the locked room.

Bypassing workers who were still taking measurements and computing estimates, she took the stairs to the second floor. She strode to the end of the hall. Stopping at the door, she studied the heavy padlock that kept her from entering the room. She'd searched for the key for three days, but with no luck. Whatever Aunt Grace had stored inside that room, she obviously wanted to keep secret.

Karessa straightened her shoulders. This was *her* house now. She wanted to know what was inside that room.

"Excuse me, Ms. Austin."

Karessa turned to see the plumber Eddy standing before her. She automatically smiled. "Yes?"

"I'm through downstairs. Would you like me to start up here?"

His question temporarily took her mind off the locked room. "Yes, please. The main bathroom is two doors down on the left. I'll be adding another small bathroom that connects to my bedroom. I'll have my contractor contact you so you two can work out the details."

"Sounds good."

He turned to walk away. The toolbox in his hand drew her attention. "Uh, wait please."

Eddy faced her again. "Ma'am?"

"Can you take off a lock?" She gestured at the padlock. "I can't find the key. It wasn't with the rest of my aunt's keys."

He stepped closer and examined the lock. "I can unscrew the hinges."

"Wonderful. Thank you."

A few minutes later, Eddy removed the hinges and pushed open the door. Karessa stepped into the bedroom . . . and stepped back in time to the early 1900s. Her extensive study of history helped her recognize the time period immediately. Chinese rugs were scattered across the wooden floor. A chenille bedspread covered the four-poster bed. A large chest of drawers sat against one wall, next to a small writing desk. The opposite wall held a dresser with a large oval mirror. Lacy white curtains covered the windows. A wooden rocker with a faded seat cushion sat near the windows.

The room was charming.

"Uh, Ms. Austin?" Eddy said. "You through with me?"

She turned and smiled at him. "Yes, thank you." Her smile faded when she noticed his wide eyes. "Is something wrong?"

"Are you okay in there?"

"Of course I'm okay. Why wouldn't I be?"

"It feels . . . funny."

Karessa noticed that Eddy stood outside the doorway. She didn't need a plumber in this bedroom, but he had no reason to think anything was wrong. "Come in, Eddy. You can see for yourself that everything is fine in here."

"No, thanks, Ms. Austin." He thumbed over his shoulder. "I'll, uh, check out that bathroom."

He skittered away much quicker than what she thought a man as large as that would be able to. How odd that he wouldn't come into the room.

Karessa shrugged and walked over to the east windows. Aunt Grace's windows gave her a view of the backyard. These windows let her look out over the front yard and would give her the morning sunlight. Karessa would much rather wake up with the sun than an alarm clock.

She'd planned to turn the large storage closet next to Aunt Grace's bedroom into her private bath since it butted up against the current bathroom. Now she wasn't sure. She wouldn't have a private bath if she moved into this bedroom, but she liked it so much better than Aunt Grace's room. This room had . . . character.

She didn't understand why it had been padlocked, or why there wasn't a thick layer of dust over everything.

Karessa threw open the windows and sniffed deeply of the rain-cooled air. A light shower an hour earlier had lowered the temperature and made the air smell fresh. She walked over to the south wall and opened those windows also. A refreshing cross-breeze made her smile. Oh, yes, she liked this room very much.

Realizing she still had several workers in her house who probably needed to talk to her, she turned to go back downstairs. She froze in place when a blur of white flashed before her eyes. It happened so quickly, she wasn't sure if she'd really seen anything.

She stood still, staring at the spot where she thought she'd seen the white blur. Nothing else appeared after several seconds. Karessa swallowed. She didn't know whether to be frightened, or ashamed of herself for letting her imagination get away from her.

Shaking her head at her own foolishness, Karessa started toward the stairs. First thing Monday morning, she'd show this room to Kevin Grayson and get his opinion on renovating it.

∾

"It didn't work!" Mary paced back and forth in front of the east windows. "We've always been able to get anyone in this house to do what we want, as long as we concentrated together. It worked with Grace. Why didn't it work with Karessa?" She stopped pacing and faced Aaron. "She's going to move into our room! I don't want that."

"You can't stop it, baby. We tried to stop her from taking the lock off the door. It didn't work." He chuckled. "That plumber certainly didn't want to come in here."

Mary scowled. "This isn't funny, Aaron. She's going to move into *our room*."

"Not if we can keep all those workers out of here. If she can't get anyone to change this room the way she wants it changed, she can't move in here."

She hadn't thought of that. Perhaps she and Aaron couldn't influence Karessa, but they could easily take care of a few men. Mary smiled. "I like the way you think."

⋈

Max waited until shortly after five o'clock before he wandered into Grayson Construction. He'd seen Kevin's pickup out front when he'd parked, along with a few other vehicles. The parking lot was now empty except for Kevin's truck. Perfect. Max wanted to be alone with Kevin while they talked.

He heard Kevin's voice on the telephone when he walked through the front door. Following the sound of the voice, he found his old friend in a small office at the back of the building. He leaned on the doorway and blatantly listened to Kevin's conversation. From the exasperated look on his college chum's face, he guessed that Kevin wasn't happy.

"So go without me. Your mother will be happier if I'm not there anyway."

Ah. Must be talking to the little woman.

"I don't know when I'll be home. It should be soon. I just have a couple more things to finish up here . . . Okay, okay. I will . . . Yeah, me too."

Kevin jabbed his fingers through his hair. "Stupid mother-in-law," he muttered as he hung up the phone.

"Problems?" Max asked.

Kevin jerked his head in Max's direction. His eyes widened before a huge grin spread over his face. "Maxwell Hennessey. What the hell are you doing here?"

Max shrugged. "Thought I'd pop in and see an old friend."

Kevin rounded the desk and pulled Max into a bear hug. "It's great to see you, man." He gestured toward the chair in front of the desk. "Sit down, sit down. You want a Coke or something?"

"Thanks, I'm fine. But it didn't sound like you are. Trouble at home?"

"Nah. I'm not exactly best friends with my mother-in-law, that's all. My wife's wonderful. I don't know how she came from such a bitchy woman." Kevin leaned back in his chair. "You married, Max?"

"Nope. Never made it down the aisle."

"I've been married for twelve years. Got three kids." He grinned devilishly. "Had a hell of a lot of fun making them, too."

Max laughed along with his old friend. He'd forgotten how easily Kevin always made him laugh.

"Seriously, what are you doing in Fort Worth?"

"Looking for work. I've had some . . . bad luck with some of my investments."

Kevin clasped his hands behind his head. "How are you with a hammer and nails?"

"Great. I did a lot of carpentry work when I got out of college."

"I just got a remodeling job today. Big Victorian. The owner wants it completely renovated. If you want work, I got it."

"Hey, man, I didn't come here begging for a job from you. I just wanted to say hi to an old friend."

"You didn't beg, I offered. You want it or not?"

"Yeah, I want it. I'm not too proud to accept a job from a friend."

"Be here Monday morning at seven."

"I will." Max stood and offered his hand to Kevin. "Thanks, man."

Kevin also stood and accepted Max's handshake. "No problem. I wish I could talk longer with you, but I gotta get home. How about if I buy you a beer after work Monday?"

"Deal."

Max kept his face composed until he slid inside his rental car. Once safely hidden by the tinted glass, he smiled.

Damn, I'm good.

Five

Max laid down his hammer and leaned his head back to try and relax the stiff muscles in his neck. He'd forgotten how hard construction work could be on the body. Max worked out regularly and figured he was in pretty good shape for forty. A weight machine couldn't compare to three straight days of manual labor.

He had to admit he liked the physical workout, and he liked the room's results because of that workout. Kevin had put him in the kitchen. He said the owner wanted this room completely gutted and modernized. That didn't surprise Max. Karessa had always loved to cook and liked all the newest gadgets. She wanted convenience, but still wanted the kitchen to have an early 1900s appearance. Thanks to the pictures and drawings supplied by her, she'd get exactly what she wanted.

He hadn't seen her. He'd been working in her home for three days, but he always left before she showed up. She hadn't officially moved into the house yet, but she did spend the nights in her great-aunt's bedroom. He'd learned that from talking with Kevin.

Between Karessa here at night, and workers in practically every room during the day, Max hadn't had the chance to search for the bond. He would. He was determined to find the bond and get out of here before he ever saw Karessa.

He didn't think his heart could stand seeing her again.

A final tug with the claw of his hammer and the last cabinet came loose from the wall. Max stood back and smiled. He pictured Karessa's drawing in his mind, the way she wanted this room to look when completed. She'd always had excellent taste. The room would be beautiful, as would the entire house.

"How's it going?" Kevin asked from behind him.

Max turned and faced his boss. "Great. I just pulled down the last cabinet. Now I can start tearing down the walls."

"You can start on the walls tomorrow. It's ten after five."

"It is?" Max glanced at his watch. He'd been so absorbed in his work, he hadn't noticed the time.

"I wish all my men worked as hard as you do."

"I like the physical work."

"Yeah, me too." He clapped Max on the shoulder. "Karessa called me about half an hour ago. She's run into some problems at her museum, so she won't be here tonight."

Max kept his face impassive so Kevin wouldn't know how his heart had kicked into high gear. "Oh?"

"Everyone else has left. As soon as you gather up your stuff, I'll lock up after you."

This was his chance . . . the chance to search the house without anyone bothering him. "Hey, man, I'd like to work a little longer. How about if I lock up for you?"

Kevin frowned slightly. "I don't think that's a good idea—"

"You can trust me, Kevin, you know that."

"It isn't you, Max. I'm responsible for this house. I think I should be the one to lock up."

Time for Plan B. "Okay, I understand that. How about if you come back in a couple of hours to lock up? I'd like to start on these walls."

Kevin rubbed his upper lip. "No, that'd be silly. I don't want to turn around and come back here once I'm home." Reaching into his jeans pocket, he pulled out a gold key on a red keychain. "Here. Stay as long as you want to. Just don't wear yourself out so you can't work tomorrow."

"No problem." Max took the key and squeezed it in his fist. "Thanks."

"Surely you have something better to do than hang around this house and work all night."

"Nope. I don't have anyone to go home to like you do."

"My wife knows a lot of single women—"

Max held up one hand to stop Kevin from saying anything else. "I appreciate the offer, but I'm not into blind dates."

"If you change your mind, let me know."

"I will. Thanks."

Max continued to clutch the key until he heard Kevin's pickup start. Moving to the window, he watched his friend drive down the lane until he could no longer see the truck.

"Yes!" he whispered.

Slipping the key into his pocket, Max picked up his hammer and left the kitchen. Even though he hadn't been able to search the house the way he wanted to, he had checked out the downstairs. The bond wouldn't be in plain sight. It had to be hidden somewhere . . . probably in some kind of secret compartment in one of the walls or within the woodwork.

He started in the living room. Standing in the middle of the room, he turned a circle, searching for anything that might be obvious. The walls were covered with a hideous pink flowered wallpaper. Karessa's great-aunt obviously had no taste when it came to

decorating. Two of the walls had already been torn down, exposing the wooden studs. Nothing hidden there. Even though Max
had been assigned to the kitchen, he'd wandered through the
house at various times to check out what the other guys were doing. So far, no one had discovered anything hidden in the walls.

He had to find the bond before someone else did.

∞

Juggling her briefcase, purse, and the bag holding her supper, Karessa turned the knob to the back door. She stepped into a war
zone. Her kitchen had been completely destroyed. She knew it
had to be torn apart to be remodeled. Still, the missing cabinets
and appliances made her blink. The room looked so empty.

She had no place to set the items about to fall out of her arms.
Making her way to the dining room, she placed everything on the
table and sighed from relief.

The sound of a hammer pounding made her frown. She'd
seen the pickup parked outside, but assumed it belonged to
Kevin. Obviously, one of his workers decided to stay late tonight.

She followed the sound to the living room. Standing in the
doorway, she watched the man currently knocking a hole in the
wall. He stood with his back to her, giving her the opportunity to
study him without his knowledge. Wavy, dark brown hair that
covered his nape. Tall, at least six feet. Broad shoulders. Trim
waist. Long legs encased in tight jeans . . . jeans that showed off a
very nice butt.

Karessa sighed. It'd been much too long since she'd touched a
man's butt.

"Hello."

He whirled around, the hammer clutched tightly in his fist.
Karessa noticed that first before her gaze shifted to his face. Her

mouth dropped open. All the blood drained from her head, leaving her dizzy. She grabbed the door facing to keep from sinking to the floor. "Max?" she whispered.

"Hey, Karessa."

She stared at him, not believing her eyes. Maxwell Hennessey was in her house? *Maxwell Hennessey* was in her house!

Karessa released the facing and clenched her hands into fists. "What the hell are you doing here?"

He lowered the hammer to his side. "Working."

"*Working?* For whom?"

"Kevin. He gave me a job."

Nothing he said made any sense. Max was a multi-millionaire. He didn't need to work at manual labor. "What do you mean, he gave you a job? You don't need the money."

"Yeah, I do. I made some bad investments, Karessa. Things have been . . . tight for me."

"They haven't been too 'tight' for you to buy a Thomas Abernathy painting."

"I bought that before . . . things went bad."

She couldn't believe she was standing here, having a calm conversation with this man. He had lied to her, betrayed her. She should be throwing heavy objects at his head, not treating him as a guest.

"I don't care about your money situation. I want you out of my house. Now."

He took two steps toward her. She took two steps back. Dropping the hammer to the floor, he ran one hand through his hair. "Karessa, I need this job."

"Oh, puh-*lease*. You can sell the Abernathy painting and live comfortably for the next five years. A piddly construction job can't pay you anywhere near what you're used to earning."

"It's a start. That's all I need."

She *would not* feel sorry for him. She'd been a victim of his deception once. That would never happen again. "You can find your start somewhere else. I don't want you here."

"You'll never see me. You're at the museum all day while I'm here. You wouldn't have known I was working here if I hadn't decided to stay late. I only decided to work late when Kevin told me you wouldn't be home tonight."

"But I *do* know you're here and I won't allow it. I'll call Kevin and tell him you aren't allowed on my property."

She turned to leave the room. She'd taken no more than a step when Max grabbed her arm. "Karessa, please don't. I really do need this job."

He turned those pleading gray eyes on her and she began to melt. He'd always had that effect on her. Knowing she couldn't let him get to her, she narrowed her eyes and lifted her chin. "Take your hand off me."

He gave her arm a gentle squeeze before releasing it. "Look, I promise you won't see me again. I'll make sure I leave before you get here at night. I won't arrive until after you leave in the morning. You'll never know I'm here."

My heart will know. She straightened her spine, ready to tell him again to get out of her house. He continued speaking before she could say a word.

"I know you're angry at me. I know I hurt you. I regret that more than I can ever tell you. But that was five years ago, Karessa. I'm a different man now. I want the chance to prove that to you."

"I have no interest in you proving *anything* to me."

"Okay, fine. But let me keep working here. After your house is finished, I'll leave Fort Worth and be out of your life forever. Deal?"

Karessa wanted to say no. She wanted to demand again that he leave her house. But if he were really hurting financially and needed this job to survive, she couldn't turn him away. "I won't see you at all? You'll come in the morning after I've left and leave before I get home?"

"I promise."

She stared into his eyes, trying to determine whether or not he told her the truth. His eyes looked sincere. However, they'd looked sincere in the past when he'd been lying to her.

She'd have to watch him *very* closely.

"All right. You can keep on working here. But I want you to leave now."

"Sure. Whatever you want." He ran one fingertip over her cheek. "Thank you, Karessa."

She stood in place, her hand pressed to her cheek, and watched him walk out the front door. That simple, unexpected touch had been enough to bring back all the yearnings he'd been able to stir in her so easily.

Tears filled her eyes. *Damn you, Max. Damn you for hurting me. Damn you for coming back into my life and making me hurt all over again.*

❦

Max tossed back a shot of Chivas and poured another one. He downed the second shot as quickly as the first and poured a third. Crossing the room, he sat on the edge of the bed and stared into the glass. Instead of seeing the amber liquid, he saw Karessa.

God, she was stunning.

Her hair had fallen almost to the middle of her back five years ago. Now, it fell to her shoulders in soft waves. It had looked tousled, as if she'd just risen from bed after a long, intense session of sex.

Max groaned as blood rushed to his cock. He set the glass of Scotch on the nightstand with a loud *thump*. *Don't think about sex, man!*

But the seed had been planted. Memories of making love with Karessa swam through his mind. Her ivory skin shiny with sweat. Full, round breasts with big pink nipples. Long torso. Legs that went on forever. A tight, wet pussy . . .

He loosened the thin towel around his waist and palmed his hardening cock. Closing his eyes, he remembered burying his shaft inside her, thrusting over and over. He remembered how she'd arch her neck and moan softly before she came. She'd wrap her legs around his waist and pull him even tighter to her. Or she'd push him down and impale herself on his cock. She'd liked the power of being in control of him—of moving the way she wanted, the way she needed, to climax.

He pumped his cock, his strokes slowly gaining speed as the memories continued. They'd made love after their first date. They'd made love *during* their first date, unable to keep their hands off each other. He'd kissed her for the first time in the restaurant over dinner. Luckily, they'd been in a dark corner behind a large potted plant. If the maitre d' had seen Max's hand on Karessa's breast, he would've thrown them out of the restaurant.

It would've been worth it.

She hadn't pulled away from him when he'd cradled her breast in his hand and thumbed her nipple. Instead, she'd parted her lips and touched his lips with her tongue. He'd loved her taking the aggressive role. He'd deepened the kiss as she slid one hand over his thigh to tickle his shaft with her fingertips.

He'd almost taken her right then.

They'd hurried through the rest of dinner and refused dessert. In his car, one more deep kiss, one more squeeze of her breast, had to satisfy Max until he could drive to Karessa's condo. He'd damned his bucket seats all the way to her home.

But once inside her condo, the dam had burst. He'd taken her against her front door with her legs wrapped tightly around his waist while he'd pounded his cock into her creamy pussy.

The first time had been quick, rough sex. The next time, he'd made love to her in her bed, urging her toward her climax with soft touches and gentle licks of his tongue before he ever entered her.

Max's breathing deepened. His strokes quickened. The orgasm snaked down his spine and grabbed his balls. He moaned deeply and closed his eyes as pleasure flowed through his body.

It took him a moment to remember how to breathe. Opening his eyes, he noticed the drops of cum on the faded carpet. He stared at the spots, wondering if the housekeeper would even notice them in this dump. He normally stayed in five-star hotels, but couldn't do that and pretend to be poor. This shabby motel had been the perfect solution.

He hated it.

Sighing deeply, Max cleaned himself with the towel, then bent over and dabbed up the evidence of his orgasm. He was beginning to hate everything about this job.

Mostly he hated himself.

Six

Aaron watched Karessa pace across the bedroom floor, then turn and pace back again. "She isn't a happy camper, Mary."

"No, she isn't." Mary chewed on her thumbnail. "She's been upset for two nights, ever since she argued with that man."

"She obviously knows him. Who do you think he is?"

"I don't know, but he's here every day, working on the house."

Karessa walked to the bed and sat on the side. Aaron sat beside her. His great-great-granddaughter seemed to sense him and Mary, to know when they were close. She didn't sense his presence now. That told him she was truly upset. "What's his name?"

"She called him Max." Mary stepped in front of Karessa. "Whatever happened between them had a profound effect on her. They must have been in love." She tilted her head to the side. "And I think she still loves him."

Aaron frowned. Rarely did he disagree with his wife, but this time he did. "She hates him."

"There's a fine line between love and hate, darling. A woman wouldn't react so strongly to a man if the feelings didn't run deep." She knelt before Karessa. "We have to help her."

"How?"

"She needs to remember how much they loved each other."

"Mary, you don't know for sure she loved him."

"Trust me, Aaron, I know. I'm a woman. I understand how she feels."

"So you're going to interfere."

"I'm going to help. There's a difference."

Aaron watched his wife lay her hands on top of their great-great-granddaughter's. Karessa jumped as if startled. Her gaze darted to Mary's face. "She sees you."

"She can't see me, but she senses me."

"Maybe we should leave her alone."

"In a minute."

Mary closed her eyes, took a deep breath, and slowly released it. Aaron had seen his wife do a similar thing many times over the last century. She touched someone when she wanted them to do her bidding. But it hadn't worked on Karessa earlier in the week when they'd tried to keep her out of their room. "Mary—"

"Shhh."

His wife left her hands on top of Karessa's for almost a full minute. Karessa didn't move the entire time. Aaron looked back and forth from Mary to Karessa. He'd never felt such strong energy in the air. The two women were truly connecting.

When Mary opened her eyes, they were glowing.

Chills slithered down Aaron's spine. He'd never seen Mary's eyes glow. "Are you okay, baby?" he asked softly.

Shaking her head, Mary lifted her hands from Karessa's. She cleared her throat. "Yes, yes, I'm fine."

Her voice sounded husky, as if she'd just awoken. "Are you sure?"

Slowly, Mary got to her feet. "We need to leave her alone now."

"What did you do?"

"She'll dream of him."

She looked at Aaron, and her eyes appeared normal once again. Aaron wished he could take her in his arms, hold her, to be sure she was truly all right. Instead, he rose from the bed and followed Mary out of the room.

{•}

Karessa no longer felt the cool air surrounding her. The sensation had been similar to the one she'd experienced the first day she walked into this house, as if she were standing directly beneath an air conditioning vent. She looked up at the ceiling. There were two vents in the room, but neither of them blew directly onto the bed. Besides, she hadn't turned on the air conditioning yet because of the construction work.

Something—or some*one*—had touched her.

Her mind was too fuzzy to concentrate now on who that someone could be. A sudden yawn made her jaw pop. She'd been reading a bit of her great-grandmother's diary every evening in bed. Tonight, she could barely keep her eyes open. All she wanted to do was sleep.

Karessa turned off the lamp and crawled between the cool sheets. An image of Max's face flashed through her mind, as it had each evening since she'd seen him in her living room. Memories swam through her head . . . memories of a time when she'd been so desperately in love . . .

{•}

Karessa closed her eyes and tilted back her head. The warm wind ruffled her hair, making her smile. What a perfect day. Comfortable temperature, gentle breeze, and the man she loved. A woman couldn't ask for much more.

She opened her eyes and gazed at Max on the blanket. He lay propped up on one elbow, chewing on a toothpick, looking at her. A crooked grin touched his lips. "Did you like the picnic?"

"Very much. It was a nice surprise." She touched her stomach. "I ate way too much."

"You're supposed to eat too much on a picnic. It's a rule."

"A rule?"

"Yeah. Just like it's a rule for the picnickee to pay the picnicker with a kiss."

Karessa struggled not to laugh. " 'Picnickee'?"

He shrugged and grinned. "You get the idea."

"Yes, I do." Karessa moved toward him on her knees. "I think it's an *excellent* idea." She took the toothpick from his mouth and tossed it to the ground. "You do realize that I probably won't stop with only one kiss."

His grin widened. "I certainly hope not."

Leaning forward, she softly kissed him. He tasted of the wine they'd drunk with their meal. Tilting her head, she slowly moved her lips over his. He cradled the back of her head in his hand and returned her kiss. The tip of his tongue touched her lips, seeking entrance into her mouth. Karessa parted her lips ever so slightly, giving him only a tiny sample of her.

Max growled deep in his throat. "Open your mouth, Karessa."

"You can be such an impatient man."

"I am when it comes to you. Let me taste you."

Their mouths were but an inch apart. Each word he spoke puffed air across her skin. The sensation made her nipples pucker. With a soft moan, she parted her lips for his tongue.

Karessa could count the number of her lovers on one hand. She'd had one guy who barely knew what he was doing, and two guys who were very good lovers. Not even the very good ones could compare to Max. He made her body sing every time they made love.

He slid his hand down her back to her buttock and squeezed it. His tongue stroked over her lips and teeth before beginning a dual with hers. She whimpered. His kisses touched not only her mouth, but every part of her body. She'd always scoffed at the term "his kisses made her melt." She no longer scoffed. Max's kisses did, indeed, make her melt.

Karessa knew in another moment, he would push her to her back so he could caress her entire body. While she loved his touch, she planned to be in control today.

When he shifted position and gently pushed on her shoulder, Karessa pulled away. "Nuh-uh."

Max's eyebrows drew together in confusion. "What do you mean, 'nuh-uh'?"

"Today we play by my rules."

"Oh, we do?" One of his dark eyebrows arched and his eyes twinkled with devilment. "What if I don't want to play by your rules?"

"You don't have a choice."

"Well, then . . ." He lay back, his hands beneath his head. "Do your worst. Or your best."

Karessa tugged up his navy T-shirt until it bunched under his arms. For a moment, she simply looked at his chest. Broad, tan, lightly dusted with dark brown hair. The hair formed a line down his flat stomach. She touched the center of his chest with one fingertip. She followed the line of hair until it disappeared into his denim shorts, then traced the line back up to his chest. Once she'd reached her starting point, she repeated the journey with her lips, dropping soft kisses on his skin.

The sudden tightening of Max's stomach muscles made her

look at him. He rose to his elbows and watched her. Deciding to give him a show, she circled his navel with the tip of her tongue while she looked into his eyes.

"Do you like that?" she asked.

"Yeah." His voice sounded rusty, as if something clogged his throat. "I like everything you do to me."

She dragged her tongue up the center of his stomach. Each of his nipples received a long lick and gentle tug with her teeth. Max's breathing became deeper, slower. His eyelids shuttered. She could no longer see the heat in those incredible gray eyes, but she knew it was there.

She traveled back down his stomach, alternating between kisses and soft licks. She stopped when she reached his navel again. Peering into his eyes, she released the snap on his shorts. She ruffled the hair beneath his navel with her finger.

"You like my happy trail?"

"Mmm, yes. Very much. I think," she said while leisurely lowering his zipper, "I'll follow it all the way to your campground."

Max chuckled. "I've never heard it called *that*."

"I thought I'd camp out for a while, see if anything comes up."

"It's already up."

She could see the outline of his hard cock through the denim. "I noticed."

Rising to her knees, Karessa gripped the waistband of Max's shorts and tugged them past his hips. Surprised at her discovery, her gaze snapped back to his face. "No briefs?"

A grin tweaked the corners of his mouth. "I figured they'd just be in the way."

She smiled. "You're so clever."

Karessa pulled his shorts down his legs and tossed them aside. His shaft lay against his stomach, fully erect. Her mouth watered with the desire to taste him.

"Take off your blouse and bra, sweetheart. Let me see those pretty tits."

She granted his request without hesitation. She'd no sooner tossed the bra to land on top of Max's shorts than he sat up and opened his mouth over one nipple.

Karessa moaned. Tunneling her fingers into his thick hair, she pulled him closer to her breast. He kneaded her other breast while he suckled her nipple. His tongue circled the hard nub, his teeth scraped across it. He took his time, switching from one nipple to the other . . . back and forth, back and forth, sucking, nipping, licking. Karessa threw back her head and arched her back, trying to get even more of her breast into his mouth. Obeying her silent cue, he suckled harder.

The orgasm shimmied down her spine and zinged through her clit. She gasped as her pussy clenched and moisture dampened her panties. Experiencing a climax but not quite sure *how*, she clasped Max's head to her breast while she tried to remember how to think.

He lifted his head, a smile on his lips. "Did you come?"

Unable to speak yet with her heart beating so hard, she nodded.

His smile widened into a cocky male grin. "Yeah?"

The obvious pride in his voice made her laugh. "You didn't just invent the cure for cancer, you know."

"You've never come from me sucking your nipples." He caressed her back and buttocks. "I wonder how many other ways I can make you come."

"Oh, so now you want to show off?"

"Yeah."

That overconfident grin of his made her laugh. "All the ways I come now are fine, thank you."

"But we just discovered something new. I think we need to experiment some more."

She reached down and clasped his hard cock. "I think we need to concentrate on a climax for *you* right now."

Max hitched in a breath when she began fondling his shaft. "Well, if you insist . . ."

৵৻

Karessa awoke with her heart pounding and her lungs struggling for air. Desire flowed through her veins like fire, making her skin damp with sweat. She'd often had dreams of Max and her making love in the past, but hadn't had one in a long time.

This hadn't been a product of her subconscious. Everything in her dream had actually happened, right down to her having a climax from him sucking her nipples.

Her clit throbbed in memory.

Rolling to her back, Karessa lifted her large T-shirt to her waist and slid her hand between her thighs. She wasn't surprised to find her labia creamy and swollen. She bit her bottom lip and moaned when she touched her clit. It had been months since she'd been with a man. Her body decided to remind her of that fact this morning.

She rubbed her clit while she raised her shirt over her breasts. A few tugs on her nipple and her toes began to curl. Her body was so hot, it wouldn't take long for her to come. One, two, three more swipes across her clit and the pleasure flowed through her body.

After the pleasure, the tears came.

Karessa pushed down her shirt and pulled the sheet over her body. An orgasm was a powerful release. So were tears. She often cried after a climax, simply because the feelings were so intense.

These tears had nothing to do with her orgasm.

She damned Max again for coming back into her life and making her want what she didn't have.

Wiping the tears from her cheeks, Karessa threw back the sheet and sat up. Enough of self-pity. It was a totally useless emotion and accomplished nothing. She was a strong, independent woman. She had money in the bank and a house that would be gorgeous after the renovation. She ran the largest museum in the Metroplex, and ran it successfully. Her body had needs, as it had demonstrated to her this morning, but she could take care of that, too. She didn't need a man to make her life complete. She certainly didn't need love. That only led to a broken heart.

With that thought, Karessa rose and headed for the bathroom. A shopping trip to one of the malls would be the perfect way to spend her Saturday.

Seven

Karessa rubbed her forehead, but it did nothing to ease her pain. She hated headaches. No amount of medicine could make this one go away. She knew that the only thing that would help was lying down in a dark room—or a bout of wild, sweaty sex. Since she didn't have a place to lie down here in the museum and sex wasn't an option, she'd been suffering for most of the morning.

Combine her pain with lack of sleep due to her erotic dreams of Max, and she was ready to snap at anyone who talked to her. Unfortunately, Joy had several things on her agenda today that needed discussing.

She jerked at the sudden snap when Joy closed her portfolio. "Okay, that's it. Go home, Karessa."

"What?"

"I see you rubbing your head. I know you're hurting. We aren't getting any work done. Go home."

"I can't. The workers are there."

"So go to your condo."

She could do that, but she didn't want to. Her condo was so . . . sterile. It had only taken a short two weeks for her to think of the Victorian as her home. "I don't want to go to my condo."

Joy frowned. "Now you're sounding childish." Rising from her chair, she rounded the desk. She picked up Karessa's purse and briefcase from the bookcase and shoved them into her boss's arms. "Go *somewhere* and lie down."

"You know, I could fire you for this abuse."

"No, you couldn't." Joy grinned. "I'm indispensable."

"That's true." Lying down sounded like a wonderful idea. They weren't getting any work done with her in pain. Shifting her purse and briefcase so she could carry them, she stood. "I'll see you tomorrow."

"Only if you're better."

"Yes, Mother," Karessa said dryly.

Once in her car, she thumped her fingers against the steering wheel while deciding where to go. Her condo would be the logical choice. No dust, no noise, no interruptions. If she went to the house, the buzz of electric saws and the pounding of hammers wouldn't let her get any rest.

Besides, she'd see Max.

He'd kept his word. She knew he was still working because she'd casually asked Kevin about him, but she never saw him. Going to the house in the middle of the day meant she would surely see him.

That would be incredibly stupid.

{❄}

"I like him."

"How can you like him?" Aaron asked. "You know Karessa doesn't."

Mary moved to Max's right side and watched him swing his

hammer. "There's something . . . good about him. And Karessa may not like him, but she loves him."

"So you think."

"So I *know*."

Mary had no doubt of Karessa's feelings for Max. The problem lay in getting Karessa and Max back together. She didn't know what had happened between them in the past. Until they got beyond that, they couldn't have a future together.

She wanted her great-great-granddaughter to be happy.

The erotic dreams seemed to be working for Karessa to help her remember Max. Maybe a few erotic memories would work for him, too.

Mary touched his shoulder. Max jerked and stopped hammering. He whipped his head in her direction, his eyes wide.

Aaron moved closer to her. "Mary, what are you doing?"

"Helping him to remember Karessa."

"He's reacting to you. That's never happened except with a member of our family."

"He'll *be* a member of our family, Aaron . . . in time."

She closed her eyes and concentrated, letting her energy flow into Max. She could feel him trying to fight it. Refusing to give up, she continued to touch him, telling him with her mind to remember how much he'd loved Karessa.

How much he *still* loved Karessa.

Mary opened her eyes when she felt him lower his arm. His chest rose and fell with a deep breath. She smiled to herself.

Gotcha.

&

Max stopped hammering when Kevin walked up to him. "It's almost noon. You wanna go with C. J. and me to grab a burger?"

Food held no appeal at all to Max right now. He didn't understand that for he rarely missed a meal. "Thanks, but I'm not hungry. I think I'll keep on working awhile."

"Suit yourself. See you later."

Max continued nailing two-by-fours into place until he noticed all was quiet in the house. The guys had left for lunch, or were eating outside beneath the huge oak tree in the backyard. That gave him time alone with his thoughts.

He couldn't help but think of Karessa since he was in her house. Usually he could push the thoughts away and focus on finding the bond. Not now. Memories filled his head and stayed there, no matter how much he tried to push them aside.

When he hit his thumb instead of a nail, Max knew it was time to take a break.

Grabbing a Pepsi from his cooler, he held it against his throbbing thumb as he walked outside to the veranda. A gentle breeze blew from the south, bringing the smell of rain. Thunderstorms were predicted for later today and the rest of the week. He hoped it poured. The rain and gray skies would remind him of his home on the Olympic Peninsula in Washington State.

He'd never planned to settle in the Pacific Northwest. In his line of business, he traveled more than he stayed home. He'd bought a condo in Florida and lived there between jobs. It had served his purpose, even though he'd always thought of Florida as one big tourist state.

When a job had taken him to Seattle, Max had immediately fallen in love with the area. The cool weather, huge trees, beautiful mountains . . . they'd all grabbed him and refused to let go.

He wondered if Karessa would like Washington.

Well, I made it for about three minutes without thinking of her.

Max popped the top of his Pepsi and took a long drink.

Karessa had always liked the outdoors. He remembered one time in particular when he'd surprised her with a picnic . . .

֍

Max closed his eyes as Karessa fondled his cock. He'd just made her come from sucking her nipples, and that had never happened. He wanted to explore other ways he could bring her to orgasm.

His vixen apparently had other ideas. She tugged his T-shirt over his head. "Lie back, Max," she whispered.

Leaving his eyes closed, he did as she commanded. He lay still, waiting for what she would do next. First, he felt the soft brush of her hair across his thighs. Next, he felt her warm breath on his balls. The tip of her tongue teased the base of his cock.

Max groaned.

That wicked tongue ran up the length of his shaft and circled the head. He opened his eyes and rose to his elbows so he could watch her. Her own eyes were closed as she continued to lick the head. She'd told him she loved performing oral sex on him, and would gladly do it every day.

That worked for him.

She lowered her head until his shaft disappeared inside her mouth. When her lips touched the base, she slid them back up to the head. She slowly repeated the journey over and over. He wanted to pump. He *needed* to pump. But the rapturous look on her face made him lie still and wait for whatever she would do next.

Torture had never felt so good.

She opened her eyes as her tongue circled the head again. "Do you want to come in my mouth?"

Max swallowed hard. "Yeah."

The tip of her tongue darted into the slit. "We're playing by my rules, remember?"

Unable to resist touching her any longer, he tunneled one hand beneath her hair and cradled the back of her head. "Your rules are to torture me?"

A mischievous twinkle lit up her eyes. "No. My rules are to make you feel *really* good."

"Coming in your mouth would make me feel *really* good."

"How about coming in my pussy?"

"Oh, yeah. I'd like that, too."

Releasing his cock, she rose to her knees and leaned forward. Her breasts barely brushed his chest. With her lips a breath away from his, she whispered, "How about licking my pussy?"

"I would *love* that."

"We could do all of the above."

"I'm in no hurry to leave."

She smiled her vixen's smile, the one that always made him hard. Since he was already hard, this time he growled. Pulling her head closer, he gave her an open-mouth, tongue-dueling kiss.

The whimper in her throat caused the blood to surge in his cock.

"Take off the rest of your clothes. I want you naked."

She stood up and unfastened her khaki shorts. They fell in a puddle at her feet, leaving her in nothing but a pair of tiny blue panties. He palmed his cock and leisurely stroked it while she hooked her fingers in the waistband of her panties.

Instead of pulling them off, she gave him that vixen smile again. "I have a surprise for you."

He waited, but she didn't say anything else. She pulled her panties down an inch. His gaze snapped to that enticing strip of skin between her navel and the top of her panties. She pulled them down another inch. "Are you ready for your surprise?"

"Yeah," he rasped.

Her panties joined her shorts on the blanket. Max's mouth dropped open. If possible, his cock became even harder. "You shaved your pussy?"

She nodded.

Max rose to his knees before her. Slipping his hands between her thighs, he pushed gently until she opened her legs. He slid his thumbs over the smooth, silky skin. "When did you do this?"

"I shaved a couple of days ago, then again this morning. I thought you might . . . like it."

"I do." He pulled apart her feminine lips with his thumbs. She was already creamy and swollen, proof of her arousal. "My God, this is sexy." Leaning forward, he swiped his tongue across her clit. He enjoyed it so much, he did it again. "I love the way you taste."

Karessa tilted her hips toward him. "Max."

He looked up at her face when he heard her breathless voice. The desire in her eyes made him want to devour her. "Lie down, sweetheart. Let me lick on this pretty pussy."

She stretched out before him, a blond goddess. Max spread her legs wide. For a moment, he simply looked at her . . . from her tousled hair, down her long torso, past her bare mound, all the way down to her toenails painted a pale pink. He made the return journey as leisurely as the first trip, until he looked into her eyes again. His heart clutched in his chest. "You're beautiful, Karessa."

He kissed her, long and deeply, before he stretched out on his stomach between her thighs. Closing his eyes, he inhaled her unique, musky fragrance. Nothing smelled better than an aroused woman.

Or tasted better.

Max liked to take his time when giving oral sex for he enjoyed it as much as Karessa. He gave her one long swipe with his tongue from her anus to her clit. She moaned and spread her thighs another inch. Slowly, he licked the length of her slit again.

"More," she breathed.

Only too happy to oblige, he suckled her clit, darted his tongue into her vagina, licked her anus. Concentrating on that sensitive bit of flesh, he pulled her buttocks apart with his thumbs and pushed his tongue deep inside her ass.

"Oh, *God*!"

Her cry made him smile to himself. She loved it when he tongue-fucked her ass. "You like that, sweetheart?"

"Yesssss."

Max had never made a woman come from licking her anus, but he wouldn't be surprised if Karessa could climax that way. She was a very passionate woman who loved sex. She'd already come from having her nipples sucked. Rarely did they make love without her having at least two orgasms.

Even if she didn't come, experimenting would be fun.

Max pushed her legs forward until her knees almost touched her breasts. "Hold your legs for me."

She hooked her hands behind her knees. The position left her pussy completely open for him.

Beautiful.

Slipping his hands beneath her buttocks, he began the gentle assault on her anus. He drove his tongue deep inside her, then pressed it flat against her. He licked back and forth, up and down, in a circle, before driving back inside her again. Each new movement made Karessa moan a bit louder. Each new movement made his cock a bit harder. He'd fantasized about sliding his shaft inside her ass for weeks.

It was time he made the fantasy a reality.

She arched her back and keened deeply. Max leaned back and watched her anus contract with her orgasm. The urge to mate pushed him past his limit. Rising to his knees, he rolled Karessa to her stomach. Her body was limp as a damp dish cloth. Good. He wanted her perfectly relaxed when he thrust inside that gorgeous ass.

Max reached for the bottle of coconut-scented massage oil he'd included in the picnic basket. Flipping up the top, he poured a generous amount over his fingertips. He parted Karessa's buttocks with one hand and slathered the oil over her anus.

She moaned softly.

"Get on your knees, Karessa."

She did as he said. Max slid his cock inside her pussy. The tight, wet warmth made him groan. He thrust slowly while he pushed his thumb into her ass. She moaned again and arched her back.

"Okay if I play a little, babe?"

"Yessss."

He grinned. He loved when she stretched out her "yes." That meant she was totally into whatever he did to her.

He continued to thrust slowly. Removing his thumb from her ass, he replaced it with two fingers. He pumped them in and out, in and out, getting her ready to accept his cock.

Several moments passed before he couldn't wait any longer. Max withdrew his fingers from her ass, his cock from her pussy. Adding more oil to the head of his shaft, he pressed it against her anus. Instead of tightening, as he'd expected, Karessa pushed her buttocks back at him.

His little vixen wanted this as much as he.

"You want me to fuck your ass, don't you?"

"Yessss."

"Hard or easy?"

"Hard. Fuck me hard, Max."

He pushed his cock all the way inside her ass. Karessa arched her back even more and tossed back her head. "Oh, *God*!"

"Am I hurting you?"

"No, no. It feels incredible."

Slipping one hand beneath her stomach, he held her tighter against him. His thrusts picked up speed until he was hammering into her. Leaning over her body, he drove his tongue into her ear. She shivered.

"This feels . . . *God* . . . so good. I love having my cock in your ass."

"Harder, Max. *Harder!*"

Karessa's breaths became choppy and uneven . . . the sign of an impending orgasm. Sliding his hand farther down her stomach, he caressed her clit. "That's it, babe. Come for me while I'm fucking your ass."

Her body bucked beneath his. The contractions of her orgasm grabbed his cock. His balls tightened. Max thrust as deeply inside her as he could and came.

Remembering how to breathe took too much concentration. Instead, he followed Karessa as she stretched out on the blanket. He lay still, his shaft still inside her, while the aftereffects of his orgasm flashed through his body. Making love with Karessa was always special. This had been . . . overwhelming.

His heart clutched in his chest again. He'd never told a woman he loved her. Feelings so strong, so powerful, had to be expressed out loud. He kissed the curve of her ear. "I love you, Karessa," he whispered.

She lifted her head and gave him a gentle smile. "I love you, too."

Eight

Karessa slipped her hands in the pockets of her slacks and stared at Max. He sat in the porch swing, his head resting on the back, his eyes closed. She took the time to study him. A few strands of gray were now mixed in his dark hair. The laugh lines at the corners of his eyes were more pronounced. Other than those two things, she saw no evidence of his aging. His stomach was still as flat as it had been five years ago, his chest and shoulders as broad. He'd always had a killer body.

The mustache was new. Full and thick, it almost covered his upper lip. Karessa had never kissed a man with a mustache. She couldn't help wondering how it would feel against her lips . . . and other, more intimate, parts of her body.

His chest rose and fell steadily as if he were asleep. He must be having a very sexy dream. His erection filled the crotch of his faded jeans.

Her mouth watered at the sight.

She cleared her throat. "Max."

Nothing. "Max," she said a bit louder.

Still nothing. Karessa wiped her palm on her slacks and touched his shoulder. His body jerked. He opened his eyes and whipped his head toward her. That laserlike silver gaze pierced her, making her catch her breath.

It should be against the law for a man to ooze so much sex appeal.

"Karessa." He frowned slightly. "What are you doing here?"

"It's my house."

"It's the middle of the day. You're usually at work."

He sat up straighter, and winced. She had no doubt his jeans had cut into his erect penis. She turned her head for a moment to give him the privacy to adjust himself. Not wanting to tell him about her headache, she gave him another reason she'd come home in the middle of the day. "I wanted to talk to Kevin about one of the upstairs rooms. I've been leaving early and getting home late, so haven't had the chance to say more than a few words to him in passing."

She saw him stand out of the corner of her eye. Deciding it must be safe to look at him again, she once more faced him.

"Kevin went out to lunch. Can I help you with something?"

She wanted to get Kevin's opinion about renovating the bedroom she liked so much. Getting Max to look at it first only made sense. Friend or not, she doubted if Kevin would have Max working for him if Max wasn't good at his job. "Come with me please."

She led the way upstairs and down the hall. Outside the door to the bedroom, that strange chill flowed over her again. She paused and looked over her shoulder at Max. He was looking up at the ceiling, a slight frown on his lips. "What's wrong?"

"I feel cold air." His gaze met hers. "You didn't turn on the A/C, did you?"

"No, I didn't."

"Weird."

With a shrug, Max reached past her to turn the doorknob. He pushed open the door and Karessa stepped across the threshold. He followed her into the room. Turning in a circle, he took in everything from the ceiling to the floor, including the furnishings. When he faced her again, a sensual light filled his eyes.

"It's sexy and feminine, just like you."

She slipped her hands in her slacks pockets, unsure how to respond to his observation. Deciding it was best to ignore it, she returned to the subject of the house. "I've thought about making it my bedroom. Aunt Grace's room is nice, but this room is . . ." She stopped, not knowing what words to use to describe how she felt about this room.

Max nodded. "I understand." He took one step closer to her. "What do you want me to tell Kevin?"

"There's a small sitting room next to this one. I'm wondering if it can be turned into a bathroom. I'd like to make a door in the wall there . . ." She pointed to the wall on her left. "So it could be my private bath."

"I doubt that would be a problem, but it depends on the plumbing. Eddy can tell you better than I can." He slipped his hands in the back pockets of his jeans. "This is the first time I've been upstairs. Kevin assigned me to the kitchen." He gazed at her again. "It doesn't look like it needs much work. It's almost as if . . ." He stopped.

Karessa knew what he'd been about to say. "It's almost as if someone lives here."

"Yeah." Walking over to the dresser, he ran his fingers along the polished wood. "No sawdust. Have you cleaned in here today?"

She shook her head. "The door was padlocked. I couldn't find the key, so the plumber unscrewed the hinges for me over a week ago, but I haven't cleaned anything. I don't know how long it had been locked up."

"Even with the door shut, dust would seep in over time."

Cool air flowed over Karessa, making her shiver. She wrapped her arms across her breasts.

"You okay?" Max asked.

She nodded. "I just had a chill."

Eyes narrowed, he walked up to her. "Are you sure that's all?"

"Of course I'm sure. I . . ." She stopped when a sharp pain passed through her forehead. She winced and pressed her hand against her temple.

"You have a headache, don't you?" Max asked.

"It isn't bad."

"Yeah, right." He stepped behind her and laid his hands on her shoulders. "Let me help—"

She jerked away from him. "I told you not to touch me."

She heard him release a heavy sigh as she faced him again. "I wasn't making a pass, Karessa. I only want to help."

"I don't need your help."

"Max?" Kevin called out. "You upstairs?"

"Yeah," Max said, his gaze still on Karessa's face.

She turned to the door. Kevin walked down the hall toward them. When he reached the doorway, he stopped in his tracks. His eyes widened and his eyebrows disappeared into his hair.

"Whoa!"

"What's wrong?" Karessa asked.

"I can't . . . go in there."

"What do you mean, you can't come in here?" Max asked. "We're in here."

"Yeah, but . . ." Eyes still wide, he quickly scanned every corner of the room. "I can't do it, man."

"I want this room renovated, Kevin."

He held up both hands, palms toward her. "Sorry, Karessa. I'll do the rest of the house, but I won't do that room."

She frowned. "But that doesn't make sense."

"I know it doesn't, but . . ." He stopped again. "Sorry."

He turned and quickly walked back down the hall toward the stairs.

Max looked at Karessa. "What the hell was that about?"

"I don't know. Eddy wouldn't come in here either. He took the hinges off so I could open the door, but wouldn't come in here with me."

She didn't understand why Max would enter this room when no one else would. Something was stopping everyone else from crossing the threshold.

"If you really want this room renovated, I'll do it."

Karessa bit her bottom lip. She hated to ask Max for anything. Perhaps some of Kevin's other employees would do the work for her. "You can't do it by yourself."

"Sure I can." He flashed her a crooked grin. "I'm good."

His teasing made her chuckle. She'd always loved his quick wit and sense of humor.

She'd loved so many things about him . . . until he'd betrayed her.

"I'll think about it. The downstairs is the most important. This can wait."

Max nodded. "Let me know when you decide."

"So you plan to be in Fort Worth awhile?"

"At least until your house is done."

She stared at him, unable to drag her gaze away. He was just so . . . *male*. He filled the room with his presence, his very essence. His height, the breadth of his shoulders, his husky body, that sexy mustache . . . everything about him oozed testosterone.

Damn hormones.

Another jab of pain in her head made her wince. Max took a step closer to her. "Karessa, let me help you. I remember when you had those headaches. A massage always helped you feel better."

Yes, it had, because a massage had always led to sex. An orgasm had been the best pain fighter she'd ever discovered. "I just need to lie down."

"The guys will start working again soon. You won't get much rest with all the noise."

"I'll be fine."

Max frowned. "You always were stubborn."

The pain kept her from responding to him. Instead, she turned toward the door. "I have to lie down."

Two feet from the doorway, a cold gust of air washed over her . . . colder than anything she'd felt so far in the house. Karessa gasped and stopped in her tracks. She didn't realize that Max was right behind her. He bumped into her back and grabbed her upper arms.

"What's wrong, Karessa?"

She drew in a sharp breath, but not from the cold. Max's hands on her quickly brought forth yearnings she'd tried to forget. How she'd love to lean back against him, have his arms slide around her waist, his hands glide up to cradle her breasts. She'd gained weight in the last five years. She wondered if Max would like her fuller breasts.

His warm breath ruffled the hair over her ear. "Karessa," he whispered as he squeezed her arms.

The feel of his cock brushing her buttocks gave her the strength to pull away from him. "Excuse me."

She hurried down the hall to her bedroom, eager to be away from Max as quickly as possible.

༄

Mary crossed her arms beneath her breasts. "I *told* you she still loves him."

"Yeah, you did." The satisfaction in her eyes made Aaron frown. "You don't have to be so smug about it."

"After a century, you should know when I'm right." She flopped down on the bed, resting on one elbow. "Unfortunately, being right isn't getting them back together."

"Don't you think Karessa's dreams are helping?" Aaron asked. He sat on the bed next to his wife, as close as he could get.

"They're helping her to remember, but they aren't helping her to forgive him."

"Maybe whatever he did to her is too much to forgive."

Mary tapped one fingernail against her teeth. "There has to be a way to find out why she's so angry at him. I'd have a better chance of helping her get over it if I knew exactly what he did. I tried to get them to stay in here so they'd talk longer, but they ignored me."

"Too bad we can't just ask them what happened between them."

"That's true."

She lay back on the bed and linked her fingers together on her stomach. Her position let Aaron clearly see the soft swell of her breasts inside her neckline. His mouth watered with the desire to run his tongue over her creamy flesh.

"Aaron, stop," Mary said softly.

He raised his gaze back to her face. Sadness filled her eyes. "Stop what?"

"We can't be together. Stop looking at me like you want to make love to me."

"I *do* want to make love to you. I want to kiss you, touch you, lick every inch of your skin . . ."

Mary abruptly sat up, her back to him and her head lowered. Aaron bent down so he could see into her face. "Mary, we can still pleasure each other."

"I know that. We've been masturbating for almost one hundred years."

"Do you think that's wrong?"

She pushed her hair back from her face and turned to look at him. "No, I don't think it's wrong. I know it pleases you when I touch myself. I enjoy looking at you, too, when you touch yourself." Tears flooded her eyes. "I'm just tired, Aaron. I want to be with *you*. I don't want to rely on my own hand for an orgasm."

Her tears made him feel helpless. "Mary—"

"They're the key, Aaron. Karessa and Max are the key to breaking the spell. I *know* that. That's why we have to get them back together."

If she felt so strongly about it, then he'd do everything he could to help. "What do you want me to do?"

Nine

June 27, 1925—He kissed me today. It was the first kiss I have ever received from a boy. I was so nervous, I did not know what to do. I was afraid he would think me foolish. He only smiled and kissed me again.

It was wonderful.

Mrs. Lewis knows how I feel about him. She helped me set up a meeting with him by telling my mother she needed my help with a project at her home. My mother gave Mrs. Lewis what I call "the look," but Mrs. Lewis did not back down like most people do. She said it would be good for me to get out of the store for a while and earn a little spending money. With so many people in the store, my mother could not refuse.

I did go to Mrs. Lewis' house and help her finish sewing her new curtains, but left long before my mother expected me back at the store. That is when I met him by the creek. We were totally alone and talked for almost an hour. He said he would meet me again the first chance he could. Then he kissed me. I thought I might faint, the feelings inside me were so strong. They became even stronger when he touched my breast.

My mother has taught me it is wrong to let a boy touch me before marriage. This did not feel wrong. I wanted him to touch me, and I would have let him touch me any way he wanted to. Being a perfect gentleman, he pulled back with a smile and said we needed to leave before my mother came looking for me.

I know she suspected something. She did not ask any questions, but I could tell by the anger in her eyes. I refuse to let her destroy my happiness. I have found the one I want to spend the rest of my life with. I will not let my mother or anyone else stop me from being with him.

I hid the money Mrs. Lewis gave me in my secret place. I know my mother searches my room. She tries to be careful, but I can tell that items have been moved. She does not like me having money of my own and has often asked how much I have. I will not tell her. I will not tell her about any of the things I have found hidden in the house.

Some of those things make me wonder all over again if she is truly my mother.

A soft knock on the door made Karessa look up from her great-grandmother's diary. "Yes?"

Max opened the door and peered inside. "Feeling better?"

"Yes, thank you."

"May I come in?" He held up two plastic bags. "I thought you might be hungry."

The scent of lemon chicken and pork chow mein drifted to her nose. Her mouth watered and her stomach growled. Her pounding head had kept her from eating any lunch.

She didn't want to accept anything from him, but her taste buds had other ideas. "What did you buy?"

He grinned. "A little of almost everything. I didn't have any lunch."

"Me either."

"So, may I come in? There isn't much of a place to eat downstairs."

That was true. The downstairs and most of the upstairs were demolished. Her room and the bedroom at the end of the hall remained the exceptions. If Max had been good enough to go out and get their supper, she could at least provide a clean place to eat it. "Come in."

He entered the room and closed the door behind him. Although spacious, Aunt Grace's bedroom seemed so much smaller with Max in it. Karessa moved over to make room for him on the bed. He sat down, one bent leg resting on the bed, and began unloading white cardboard containers from the sacks.

It seemed so right to have him in her bedroom.

She looked down at the diary still open on her lap. Thinking about her few months with Max hurt because of the way their relationship had ended, but she also had many fond memories from their time together. She'd loved him desperately, and had no doubt that he'd loved her, too . . . at least, in his own way.

What happened between them had taught her a lot about men and love. She didn't trust as quickly now. It made it easier for her to determine whether or not to give a man more than one date.

It also made life lonely.

Max held out a bottle of water to her and a long, wrapped straw. "Here you go. I stopped at the convenience store a couple of miles from here so I could get a straw that would fit in your bottle."

He remembered she liked to drink from a straw. The knowledge made her swallow hard. It was a simple thing, but something that had been important to her and he remembered. "Thank you."

His smile made her breath catch. Dropping her gaze from his handsome face, she reached for one of the white containers. She opened it to find her favorite—lemon chicken.

Max handed her a plastic fork as he peered into her container. "Figures you'd find the lemon chicken right off the bat."

"I have a good nose."

"At least save me a bite."

"Maybe," she said with a grin.

He opened another container and scooped up a forkful of broccoli and beef. "I guess I should've picked up some paper plates."

"This is fine. It's like a picnic."

She looked at him when she realized what she'd said. His eyes narrowed and turned sultry. "Picnics can be a lot of fun."

Karessa cleared her throat and took another bite of lemon chicken, deciding it would be better to say nothing to that comment.

Max ate silently for a few moments before he gestured to the diary. "Whatcha reading?"

"My great-grandmother's diary."

He paused in the process of opening another container. "Really?"

Karessa nodded. "It was among the papers from Aunt Grace. I remember her mentioning it several years ago. She never read it. I can't imagine why not. It's part of our family's history."

"Your Aunt Grace was a bit of a rebel."

"You're telling me?"

Max chuckled. "I liked her. She was wild and fun and didn't worry about what anyone thought of her. She followed her desires, no matter where they took her."

"Yes, she did."

She couldn't help the sad note that crept into her voice. Max must have noticed it. He lightly touched her knee. "You miss her, don't you?"

"Very much."

"Look at it this way—she's driving everyone crazy in heaven."

The mental picture of Aunt Grace telling God exactly what to do made her laugh. "I have no doubt of that."

She took another bite of her chicken. Max nudged her container with his fork. "You really aren't going to share that, are you?"

"Only if you'll share your pork chow mein."

"Deal."

She switched containers with him and dug into the noodles and meat dish. She'd taken two bites before she realized how intimate it was to share food with him.

The rumble of thunder startled her. "Is it raining?"

"It wasn't when I came in, but there were a lot of dark clouds in the sky."

"I haven't turned on a TV in days, so I haven't watched the weather or the news. I've no idea what's happening in the world."

"Same old stuff. You haven't missed much by not watching the news. I'd imagine your great-grandmother's diary is a lot more interesting than anything on TV."

"I'm enjoying it very much." Karessa set her container on the nightstand and turned the diary toward Max. "Here. Read this sentence."

Max wiped his hands with a napkin before taking the book from her. "'Some of those things make me wonder all over again if she is truly my mother.'" Frowning, he looked back at Karessa. "She doesn't think her mother is really her mother?"

"She's written that several times in the diary, at least in what I've read so far. I'm eager to find out if that's actually true."

He laid the book on the bed. "If it *is* true, then your ancestors are completely different than you've believed your entire life."

"I hadn't thought about that."

"Does that bother you?"

Karessa considered his question for a moment. "No. I didn't personally know any of my ancestors earlier than my grandparents anyway. I've always been interested in my family history, but if I find out my great-great-grandparents were other than who I thought they were, it won't make any difference to me now."

A frigid gust blew over Karessa and she shivered. "Did you feel that cold air?"

"Yeah." Max frowned again as he looked around the room. "I've got to find that draft. I can't figure out why there would be cold air in this house when it was eighty degrees today."

Thunder rumbled again, closer this time. Max closed his empty container. "Sounds like that's my cue to get out of here. If it starts raining, my truck will get stuck in the mud."

"Thank you for bringing supper."

He smiled. "My pleasure. I'll put the rest of it in your refrigerator. The egg rolls are still in the sack. I figure you'll have one about . . . nine o'clock, right?"

"You remember a lot about my habits."

His smile faded. "Yes, I do," he said softly. "You might be surprised at all the things I remember about you, Karessa."

The tenderness in his voice made her want to reach out to him. Instead, she handed him her empty container and water bottle. "Good night."

He stared at her for a long moment before standing. "Good night."

At the door, he turned to face her. "This was nice. Thank you for having dinner with me." He opened the door, but didn't step across the threshold. "I want you to know I regret hurting you. If I could go back, I'd do everything differently."

"But we can't go back, can we?" Karessa whispered.

"No, we can't. I'm sorry about that. I'm sorrier than I can ever tell you."

She watched him go through a blur of tears. She was sorry, too . . . sorry that the lure of riches had meant more to Max than her love.

ഉ‑

A flash of lightning lit up the dark sky outside the dining room. Max glanced out the window at the churning clouds. If they ever opened up, it would rain buckets.

"Hey, Max."

He turned at the sound of Kevin's voice. "Yeah?"

"All of Tarrant County is under a tornado watch. I don't want to take any chances with my guys' safety, so I'm letting everyone go early."

"Sounds like a good idea."

"You wanna lock up for me?"

"Sure."

"Thanks. My wife freaks at thunderstorms. I gotta get home and protect her." He bobbled his eyebrows and grinned devilishly. "She's always *really* appreciative of my protection." He clapped Max on the shoulder. "Finish up and get out of here. I'll see you Monday."

"Okay."

Max thought about Kevin's words as he began gathering up his tools. Kevin's wife was afraid of thunderstorms. Karessa loved them. She wasn't crazy about lightning, but the more thunder and rain, the better. He could remember a couple of times when they'd lain together in bed after making love and listened to the storm raging around them.

He missed that closeness, that intimacy, with a woman. He could get sex anywhere. Making love to a woman was totally different than having sex. He didn't think he'd ever "made love" to any woman but Karessa.

It would be so easy to fall in love with her again. Knowing that she wouldn't return his feelings hurt all the way to his soul.

Sticking to their agreement hadn't been easy. He couldn't help being around her when she came home early. He also couldn't help worrying about her, like on Tuesday afternoon when she had a headache. All he'd wanted to do was take care of her. Chinese food had always made her feel better.

In the past, Chinese food had always been followed by lovemaking. Hell, *everything* had been followed by lovemaking. Karessa was an incredibly passionate woman.

Max sighed heavily as he dropped the hammer in his toolbox. He needed to get out of here. Being around Karessa and not having her was slowly eating away at him. He had to find that bond and get out of Fort Worth . . . and out of her life for good.

He had the perfect opportunity now to search. No one else was in the house. Karessa wouldn't be home for hours. Some rumbles of thunder and flashes of lightning wouldn't frighten him away.

Grabbing his hammer again, Max headed for the stairs and the bedroom at the end of the hall.

He stopped two feet past the doorway and looked at every corner, every wall. The bond had to be hidden in this room. It's the only room in the house that had been padlocked, meaning *something* of value was in here.

Starting at the wall to his left, Max began tapping the wooden boards, searching for a hollow sound. There could be a false wall, or even a secret hiding place behind one of the boards.

He jumped at a crack of thunder. A moment later, the skies finally opened up. It sounded like large hail hitting the roof instead of raindrops. At least with the horrible weather, he could be assured that Karessa wouldn't be home early.

There. Max couldn't be sure over the sound of the pouring rain, but that tap sounded different from the others. This could be it, the break he'd been wanting for two weeks. He tapped again, a bit harder.

"What are you doing, Max?"

Ten

Max dropped his hammer and whirled around. Karessa stood in the doorway, water dripping from her hair and clothes. She'd obviously gotten caught in the rain.

Heart pounding at being caught, he bent over to retrieve his hammer. "Hey, Karessa."

"I asked you what you're doing."

He took his time standing so he could think of a good reason for him to be in this room. "Checking out the wall. You said you wanted a door here."

"I thought you were working in the dining room."

"I am." He shrugged. "I just thought I'd take a look in here." Before she could question him further, he quickly continued. "Looks like you could use some dry clothes."

She pushed her wet bangs back from her forehead. "It's pouring. I'm really sorry I didn't have Kevin renovate the garage first."

Lightning flashed outside the window, followed by a loud clap of thunder. He could see Karessa shiver. Despite the warm house, she had to be cold in her damp clothes. "Go ahead and change your clothes, Karessa. I'll get out of here."

More lightning flashed. Karessa bit her bottom lip as she gazed at the window. "I think the storm is getting worse."

"Kevin said there's a tornado watch for Tarrant County."

She looked back at him. "You can't go out in this, Max. You'll be soaked before you get three steps away from the house. You'd better wait until the rain dies down."

He'd never refuse an opportunity to be alone with her. "All right." He gripped the handle of his hammer. "I can start on the door for you, if you want."

"No, not now."

She rubbed her forehead. Her action made Max notice the pinched look around her mouth, the darkness beneath her eyes. He hadn't noticed those signs earlier with his heart beating so hard. "Does your head hurt again?"

"A little."

"I'd say more than a little."

"I'm fine," she said, her tone sharp.

Max knew better than to push. He remained silent while she rotated her head on her neck and released a heavy breath. "I'm sorry, Max. I didn't mean to snap at you. It's been a hell of a week."

"No problem."

"I'm gonna change and lie down. Don't work in here right now, okay?"

"Sure. I'll go back to the dining room."

He watched her walk down the hall and into her bedroom, closing the door behind her. With a glance at the wall, he left the room. There would be time later to investigate what might be behind that wall.

⋈

"What are you doing, Mary?"

His wife leaned over the railing as she watched Max descend the steps. "Nothing, darling."

"Don't give me that innocent act. I've known you for over one hundred years."

She faced him. A mischievous smile lit up her face. "They're getting closer."

"Thanks to you. The storm is a lot more intense in here than it is outside."

"I only made it seem more intense for Karessa and Max. If they walk out to the veranda, they'll discover it isn't raining as hard as they think it is."

"But they won't walk out onto the veranda because they *do* believe the storm is worse than it actually is."

Mary grinned. "I know."

Aaron couldn't help chuckling. When his wife put her mind to something, there was no stopping her. "So, what's next? A tornado?"

"I can't change the weather, Aaron."

"But you can make them *think* there's a tornado."

"If I have to."

"I'm glad you're on my side, sweetheart."

〄

Karessa had been in her bedroom for over an hour. Max figured she was probably taking a nap to try and get rid of her headache.

Wanting to be quiet so as not to disturb her, he had returned to painting the kitchen instead of working in the dining room. The lack of any noise from upstairs bothered him. The storm still raged outside, but he couldn't hear anything inside the house.

He needed to know for sure that she was all right.

He stood outside her bedroom and pressed his ear to the

door. Nothing. Max debated with himself for a moment about invading her privacy. Worry overruled etiquette. Turning the doorknob, he slowly pushed open the door.

Karessa lay on her back, one arm covering her eyes. He thought she was asleep, until she moved her arm and wiped her eyes with her hands.

Seeing her tears made his heart clutch in his chest.

"Hey," he said softly.

She turned her head his direction. "Hey."

"Still hurting?"

"Yeah."

Sympathy welled up inside him. He had to help her. She might try to push him away, but he was determined to do whatever he could to help her.

Max stepped into the room and closed the door behind him. She watched him with suspicion in her eyes as he walked toward her. "What are you doing?" she asked.

"I'm gonna help you get rid of your headache. Turn over."

"You don't have to—"

"Don't argue with me, Karessa. A massage always helped you. Now turn over on your stomach."

A frown formed between her eyebrows, but she didn't argue. She rolled to her stomach, her face turned away from him.

Max sat on the side of the bed and laid his hands on Karessa's shoulder blades. One touch and he had no doubt why her head hurt.

"You're so tight." He pressed into the blades with his thumbs. She groaned. "Too much stress lately?"

"New exhibits."

He knew Karessa always worried about how the public would react to a new exhibit. Max thought she worried over nothing. All the museum's exhibits were well received and very popular. Her worrying was probably what made The Gage-Austin so popular and successful.

Success shouldn't make her suffer.

He slid his hands up to her shoulders. They felt like bricks instead of flesh. "Jesus, Karessa, don't you ever relax?"

"Rarely."

"That's apparent. I think you need some time on a tropical island somewhere with no phones and no obligations."

"Mmm, sounds good. When can I leave?"

Max chuckled. "As soon as I turn your body into a pile of mush."

Her cell phone chirped from the nightstand. Max felt her tense as if she were going to raise up to answer it. He pressed harder on her shoulders. "Uh-uh. Ignore it."

"But it might be—"

"I'm not letting you up. You can check the voicemail later."

"Don't pull your macho shit on me, Max."

He chuckled again. "Such language."

"Max—"

"Straighten your neck so I can get to it."

He grinned at her huff of breath. She'd never liked it when his opinion differed from hers. Tough. This was for her own good. If he had to pull his macho shit on her, he would.

She straightened her neck and propped her forehead on the pillow. "There. Are you happy?"

"Ecstatic, except your hair's in the way. You have one of those hair clip things?"

"In the bathroom, second drawer on the right."

"Lotion?"

"On the dress— Why do you want lotion?"

"Be right back," he said, ignoring her question.

When Max returned to the bedroom, he removed his work boots and left them by the door. The best way to work on Karessa would be to straddle her, and he didn't want to get her bedspread dirty.

Climbing back on the bed, Max gathered up Karessa's hair and clipped it high on her head. She wore a floppy T-shirt with a loose neck. He tugged it away from her neck before reaching for the bottle of lotion. Pouring a liberal amount in his palm, he rubbed his hands together to distribute the rose-scented liquid. He pressed his thumbs into her muscles as he spread the lotion over her shoulders and neck.

Her back rose and fell with a deep breath. "That's nice."

"I'm glad you approve."

"I shouldn't let you do this."

"Why not? I've given you lots of massages."

"I'm still angry at you."

"I know," he said softly.

"So why are you doing this?"

"Because I care."

She gave no response to his comment. That didn't surprise him. He doubted if Karessa would ever believe he cared for her, especially how deeply he cared.

He wanted to work on her back as well as her neck and shoulders, but the neckline of her shirt wouldn't stretch enough to let him do that. He poured more lotion in his hands, then ran them up under her shirt.

"Max!"

She started to raise her torso off the bed. One firm hand in the middle of her back stopped her. "Calm down. I'm not making a move on you."

Deep pressure with his thumbs made her moan. "Your whole body is one big knot. You need to soak in a hot tub."

"The best I can do now is a bathtub."

"That's probably a good idea, after I work on you some more." He slid his hands all the way up her back, stopping only long enough to unhook her bra. Her body tightened when he unfastened it, but he disregarded her reaction and continued the massage. Up and down, side to side, he kneaded her flesh until the stiffness began to melt away.

Touching her was causing a completely different stiffness in his body.

Ignoring his growing erection, Max pushed her shirt up to her shoulder blades. A gentle downward tug on her jersey pants gave him access to her lower back. Her skin was already smooth; the lotion made it even softer. He hadn't touched her in five years, and planned to savor the feel of her flesh beneath his hands as long as he could.

Her breathing grew deeper . . . the sign of her beginning arousal. His massage was apparently affecting her as much as him. Max ran his hands all the way up to her neck, then made the return journey to her low back. He repeated the process over and over, dipping a bit farther inside her pants each time.

On the last pass, he palmed her buttocks. Karessa shifted on the bed, spreading her legs another inch. Taking that as a sign that she wanted more of his touch, he slid one thumb between her buttocks. She clutched the pillow and lifted her ass a few inches off the bed.

"You want this, don't you?" he asked as he circled her anus with his thumb.

She didn't answer with words, but her breathing increased. Max tugged her pants and panties down her legs to her knees.

The sight of her ass made him groan. It was larger, fuller, than the last time he'd been with her. He could tell she'd gained weight. It seemed to be focused mainly in her breasts and ass.

Perfect.

His own breathing now as erratic as hers, Max pressed one hand against his bulging zipper while he caressed her anus. Dipping his thumb down to her pussy, he collected her cream and spread it over the puckered hole. Karessa whimpered. She began to pump her hips in time with his movements. Each time she raised her hips, his thumb slipped a bit farther inside her ass.

Touching her like this made his head swim, but it wasn't enough. Stretching out on his stomach, Max spread her buttocks wide and licked her anus.

"Yes," Karessa moaned. "Like that."

Her musky, womanly scent drifted to his nose as he moved his tongue around the small hole. He'd never been with a woman who smelled as sexy as Karessa. Or tasted as good. He made one pass over her labia with his tongue before darting it inside her ass.

"Mmm. That feels good."

To him, too. He'd be happy to tongue-fuck her ass all night long. He wanted to make her come over and over and over . . .

Karessa lifted her hips another few inches. "More. Oh, more, please!"

All too happy to comply with her wish, Max thrust his tongue harder, faster, into her ass as he pushed two fingers into her creamy pussy. Karessa froze for a moment, then moaned loudly and trembled. The walls of her pussy clamped onto his fingers, expanding and contracting through her orgasm.

Max gave her anus one last lick before he rose to his knees and flipped Karessa to her back. Her eyelids drooped. A satisfied smile touched her lips. She might be satisfied, but his cock was as hard as the handle of his hammer.

His gaze passed over her bare skin. With one finger, he touched the smooth flesh of her mound. "You still shave your pussy."

She nodded. "I like it this way."

Cradling her mound, he slid his fingers over her wet labia. "So do I." He watched her eyes drift closed while he touched her. "It's very sexy."

She opened her eyes again when he tugged her pants and panties off her legs. One jerk and his T-shirt joined her clothes on the floor. Looking into her eyes, he unbuckled his belt and unfastened his jeans. Her gaze dropped to his pelvis when he pushed his jeans and briefs past his hips.

His cock jerked when she licked her lips.

He'd love to feel that warm mouth wrapped around his shaft. Not now. Now, he needed to fuck her. Not able to wait one more second, he stretched out on top of Karessa and entered her with one stroke.

It was like coming home. He'd been with women—a lot of women. No other woman had ever fit so right in his arms. No other woman had ever made him feel whole, as if they were truly part of each other.

No other woman had ever made him feel love so deeply.

He kissed her. Her lips softened beneath his and parted ever so slightly. Slipping one hand behind her neck, he tilted his head to deepen the kiss. His tongue stroked her lips, her teeth, her tongue. He began to move his hips, driving his shaft into her creamy pussy. She responded eagerly, her arms wrapping around his neck while her hips rose to meet his hard thrusts.

Max knew he'd come much too soon if he kept up the frantic

pace. Holding Karessa tightly, he rolled to his back. "Ride me, sweetheart."

She pushed herself into a sitting position. Max inhaled sharply. Her new position buried his cock inside her, all the way to his balls. It wouldn't take more than a few thrusts for him to come.

Karessa pulled off her shirt and tossed it to the floor. Her bra followed. Max stared at full, creamy breasts with big pink nipples. Cradling the globes in his hands, he ran his thumbs over the hard nubs. "You're bigger."

"Mmm-hmm."

He pushed her breasts together and squeezed them. "They're beautiful." He looked up into her eyes. "*You're* beautiful."

She lifted her hips until only his head remained inside, then lowered herself to take all of him again. Max continued to knead her breasts as she rode him. Her movements were easy at first, but soon gained in speed. He wanted to let her control their love-making. The need to pump overruled his good intentions. Holding her waist, he lifted his hips to meet each of her movements. Pleasure shimmied down his spine, straight into his balls.

Before it could peak, Karessa threw back her head and arched her back. Her pussy grabbed his cock, milking it as she came.

Her orgasm brought on his own climax. Max shoved his cock as far inside her as he could and let the pleasure engulf him.

Seconds might have passed, or maybe minutes, while Max tried to breathe normally again. He watched Karessa's body, knowing the aftershocks of her orgasm still gripped her. She ran her hands up her thighs, over her stomach and breasts, and up into her hair. The clip fell silently to the bed. She shifted her body, drawing a soft groan from him.

The sound must have penetrated her senses, bringing her back to him. Lowering her head, she gave him her vixen's smile.

"Very nice."

Max squeezed her thighs. "Very."

Leaning forward, she braced her hands on his chest. "Now that the pressure is off, so to speak, don't you think it's time you told me the real reason you're here?"

Eleven

Guilt filled his eyes before he was able to mask it. Karessa waited for the excuse she knew he would give her.

"What do you mean, the real reason I'm here? I'm working for Kevin."

"Why?"

"I've developed a fondness for food. I like to eat."

"And that's the only reason?"

"What other reason could there be?"

Smiling without a trace of humor, Karessa shook her head. "Ah, Max. You were always so good at answering a question with a question." Her smile quickly vanished. "I don't like it. And I don't believe you lost all your money in bad investments. You're too smart to put all your eggs in one basket. You may have made some bad investments, but there's no way you're so poor you need to be working at a construction job to eat. There's something here, in this house, you want."

He lifted his hips. "Yeah. I want *you*."

"You can't distract me with sex, Max. I want the truth *now*."

She stared into his eyes, watching the different emotions flash through them. She saw guilt again, then concentration as if he were trying to think up another excuse. Then she saw acceptance. That's when she knew he would tell her the truth.

He rubbed one hand over his face. "I think there's a bond hidden in your house."

"A bond."

"Yeah. A bearer bond, worth about one hundred seventy-six million."

The amount staggered her. Her mouth dropped open. "One hundred seven— Are you sure?"

"Of the worth? Not exactly, but that's close. Am I sure it's here? All the research points to this house."

She should have known he was searching for treasure again. He hadn't come back to Fort Worth, to *her*. He'd come back for more riches.

It shouldn't hurt so much. Her heart should have hardened after the last time he'd trampled on it. But the heart could be incredibly stupid. She'd never gotten over Max, not completely. A part of her still loved him.

A bigger part of her wished he loved her, too.

"Well, I can certainly understand why you would pretend to be poor so you could work in this house. That's quite a prize."

He ran his hands over her thighs. "After what we just shared, the prize doesn't seem as important."

Karessa lifted her hips so his cock could slip out of her. "What did we share?" she asked as she climbed off the bed.

"We made love."

She laughed while slipping on her pants. "We didn't make love. We fucked."

Scowling, Max propped up on one elbow. "Don't degrade what we did, Karessa."

"I'm not degrading it. I'm simply stating a fact." Not bothering with a bra, she pulled her T-shirt over her head. "You're very good in bed, Max. I needed a man and I used you." She glanced at him in time to see him wince. "Does that make you feel like a whore? Well, now you know how I felt when you fucked me to steal the map from the museum."

He scrambled off the bed, tugging up his briefs and jeans as he stood. "I didn't steal that map."

Karessa rolled her eyes. "Oh, excuse me. That's right. You didn't really 'steal' it. You only 'borrowed' it long enough to make a copy."

He huffed out a breath and ran his fingers through his hair, but said nothing.

"What, no comeback? No justification for being a thief? At least tell me it was worth it. Tell me that map led to the treasure you just *had* to have."

"No, it didn't lead to any treasure."

"So those months of taking advantage of me were for nothing."

"I didn't take advantage of you. Karessa, I loved you. I *still* love you."

She threw up one hand toward him, palm forward. "Don't you *dare* tell me you love me. You have no idea what it means to love someone."

"I know I love you, and always will."

Instead of his words bringing joy, they drove the knife a bit farther into her heart. "Forgive me if I don't believe you."

He took a step closer to her. "Karessa—"

"I want you to go now, but come back tomorrow morning. Taking that bond off my property would be grand theft, Max. Do you realize that? But I don't care. I'll help you find it and hand it to you in order to get you out of my life."

୧୬

"You might as well stop the storm, Mary. It isn't working anymore."

"I know."

The sadness in her voice tore at Aaron's heart. The tears shimmering in her eyes made him long to draw her into his arms and comfort her.

The sound of a raging storm disappeared, to be replaced with the gentle patter of raindrops. Aaron stood next to his wife and watched Max walk out of the house. Her plan hadn't worked. He didn't doubt that Karessa and Max had made love in her bedroom, although he and Mary made sure they were as far away as they could get in order to give the couple privacy. Yet they had still argued. Whatever had happened between them in the past must be too much for Karessa to forgive.

"What now?" Mary asked in a soft voice.

"I don't know, sweetheart."

She turned to face him. Tears still glimmered in her eyes, but he also saw determination. "I won't give up, Aaron. They're the key to us being together."

"There's nothing else you can do, Mary."

"There's *something*. I just haven't figured it out yet. But I will. I promise you I will."

୧୬

The air smelled fresh from last night's rain. Karessa inhaled deeply before taking a sip of her coffee. She'd come out to the veranda to enjoy the morning. Now sitting in the porch swing, she let her gaze sweep the acres of oak and pecan trees that she owned. The view was peaceful, comforting.

Unlike her emotions.

Her eyes still burned from crying and lack of sleep. She was angry at herself for letting Max get to her. She should have thrown him out of her house the very first day. But no, she had to fall for his sob story.

What a wimp.

She'd learned her lesson. Deep inside, she'd always hoped that Max would come back to her. She'd loved him enough to forgive him, to give him another chance. No more. She'd help him find his precious bond. She didn't care about the money. She didn't *need* the money. She just wanted him gone.

The sound of his pickup made her heart lurch. She hated that the knowledge she would see him soon made her body heat with desire.

Damn the man for being such an incredible lover.

She took another sip of coffee while he parked his truck. She watched him climb out of the black vehicle and saunter toward her. Her gaze fell to the impressive bulge behind his fly. Those tight, faded jeans left nothing to the imagination. Of course, she didn't need her imagination. She knew exactly how his cock looked, felt, tasted . . .

"Good morning," he said once he stood at the bottom of the steps.

Karessa cleared her throat. Damn hormones. "Good morning. There's coffee inside, if you want some."

"I'm fine." He climbed up one step, then stopped. "May I join you?"

Karessa nodded. Max sat beside her and stretched his legs out in front of him. She took another sip of her coffee before setting the mug on the arm of the swing. It was time to give up on silly fantasies and get down to business. She wanted to get back to her life . . . a life without Max.

"I spent a lot of time last night reading my great-grandmother's diary. I think we'll find the location of the bond in it."

"Karessa, you don't have to do this. I'll leave and—"

"No, we're going to do this. It would be a shame for you to have come all this way and not find your treasure."

"Damn it, you mean more to me than any treasure."

Ignoring his declaration, Karessa opened the diary. "Let me read part of this to you. It's dated August 2, 1925. 'I know my mother has been searching my room again. So far, she has not found this book, or the other treasures I've hidden. I must make sure she does not. I want to keep writing down my thoughts, my feelings, but I must be more careful.'" She looked up at Max. "This is where she starts writing poems."

"Poems?"

She nodded. "I assume she did that in order to hide things from her mother. This is the first one:

> *A bond broken, victim of deception,*
>   *The lead to a brand-new start.*
> *Casual search, an image perfection,*
>   *A heinous conceited art.*
> *Documented silver in the reflection,*
>   *Eternal never-ending see.*
> *Faithful perform careful introspection,*
>   *A turn around is the key."*

Max frowned slightly. "Do you understand what that means?"

"No, but it's important. She wrote that she had hidden treasures. Perhaps the bond is one of those treasures."

"And perhaps the treasure is a fancy comb. She was a teenager when she wrote that."

"It's pretty profound for a teenager." She closed the diary. "I assume you've searched for the bond."

"A little. There are usually too many people around for me to search very much."

"Do you have an idea where it might be?"

"It could be in the bedroom that was locked. There had to

be something important in there or it wouldn't have been locked."

"True. So, let's go look."

She stood and headed for the front door, not bothering to see if he followed her. She had no doubt he would.

"Let me grab my toolbox, Karessa."

She waited for him at the foot of the stairs while he went into the dining room. Toolbox in hand, he followed her up the stairs to the bedroom at the end of the hall.

{∞}

Aaron watched Karessa and Max approach the bedroom. "We know where that bond is."

"But there's no way to tell them." Mary turned to him, her eyes wide and shining with excitement. "Wouldn't it be wonderful if they found the bond *today*? You do realize what today is, don't you?"

"Of course I do. But I don't think finding the bond will bring them back together, Mary. She's too angry at him."

She stepped to the side when Karessa and Max entered the bedroom. "Eva killed us on this day. They'll find the bond and it'll bring them back together, which will let us finally be together."

"I wouldn't disappoint you for anything, you know that, but I'm not as sure as you."

"Trust me, Aaron. I know I'm right."

{∞}

Karessa knelt on the floor and sat back on her heels. She didn't want to be in Max's way, but she intended to study everything he did. Hammer in hand, he stepped up to the wall next to the dresser. "You think it's in the wall?"

"It could be. I thought I heard a hollow sound yesterday when I tapped on this board."

"You mean, like a secret compartment?"

"Yeah."

Slowly, he moved down the board, gently tapping it with his hammer. Six inches from the floor, Karessa heard a distinct difference in the sound. She looked up as Max gazed at her. Silently, she nodded.

He maneuvered the claw into the edge of the board. The wood began to splinter as he tugged on it. He stopped and gazed at Karessa again.

"Go ahead. The board can be replaced."

Another tug with the claw and the board broke. Max tugged on the pieces until they fell to the floor. Karessa leaned forward and looked inside the wall at the same time as he.

Nothing. The wall was empty.

Max sat down, one foot resting on the floor. Karessa could clearly see the frustration in his eyes. "It's like a sickness with you, isn't it?"

He looked at her, his eyebrows drawn together in a frown. "What?"

"Treasure hunting. You're addicted to it, just like someone who smokes or drinks or gambles. The adrenaline rush gets you high."

He huffed out a breath and rubbed his mustache, yet didn't respond to her comment.

"What now?" she asked.

"I don't know." Rising to his feet, he offered her his hand to help her stand. She accepted it and let him tug her to her feet. "I have this gut feeling the bond is in this room."

"Then we'll keep looking."

Karessa walked over to the bed and sat down. Picking up the diary that she'd laid there earlier, she opened it to the next passage.

"My great-grandmother didn't write any more poems for several pages." She glanced at Max when he sat beside her, then returned her attention to the diary. "This is the next one:

> *Reach for one who reaches for you,*
> *Gently touching, one becomes two.*
> *Seeking that which seems invisible,*
> *Breaking could be apprehensible.*
> *Search with your heart and all will be clear,*
> *The dark-haired hero saves the brilliant fair hair."*

"May I see that?" Max asked.

Karessa handed the book to him. She waited while he reread the poem. "What do you think?"

"Hell, I don't know. I was never good at riddles."

"Me either. I guess we need to . . ."

Karessa stopped when a bright light hit her eyes. The sun shone through the window and reflected off the dresser's mirror. Blinking quickly, she moved her head a few inches to the side. "Wow, the sun is bright this morning."

Max looked up from the diary. His gaze traveled from her face to the mirror and back again. "The sun?"

"Yeah. The light reflected off the mirror and hit me right in the eyes."

"The light reflected . . ." He stopped. His eyes widened slightly, then he looked back at the diary. "'Seeking that which seems invisible, breaking could be apprehensible.'" He flipped back through the pages. "Where's that poem you read me this morning?"

"Here." She found the spot in the diary for him. "What is it?"

"'Documented silver in the reflection.' She's written about a reflection. A mirror has a reflection. And it's supposed to be bad luck, or 'apprehensible' to break a mirror."

Karessa inhaled sharply. "It's in the dresser."

"It's in the mirror." He continued to read the first passage. "'A turn around is the key.'" He raised his gaze back to Karessa's face. "It's *behind* the mirror."

Twelve

The heightened senses. The rush of blood to the brain. The instant erection. The sweaty palms. All the emotions that hit Max at once when he was about to find his treasure didn't happen. He didn't understand that. He always felt as if he'd soared to the highest peak of a mountain when he held the treasure in his hand.

Perhaps the high would hit him once he actually held the bond.

He pulled the dresser away from the wall, far enough so he and Karessa could step behind it. A weathered, warped piece of wood covered the back of the mirror. There was no telling how long that piece of wood had been in place.

"Do you need the hammer?" Karessa asked.

"Yeah."

Working carefully, Max pried the wood away from the dresser until he could slip the claw behind the nail heads. Karessa stood close to him, accepting the nails in her outstretched hand as he removed them.

He dropped the last nail into Karessa's palm. Gently, he pulled the wood away from the mirror.

A yellowed envelope fell to the floor.

He stared at it, unable to comprehend yet that he'd actually found the bond. Setting the piece of wood against the wall, he knelt and reached for the envelope. He stopped four inches from it and looked up at Karessa. She stood with her arms crossed over her stomach, staring at his face.

Tears glistened in her eyes.

"Looks like you found it," she said, her voice raspy.

"Yeah."

He continued to look at her, making no move to pick up the envelope. She frowned slightly. "Why are you waiting? Pick it up. It's what you want."

Releasing a sigh, Max picked up the envelope and stood. He held it in his right hand and tapped it against the palm of his left. He felt nothing. There was still no excitement, no blood rush, no pounding heart, no erection. He held a fortune in his hand, yet felt only disgust at himself.

Karessa was right. Hunting for treasure was an addiction. Or it had been . . . until now.

This was crazy. He should be salivating with the knowledge that he held a fortune. But he didn't want the bond. He only wanted Karessa.

"Here." He held the envelope out to her.

Her frown deepened. "What?"

"I don't want it. It belongs to you."

Her mouth slackened, then her eyes narrowed. "What are you doing, Max?"

"The bond belonged to your great-grandmother. We found it in your house. It's legally yours."

She hesitated before taking the envelope from him. "I don't understand."

"I'm doing the right thing. Possibly for the first time in my life." Max hooked his thumbs into the front pockets of his jeans. "You're right, Karessa. I did have an addiction. I fucked up five years ago when I followed that addiction instead of my heart.

I never should have hurt you. I've regretted that every day since I left you." He let his gaze travel over her face . . . the face he'd seen every night in his dreams for five years. "God, I love you."

"Max—"

"I know you don't believe me. I understand that. And this . . ." He motioned toward the envelope. "isn't a con. I'm not trying to get you to feel sorry for me. I'm simply being honest." Hoping she would accept his touch, he reached out and slid one hand beneath her hair. "I don't need any more money. I could blow money like crazy and not spend what I've already made. Take the bond and cash it. Use it to add to your museum, or pay for the renovations to this house. Build five more houses just like it in different cities. Go on an around-the-world cruise. Whatever you want to do."

She remained silent for several moments. "Why are you doing this?"

"Because I love you," he said without a hint of hesitation.

She stared into his eyes, clearly not sure whether or not to believe him. Words were easy. Perhaps she needed a different way to convince her of his feelings.

Max lowered his head until his lips touched hers. He kissed her softly, tenderly, trying to show her how very much he cared. When she didn't pull away from him, he slipped his other arm around her waist and pulled her against him. He deepened the kiss, using his tongue to circle the outline of her lips before dipping it inside her mouth.

A soft moan from her throat sent blood rushing to his cock.

Max stopped the kiss and rested his forehead against hers. "Now *that's* an addiction I'd gladly live with for the rest of my life."

She pulled back and looked into his eyes. "Just like that? No more hunger for the treasure hunt?"

"The only hunger I have is for you."

Karessa wanted to believe him. She desperately wanted to believe him. Sharing her life with Max had been her dream five years ago. That dream had never completely died. But she had a hard time believing he could be "cured" of his addiction so quickly.

Stepping out of his arms, she held up the envelope so he could clearly see it. "We haven't opened the envelope yet. The bond might not be in here."

"That's true."

She raised the envelope a bit higher and gripped it with both hands. "So I could tear it in two, right now."

"You could. It's yours. You can do whatever you want."

No fear flashed through his eyes, no sign of anxiety. He truly didn't care if she tore the envelope in two.

"Max, are you serious? You'd let me tear this envelope, knowing there might be a bond in it worth millions?"

"There is no 'letting' you do anything, Karessa. I said the bond is yours and I meant that. I only want *you,* nothing else."

The love and sincerity in his eyes convinced her he was telling the truth. Tears sprang to her eyes again. This time, they were tears of happiness. "You really do love me?"

He smiled. "With all my heart."

Karessa wrapped her arms around his neck and hugged him tightly. "I love you, too," she whispered.

❧

"Aaron, I feel funny."

"Yeah, me, too."

"What's happening to us?"

"I don't know."

"Aaron!"

❧

Max saw the two people materialize behind Karessa. "Jesus!" He immediately tugged Karessa behind him to protect her. "Who the hell are you?"

"You can see us?" the man asked.

"Yeah, I can see you." He gazed at the two people, noting their old-fashioned clothing. They looked like they'd stepped out of the early 1900s. "Who are you?"

The couple looked at each other. Max saw the woman's eyes fill with tears before she smiled at the man. "Aaron, it worked! I told you it would."

He held out a hand to her. She moved her hand slowly toward it, almost as if she were afraid to touch him. When she laid her hand in his, she audibly gasped.

"I can touch you," she whispered.

The man drew her into his arms. Max looked at Karessa. The confusion on her face told him she had no idea what was happening, either. "Who are these people?"

"I don't know. She called him 'Aaron.'"

"Yeah, well, that doesn't tell me anything." He looked back at the couple. "Excuse me for bothering you two, but who are you?"

Aaron released the woman after kissing her softly. "I know you have a lot of questions, Max."

"To put it mildly. And how do you know my name?"

He looked at Karessa. "We're your great-great-grandparents, Karessa."

Her mouth dropped open. "My . . . What?"

"We'll explain everything to you, I promise. But first . . ." He lifted the woman's hand to his mouth and kissed the back. "Mary and I need to . . . talk."

With that comment, they disappeared.

Max blinked. "Well, that was . . . interesting."

"Did we just see two people who claimed to be my great-great-grandparents?"

"Yeah, we did."

Karessa crossed her arms over her breasts. "Okay, I am officially freaked now."

"Don't be freaked."

"Max, they're *ghosts*! I have ghosts in my house."

"Hey." He took her in his arms and held her tightly to him. "It's okay, Karessa. They won't hurt you."

She wrapped her arms around his waist. "You probably think I'm silly."

"No, I don't think you're silly."

"Aren't you afraid at all?"

"Not really. Maybe I should be freaked, like you said, but it makes sense for ghosts to be here."

She raised her head from his chest and looked at him. "Why?"

"Haven't you sensed their presence?"

"I've sensed . . . something."

"So have I. I think they wanted us back together."

"What difference would it make to them?"

"I don't know. I guess we'll have to ask them."

A sexy moan filled the air. Karessa's eyes widened. "What was that?"

Max grinned. "I didn't think that guy had a 'talk' look in his eyes. He had more of an 'I-gotta-jump-her-bones' look."

"Do you think they're making love?"

"Absolutely."

"But ghosts can't make love."

"Who says?"

Another, louder, moan filled the air. Max released Karessa and took her hand. "Let's leave them alone."

He led her to her bedroom. After shutting the door, he tugged her to the bed. Lying on his back, he drew her into his arms. She snuggled up to his side, one leg between his.

"Feel better now?" he asked.

"Mmm-hmm."

"Still scared?"

"No. I think you're right, that they're . . . friendly. I mean, they could've hurt me a long time ago if they'd wanted to, right?"

"Right." He kissed the top of her head. "They'll talk to us later, I'm sure of it."

Her hand lazily caressed his chest. Content, he simply held her for several moments before speaking again.

"Marry me, Karessa."

Her hand stilled. Max continued before she could say anything. "Don't say yes or no until you talk to your lawyer about a prenup. I have no intention of us ever divorcing, but your assets need to be protected. I don't want you believing that I want to marry you simply to get that bond, or the museum, or anything else of value you own."

She tilted her head on his shoulder. "And to protect your assets, too?"

"No. Anything I own is yours. That's the way I want it."

"Maybe that's what I want, too."

Tilting up her chin, he kissed her softly. "Please, sweetheart. Talk to your lawyer. You're a wealthy woman. It's the smart thing to do."

He enjoyed the kiss so much, he kissed her again. And again. On the third kiss, he rolled her to her back. He deepened the kiss as he cradled one breast in his hand. A brush of his thumb made her nipple stand up as if begging for more.

Max was only too happy to give her more.

"I want to be inside you," he whispered against her ear.

Karessa rose from the bed. Max propped up on one elbow and watched her undress. With each article of clothing that fell to the floor, his cock got a bit harder.

She stood nude before him . . . legs parted, breasts thrust forward, hands lifting her hair from her neck. A Roman goddess couldn't be as beautiful as Karessa looked right now.

"You take my breath away," he said, his voice husky.

That vixen smile he loved tilted up the corners of her mouth. "You're wearing way too many clothes."

"I can fix that."

Max scrambled off the bed while Karessa climbed up to the middle on her knees. Mere seconds later, he was as nude as she.

A devilish light twinkled in her eyes. "That's quite a boner you have there."

He stroked his hard cock. "The better to fuck you with, my dear," he growled.

Karessa laughed at his Big Bad Wolf imitation, but the laughter quickly faded from her voice. "Make love to me, Max."

He returned to the bed, moving on his knees to within a few inches of her. Taking her hands in his, he linked their fingers together. He held their hands out from their bodies as he leaned closer and kissed her.

The barest mingling of breaths. A brush of tongue. A gentle nibble on her bottom lip. Max didn't simply kiss her; he worshipped her mouth. He moved his mouth one way, then the other. Seconds passed, perhaps minutes, as he continued to kiss her every way he possibly could.

She tightened her fingers on his when the kiss ended. "Wow," she breathed.

Max nipped the skin beneath her ear. "I love kissing you."

"And you do it so well."

"Then I'll do it some more."

He covered her lips with his again. Releasing her hands, he wrapped his arms around her and slowly lowered her to the bed. She clasped his back as he stretched out on top of her. He slid his cock inside her pussy with one long stroke.

The silken glide. The snug clasp of her flesh around his shaft. The soft sucking sound her pussy made when he withdrew his cock. Max pumped into her slowly, building their pleasure a little at a time. She'd asked him to make love to her, and that's exactly what he planned to do. He didn't increase the speed of his thrusts, not even when Karessa's fingernails dug into his butt.

"Harder, Max."

He darted his tongue into her ear, and smiled when he felt her shiver. "No. Nice and easy, Karessa." He cradled her cheek and kissed her. "Let me love you nice and easy."

He watched her as he continued moving inside her. Her eyes drifted closed. Her mouth slackened. Her neck arched. Seeing that long column of ivory skin made Max long to bite, to suck. Wrapping his hand in her hair, he tilted her head farther back and bit her neck. He soothed the bite with his tongue, then nipped her again.

"*Max*! Oh, *yes*!"

The walls of her pussy clamped around his cock. Her climax sent him over the edge with her. Slipping one hand beneath her buttocks, he held her tightly to him while the pleasure slithered down his spine and into his balls.

Karessa slid her hands up and down Max's spine. A fine sheen of perspiration coated his skin. She could feel his heart pounding against her breasts, his warm breath on her neck. The closeness, the sharing of their bodies, their hearts . . . she'd missed it so much.

He raised his head and smiled at her. "Hi."

She returned his smile. "Hi."

"Do you have any idea how much I love sex?"

His goofy grin made her laugh. "Probably as much as I do."

"Then I think we'll have a long and happy life together."

She lightly ran her fingernails down his back. "I have no doubt of that."

Karessa sighed when he kissed her. The man certainly knew how to use his tongue to its best advantage . . . in more ways than one.

He dropped a peck on the tip of her nose. "Do you think we should get dressed and look for the ghosts?"

"I guess we should. Darn it."

Max chuckled. "I promise we'll make love again today. Probably more than once."

Karessa grinned. "Goody."

He swiped his tongue across both her nipples before he rose from the bed. Rolling to her side, she watched him pull on his clothes. After he fastened his jeans, he kissed her once more. "I'll be right back."

Once he'd left the room, Karessa's gaze fell to the yellowed envelope she'd laid on the nightstand. Curiosity made her reach for it. Sitting up, she slid her thumb beneath the flap and withdrew the contents.

Thirteen

Mary sighed when Aaron's tongue slid over her clit. She'd love to lie here all day and make love, but knew they had to talk to Karessa and Max. Tunneling her fingers into his hair, she tugged gently. "Aaron, stop."

"Uh-uh. Not until you come again."

"I've already come three times." She tugged a bit harder, until he raised his head. "We've been making love for almost two hours."

He grinned devilishly. "Damn, I'm good."

Mary laughed. "Yes, you definitely are. But we have to talk to Karessa and Max. They have to be wondering where we are."

"I hate it when you spoil my fun."

He rose from the bed and helped Mary to stand. Her legs felt like limp noodles. She grabbed his arms to keep from falling.

"You okay, sweetheart?" Aaron asked, concern in his voice.

"I'm fine. Just weak. I'm not used to having so many orgasms in such a short time."

"We have a lot of time to make up for."

"Not all in one day, Aaron."

"You're determined to spoil my fun, aren't you?"

She pulled his head down so she could kiss him. "We'll have more fun later, all right? Let's get dressed and talk to Karessa and Max."

{∘}

Hand in hand, Mary and Aaron walked down the stairs. A knock on Karessa's bedroom door had produced no response, so Mary suggested they check downstairs. They followed the sound of conversation to the veranda. She spotted them first, sitting on the swing.

Max stood. "Hello again."

"Hello." Mary smiled to herself. She liked Max's manners. He would be so good to Karessa.

Her gaze slid to Karessa's face. It was almost like looking into a mirror. There were subtle differences in their looks, but even if Mary hadn't been sure of Karessa's identity, she'd know they were related.

Mary tugged Aaron closer to the swing. "We have so much to tell you, it's hard to know where to start."

"Mary, here, sit next to Karessa. I'll get a couple of folding chairs for Aaron and me."

"I'll help you," Aaron said.

Once the men left, Mary sat on the swing next to her great-great-granddaughter. "I can feel your tension. Are you afraid of me?"

"I'm . . . cautious."

"I understand that. Finding two ghosts in your house must be mind-boggling."

"It was, but Max told me I shouldn't be afraid."

"Max is a wonderful man, Karessa. He loves you deeply. Don't ever doubt that."

"How do you know?"

"I just do. Trust me, please." She straightened her skirt over her legs. "I'm sure you're confused about a lot of things."

Karessa chuckled. "Yeah, you could say that. You two look . . . human."

"I can't explain that part. I assume it's so we can communicate with you."

Max and Aaron stepped back outside, each carrying a folding chair. Mary remained silent until the men had set up their chairs and sat down, then she looked back at Karessa. "Would you like to ask questions, or should I simply start talking?"

"I do have a question. You said your name is Mary and you're my great-great-grandmother. But her name was Eva."

"I *am* your great-great-grandmother." She glanced at Aaron, unsure whether or not to be brutally honest with Karessa. His nod gave her the encouragement to continue. "Eva shot Aaron and me on this day in 1910."

Karessa gasped. "She *shot* . . . Why?"

"Because she was obsessed with Aaron and wanted him for herself. She shot us and took our baby to raise as her own."

"Katie?"

Mary nodded. "You've been reading her diary. Have you finished it?"

"Not yet."

"Katie always suspected Eva wasn't her birth mother, but could never prove it. Eva had bewitched practically everyone in the whole town. No one ever looked for us after we died. Aaron and I couldn't figure out why, until we found Eva's book of spells."

"Book of spells?" Max asked.

"She was a witch. Katie looked for the book, but could never find it. Eva kept it well hidden." She turned back to Karessa. "She had the book with her in the carriage house the night she died. Aaron and I don't know exactly what happened since we could never leave the house, but a fire started in the carriage house in 1928. That's how Eva was killed, in the fire. It was a horrible way to die."

"After what she did to us, she deserved to die a horrible death," Aaron said bitterly.

"No one deserves to die so painfully, darling."

Aaron looked at Max. "Mary always sees the good in people."

Max shifted his gaze from Aaron to Karessa. "Sounds like her great-great-granddaughter inherited that trait."

Karessa smiled at Max, then turned back to Mary. "You mentioned a carriage house?"

"Yes. This house became Katie's after Eva's death, but she decided not to rebuild the carriage house after the fire. Of course, by that time, automobiles were used for travel more than horses and a carriage house wasn't necessary."

Karessa rubbed her forehead. "This is all . . . It's a lot to try and absorb."

"I know, but Aaron and I want you to know everything."

"And you've been here all this time? Ever since you . . . died?"

"Yes. She put a curse on us that we'd be bound to this house forever, unable to touch each other. We don't know how, but the curse was broken when you and Max declared your love."

Karessa and Max looked at each other. Mary smiled at the obvious love—and lust—in their eyes. They were made for each other, just like Aaron and her.

"So, what happens to you now?" Max asked.

"We don't know for sure," Aaron said. "We're . . . in limbo, ess you'd call it."

"We do know that we won't stay here," Mary continued. "This is your house, Karessa. Aaron and I don't belong here anymore."

"But you won't go yet, will you? I still have so many questions. How many people get to actually talk to their great-great-grandparents?"

"I'm sure we can stay awhile longer." Mary smiled. "What else would you like to know?"

⟨⟩

Karessa jotted down the last thing Mary told her. She'd been writing for well over an hour. Her hand throbbed from writer's cramp, but she wasn't about to stop. She wanted every bit of information she could get about her ancestors before Mary and Aaron left.

Shortly before eleven o'clock, her stomach reminded her quite loudly that she hadn't eaten anything today. Embarrassed by her rumbling tummy, she glanced up at Mary.

Her great-great-grandmother smiled. "You are hungry."

"Starved." She bit her bottom lip. "Can you . . . eat?"

Mary shook her head. "No. But Aaron and I can take a walk among the trees while you and Max have lunch. We haven't been able to step off the veranda for many years."

"Actually, Mary," Aaron said, "it's time for us to go."

"Oh, no, not yet." Karessa clutched her notebook. "I still have questions."

"I'm afraid we don't have a choice, Karessa. Mary and I are being . . . called." He stood and held out a hand to his wife. "We have to go, sweetheart. Are you ready?"

She placed her hand in his. "As long as I'm with you, I'm ready for anything."

Tears sprang to Karessa's eyes. She could almost feel the love these two people shared. She stood as Mary did, and so did Max. "May I hug you?"

Mary smiled tenderly. "I insist on it."

Karessa hugged her fiercely, then faced Aaron. He gave her a loving smile before hugging her, too. Turning to Max, he held out his hand. "Take care of her."

"I plan to," Max said, shaking Aaron's hand.

Karessa leaned back against Max's chest when he slipped his arms around her waist. She watched Mary and Aaron climb down the steps and walk toward the grove of trees. Tiny stars glittered around them. Slowly, her great-great-grandparents faded from view until they disappeared. The stars floated in the air a few seconds, then whooshed up toward the sky.

Max kissed her temple. "I wish they could've stayed longer."

"So do I."

"They didn't have a choice, babe. They had to go when they were called. But they're together. That's what counts."

Her tummy rumbled again. Max chuckled in her ear. "I think I'd better feed you before your stomach starts registering on the Richter scale."

∞

Karessa spread lotion over her hands as she watched Max undress for bed. She couldn't help the sigh that escaped her lips when he pushed his briefs past his hips. The man was so gorgeous.

He slid between the sheets, facing her, and bunched up his pillow under his head. Amusement twinkled in his eyes. "I heard that sigh. Were you ogling my body?"

"Yes."

"Good." Hooking the top sheet with one finger, he pulled it down to her waist. "That means I can ogle yours, too."

"Before we get past the ogling stage, I need to talk to you."

He cradled one bare breast. "Can I suck on your nipples first?"

"No."

"Damn." He released her breast and shifted his head on his pillow. "Okay, talk."

She picked up the envelope containing the bond from the nightstand and held it out to him. "Open it."

Max frowned. "I don't need to open it. The bond is yours."

"Please. I want you to see what's inside."

He hesitated several moments before sitting up and taking the envelope from her. Karessa watched him withdraw the antique bond and unfold it. He read over it, then refolded it and put it back inside the envelope.

"Okay, I saw what's inside. I don't care."

"Did you notice the name of the railroad?"

"Yeah. Tanner and Watson. Why?"

"Tanner and Watson was a small railroad that was bought out by another railroad."

"And that one was bought out by a major transportation company, which was eventually acquired by Tharwood Energy."

"Right. If this bond had been issued by Tanner and Watson, it probably would be worth close to $176 million. But the name of the railroad on my bond is *Tonner* and Watson."

"*Tonner* and Watson?" Max asked, confusion in his voice.

"A smaller railroad that went out of business in 1904. The owner disappeared with all the investors' money."

"Which means . . ."

"That bond is worthless."

Max tapped the envelope against his palm. "Worthless."

Karessa nodded. "Worthless as far as money. It's important to me because I'll put it on display at the museum."

"And you know all this . . . how?"

"I run a museum, Max. I've studied history extensively, especially Texas history."

Max sat up straighter on the bed. "So this bond will make a great exhibit in your museum, but nothing else."

"Right."

He handed the envelope back to her. "I'm glad."

That wasn't exactly what she expected him to say. "You're *glad* the bond is worthless?"

"Yeah. Now you know for sure I want to marry you because I love you, not because of your money."

She opened her mouth to speak, but he continued before she had the chance to say anything. "I know you had doubts about me. Maybe you still do. But I'll spend the rest of my life proving how very much I love you. I promise you that."

Karessa believed him. The love shining in his eyes was all the proof she needed of his feelings. "I love you, Max," she whispered.

He smiled. "I like the way that sounds." Leaning forward, he kissed her softly. "I also like the way Karessa Hennessey sounds. Any chance we can make this a short engagement?"

"I have a couple of conditions about this engagement."

One eyebrow arched. "Conditions?"

"I want to borrow your Thomas Abernathy painting to display with his other paintings at the museum."

"Deal."

"And . . ."

Max frowned. "There's more?"

Karessa nodded. "When you gave me a massage last night, you mentioned me needing time on a tropical island. I want to go to some fabulous resort and be totally pampered on our honeymoon."

He smiled. "Deal on that one, too."

"In that case . . ." Wrapping her arms around his neck, Karessa tugged him closer to her. "I think a short engagement is an excellent idea."

~

Lynn LaFleur

Lynn LaFleur was born and raised in a small town in Texas close to the Dallas/Fort Worth area. After living in various places on the West Coast for twenty-one years, she is back in Texas, seventeen miles from her hometown. Lynn also publishes with Ellora's Cave and when not writing at every possible moment, she loves reading, sewing, gardening, and learning new things on the computer.